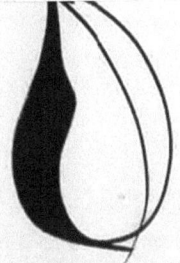

Gilded
Amaryllis

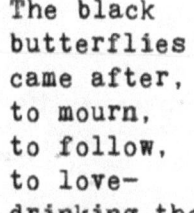

The black
butterflies
came after,
to mourn,
to follow,
to love—
drinking the silence
that used to be her name.

Poetry and Art

Dana Krystle

Website: www.danakrystle.com
Email: danakhalifa@live.com

Gilded Amaryllis: *A companion book for the novel titled- Grieving Amaryllis: Mirrors and Shadows*

An art & poetry companion book.
Dana Krystle- 2025

*'This work may contain material of a highly sensitive nature including **"suicide, eating disorders, depression"** that may be triggering for some individuals'.*

About the book concept :

Gilded Amaryllis is a companion book for a novel I wrote in 2025 called *Grieving Amaryllis*, this book is a combination of all the images I used to inspire and write the novel. Photography of the locations, concept materials, character research and landscapes are presented in this art book in a form of collage and digital juxtaposition.

The main poem was written before writing the novel itself, and from then on the story unfolded, however in this book, most of the poetry came after writing and publishing the novel itself, the poetry verses and stanzas are a depiction of the scenes and how the characters were interacting with each other, with a small poetic expression on how they felt at that moment.

A few excerpts of the novel were added in this book, including the official song that was composed exclusively for the novel titled - Gilded Amaryllis.

This book is a companion book and is an attempt to create and extend the world of the original novel (Grieving Amaryllis) in hopes of having a sort of experimental art work in a book companion format to go hand in hand with the same world building and themes.

Complete Silence.

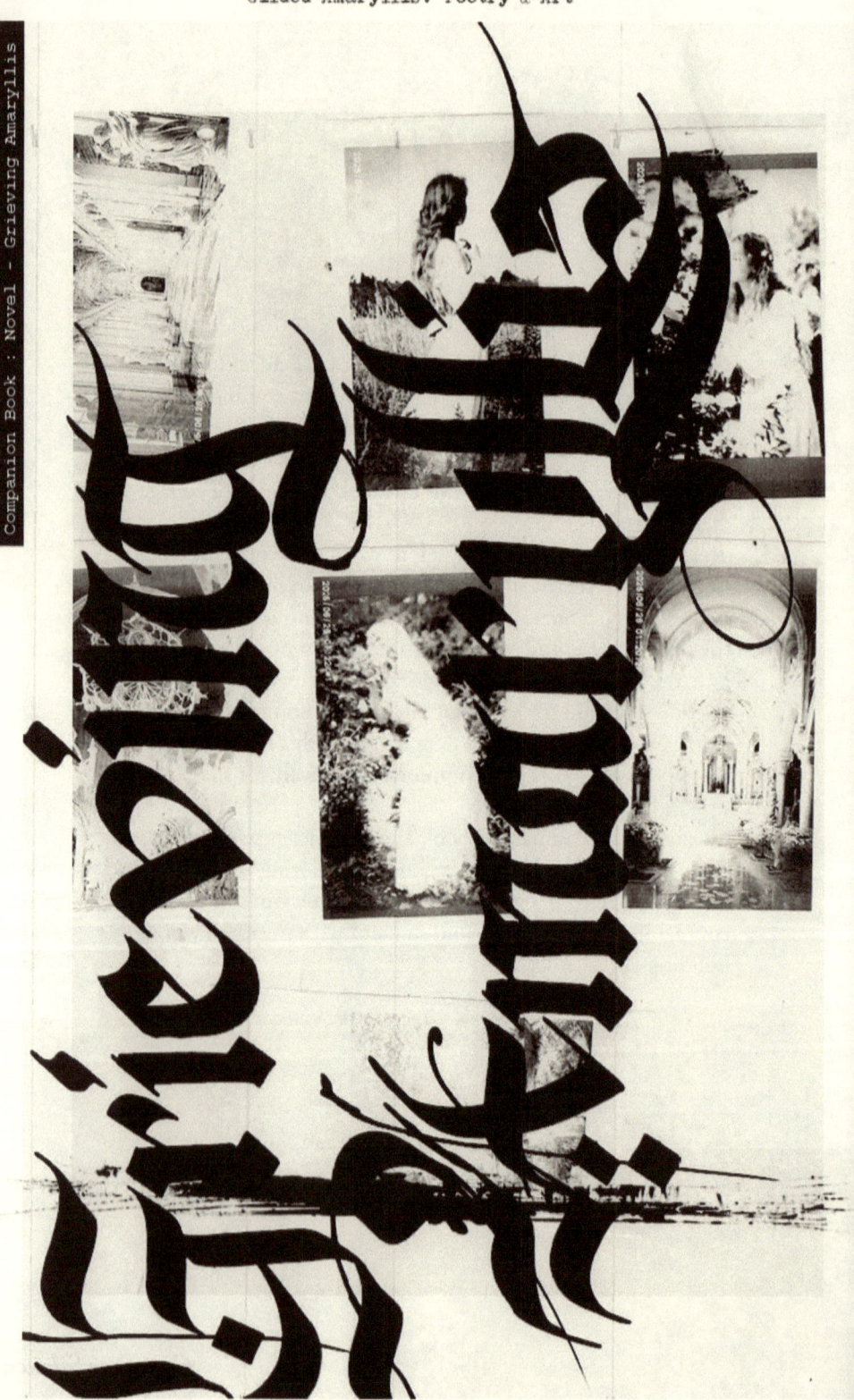

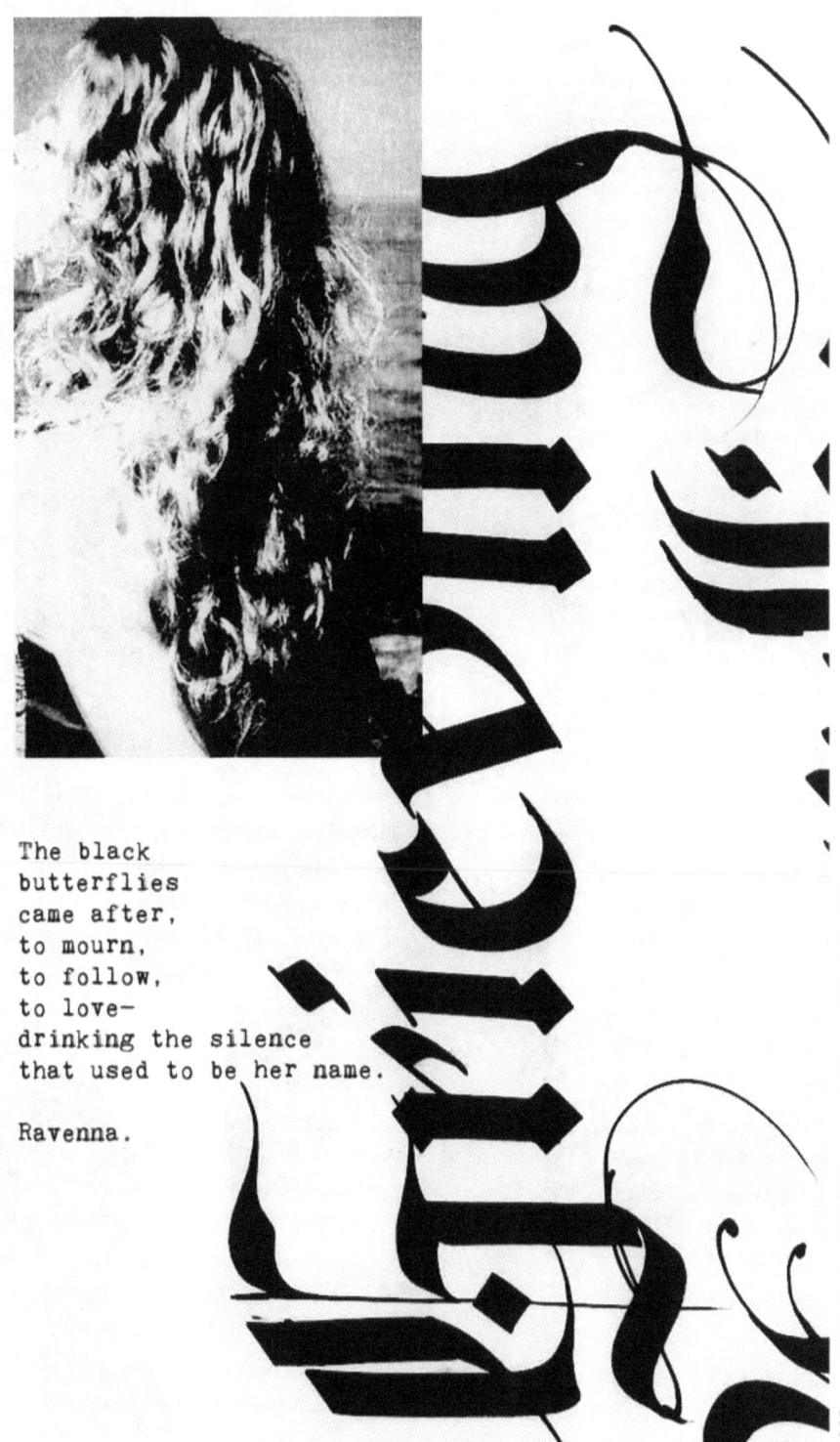

The black
butterflies
came after,
to mourn,
to follow,
to love—
drinking the silence
that used to be her name.

Ravenna.

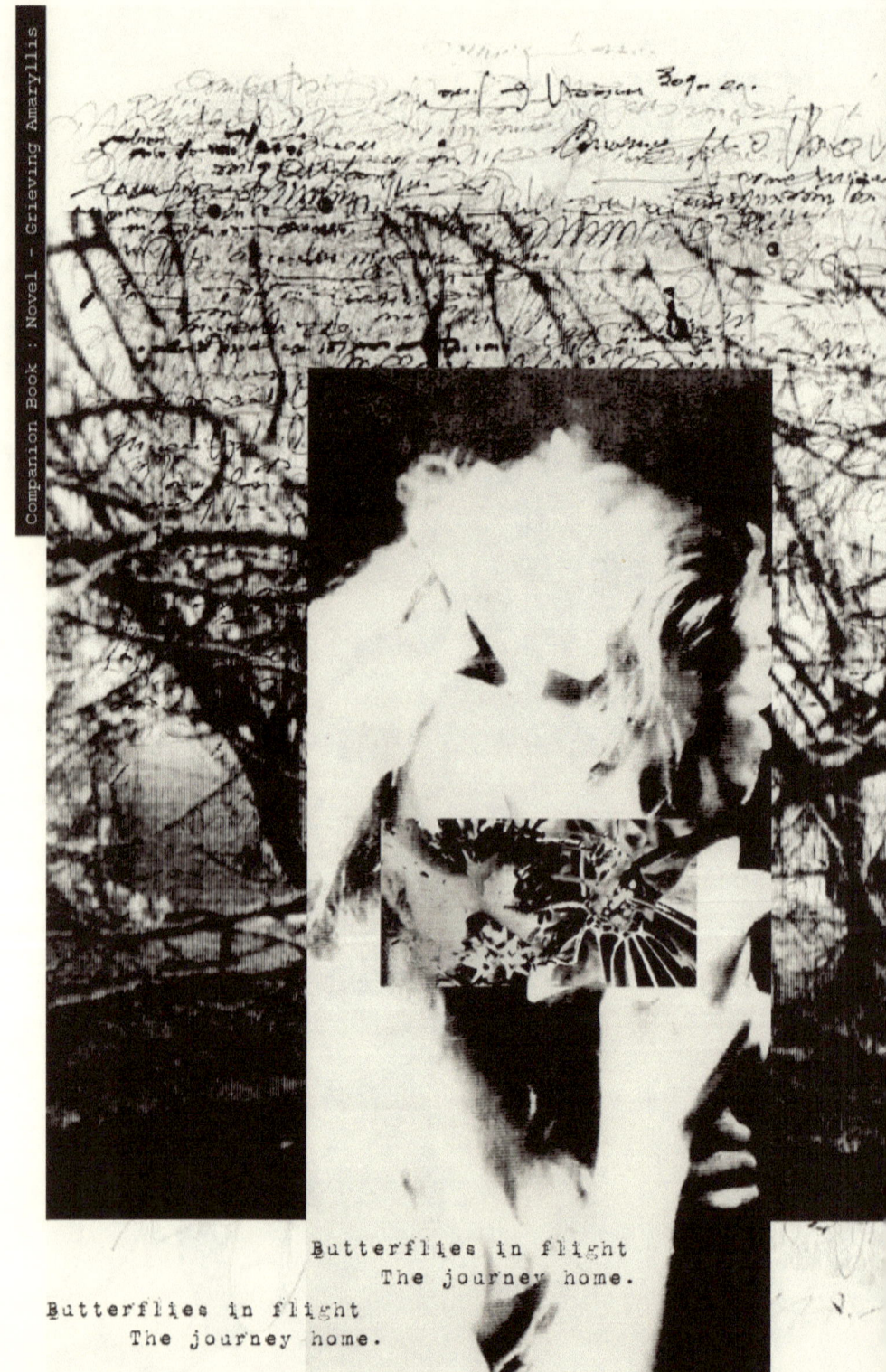

Butterflies in flight
The journey home.

Butterflies in flight
The journey home.

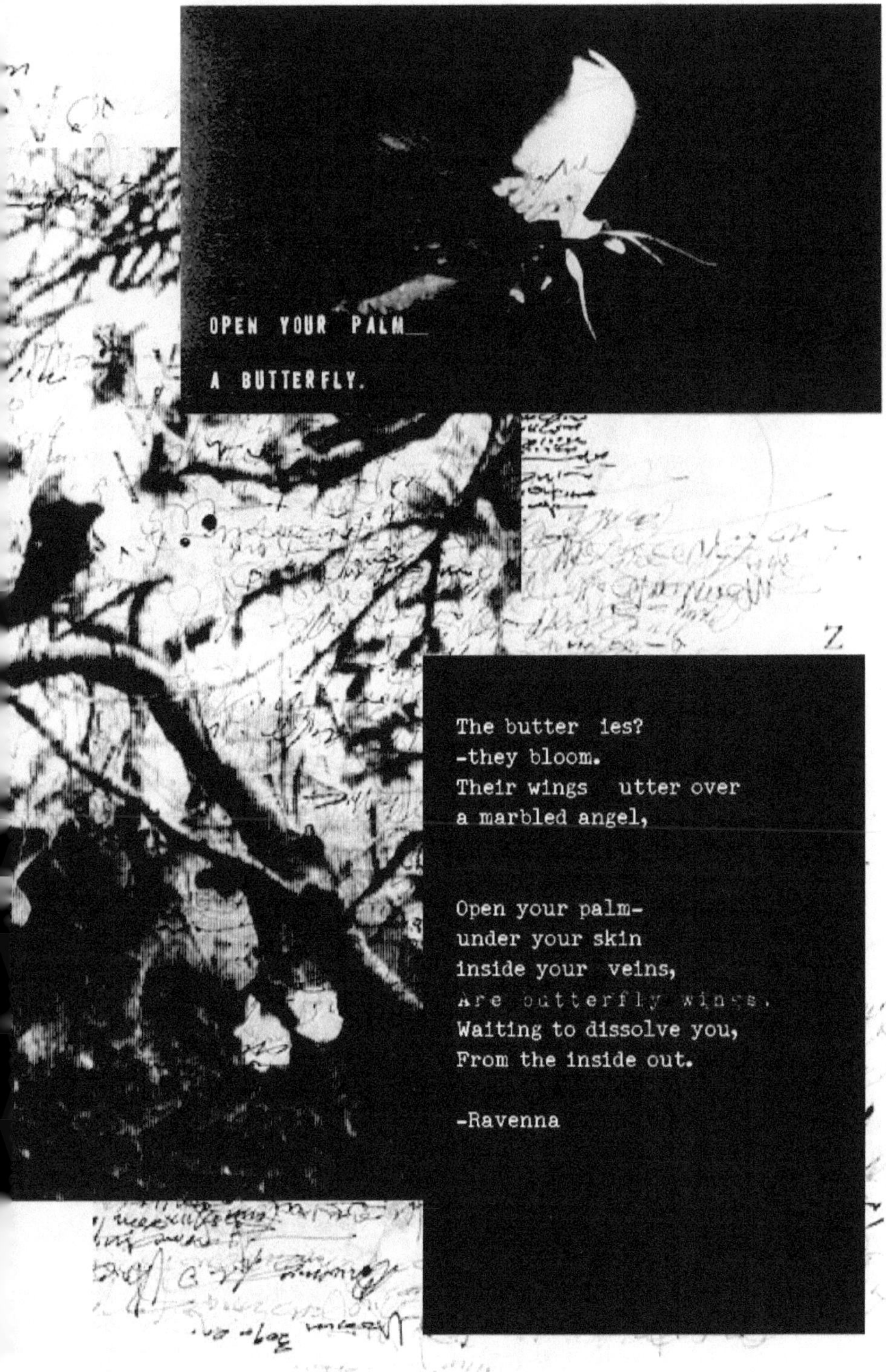

OPEN YOUR PALM_

A BUTTERFLY.

The butter ies?
-they bloom.
Their wings   utter over
a marbled angel,

Open your palm-
under your skin
inside your veins,
Are butterfly wings.
Waiting to dissolve you,
From the inside out.

-Ravenna

They threw belladonnas
Where the handle split her nape,
Her blood gorging
on copper-scented rain.
Sky-blue pastel—
a mockery
of daylight
She whispered:

"Forgive me."

Love was in his axe-
Niccolo

2025 : GRIEVING AMARYLLIS : MIRRORS AND SHADOWS

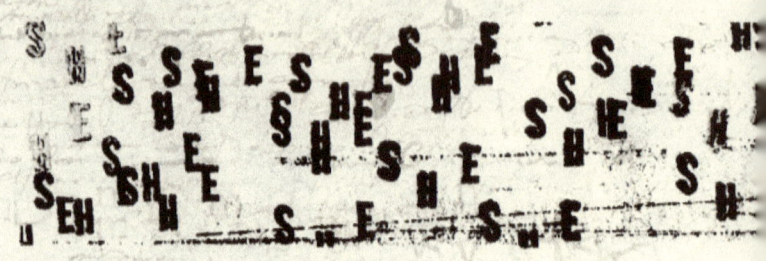

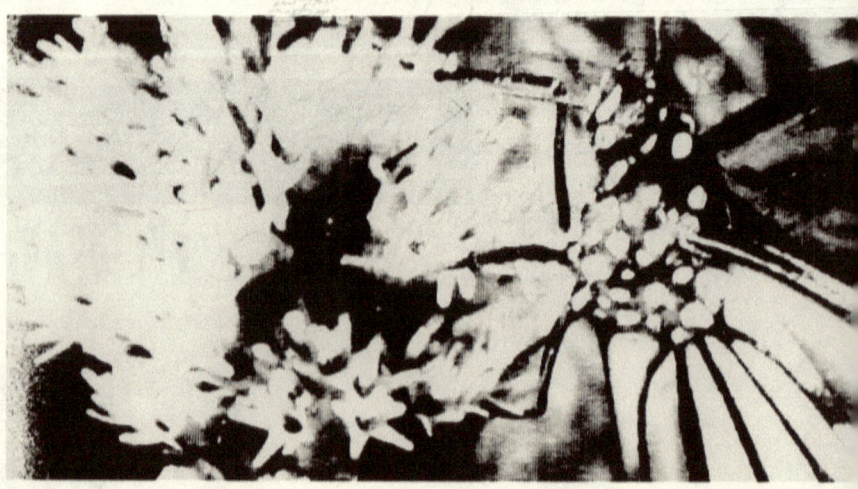

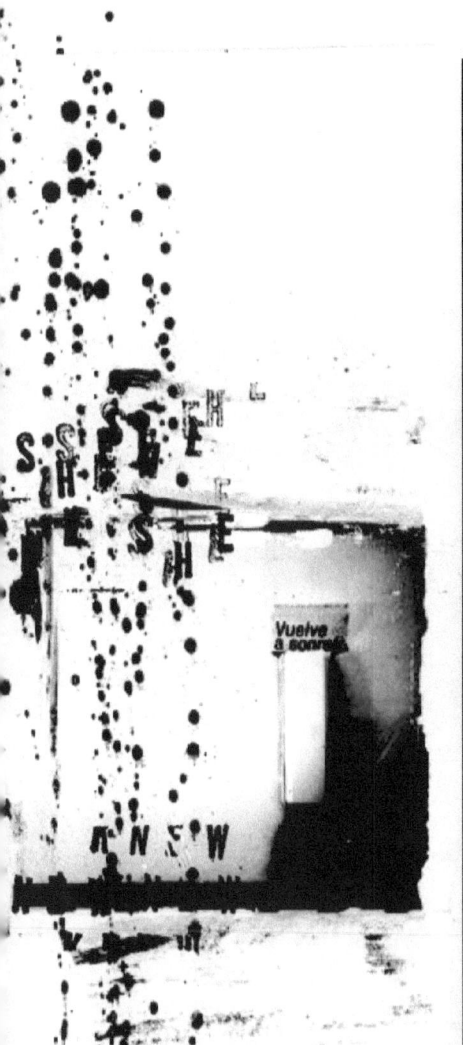

[Niccolo's note]

You were my vice and
my virtue,
The reason I was alive,
The reason to live,
The reason to die.
My everything, My only one
You were the one I dreamt;
About, Of, for...
At night.
The one who filled a hole
Inside my chest, I had no
idea how to fill.
You were THE REASON I WOKE
UP, In the morning, and THE
REASON I COULD SLEEP, at
night.
HEAVEN WAS WITH ME, BECAUSE
YOU WERE SO NEAR.
The reason I forgot hell for
a while, and it was all
because of you.
It was all for you,
Everything was all for you,
...
I LOVED YOU,
...
And I probably still do.

2025 : GRIEVING AMARYLLIS : MIRRORS AND SHADOWS

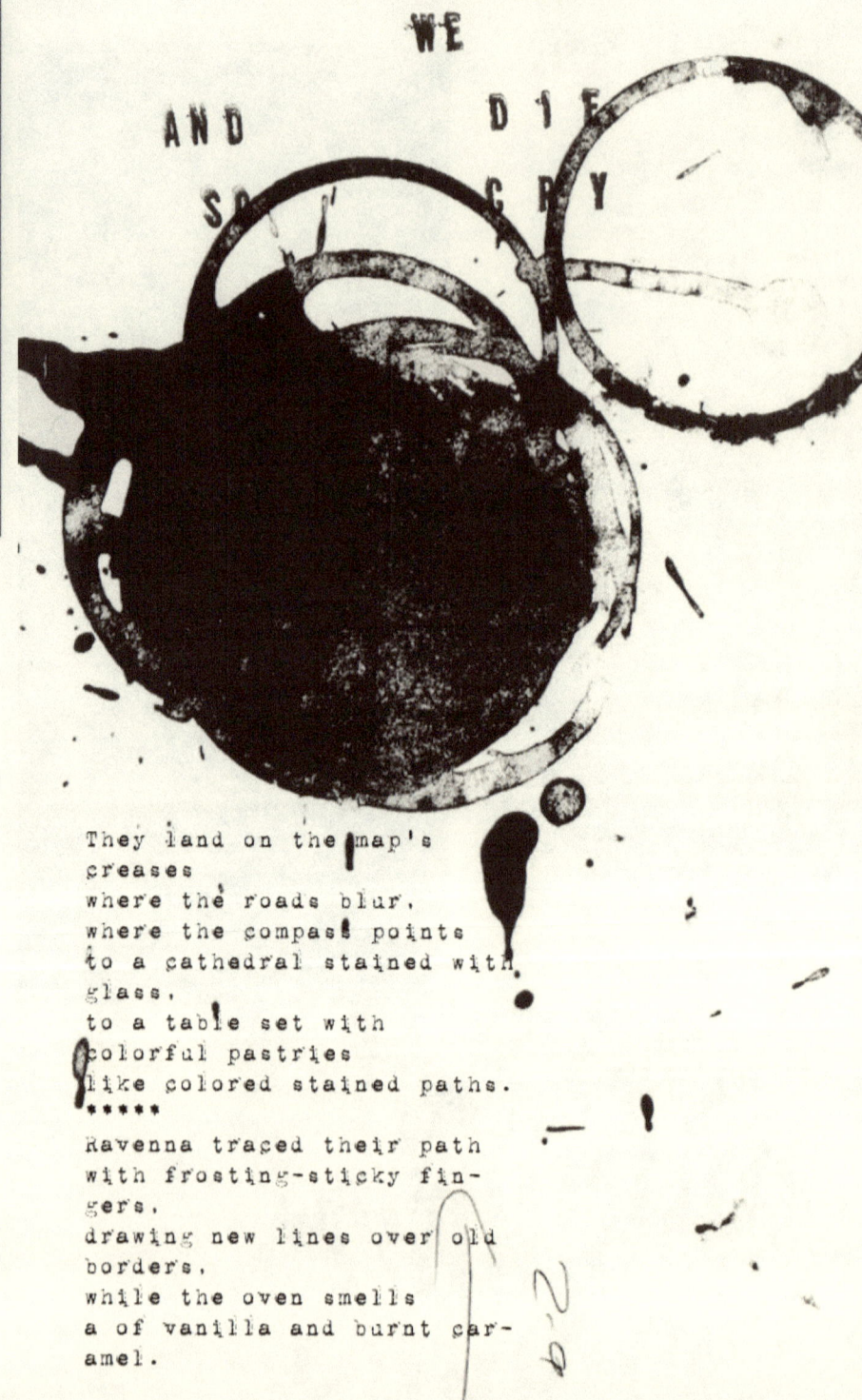

WE

AND DIE

SO CRY

They land on the map's
creases
where the roads blur,
where the compass points
to a cathedral stained with
glass,
to a table set with
colorful pastries
like colored stained paths.
* * * * *
Ravenna traced their path
with frosting-sticky fin-
gers,
drawing new lines over old
borders,
while the oven smells
a of vanilla and burnt car-
amel.

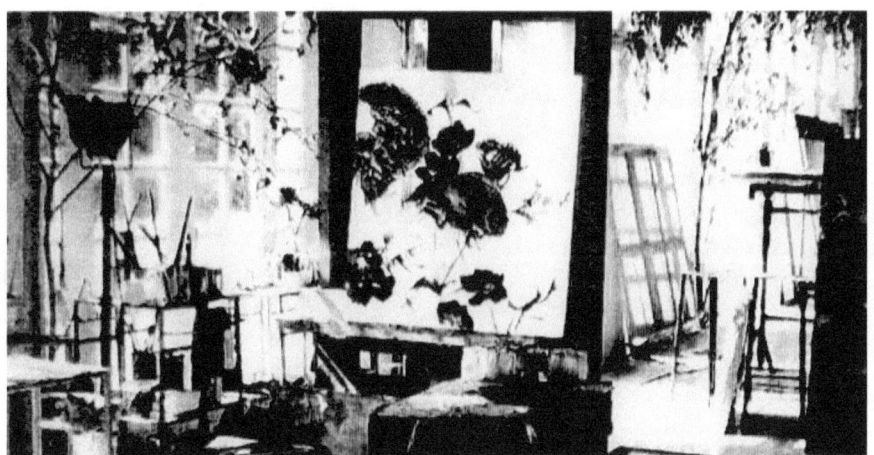

Ravenna's workshop- 2023

THE SOUL

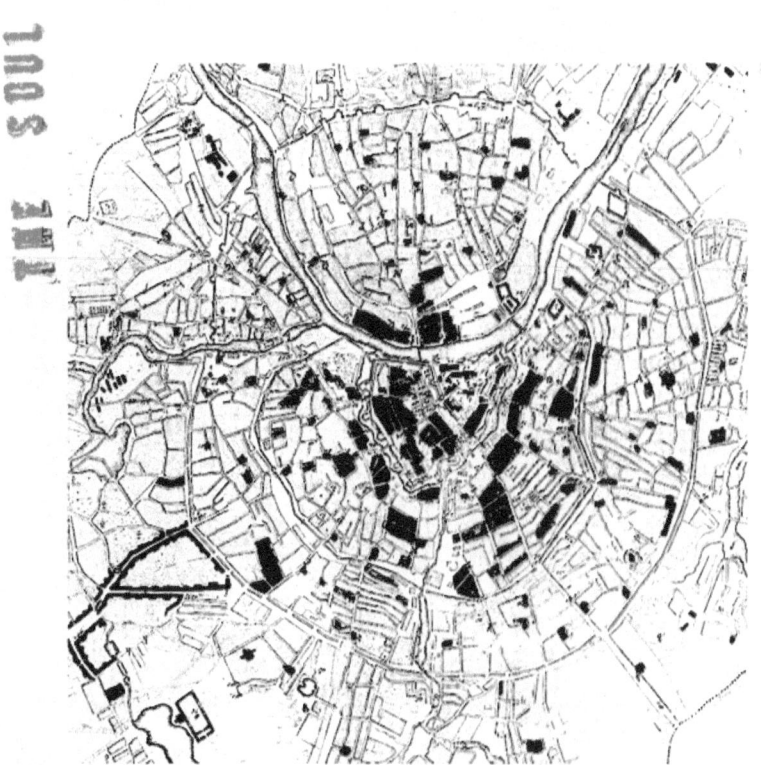

Map of City-A

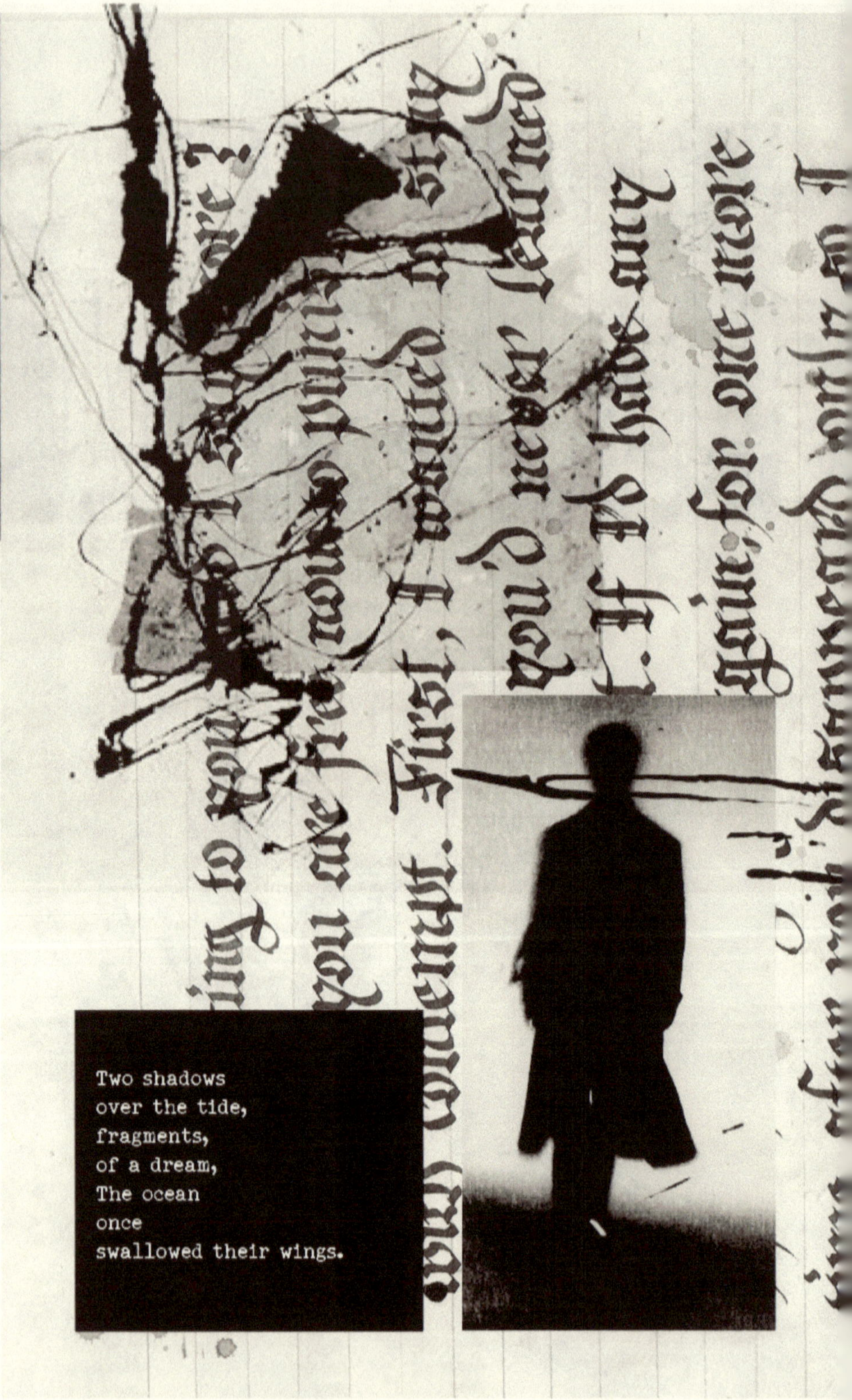

Two shadows
over the tide,
fragments,
of a dream,
The ocean
once
swallowed their wings.

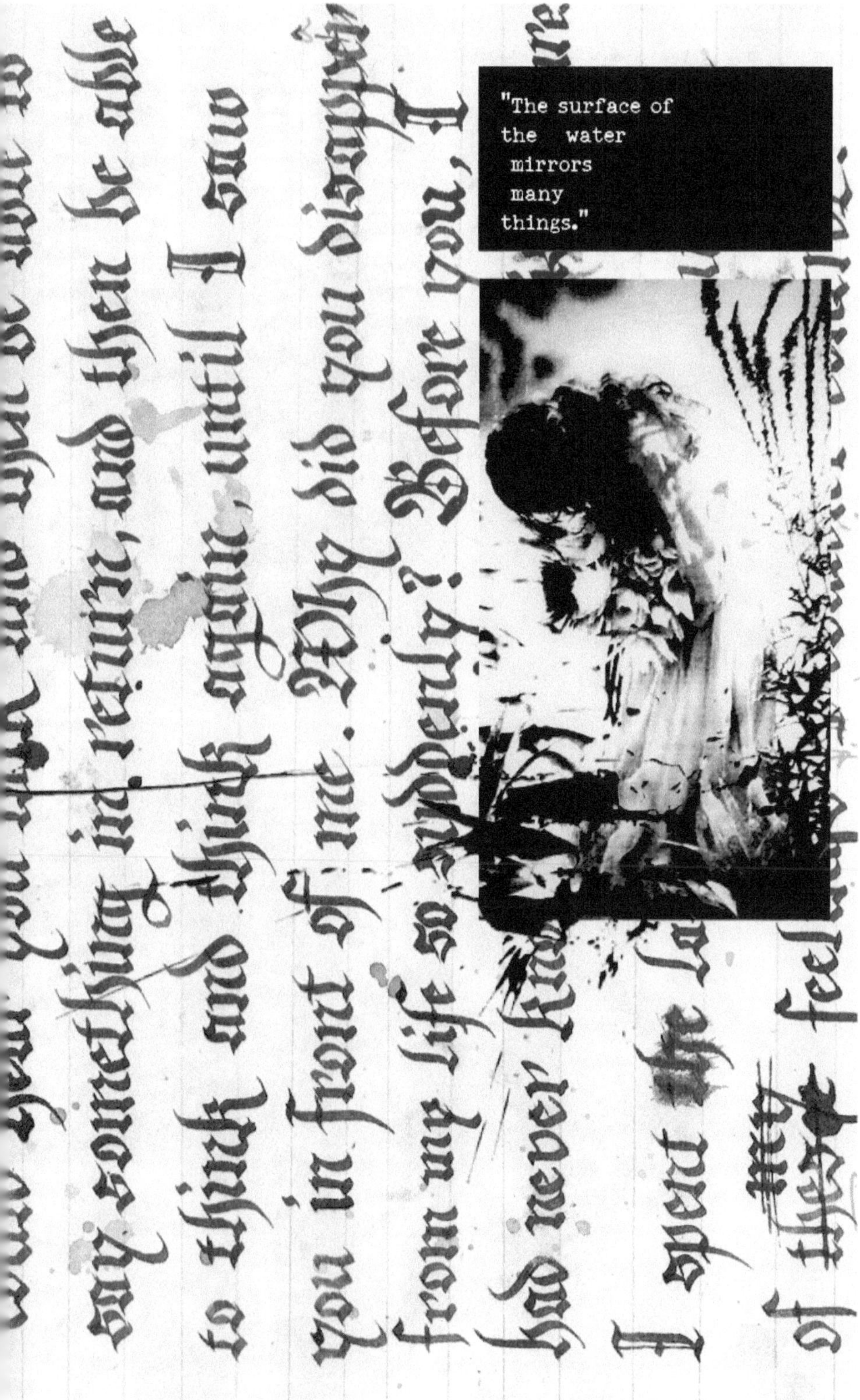

"The surface of
the   water
  mirrors
   many
  things."

say something, or return, and then be able to think and think again, until I saw you in front of me. Why did you disappear so suddenly? Before you, I from my life so suddenly had never knew I spent the la feel of these

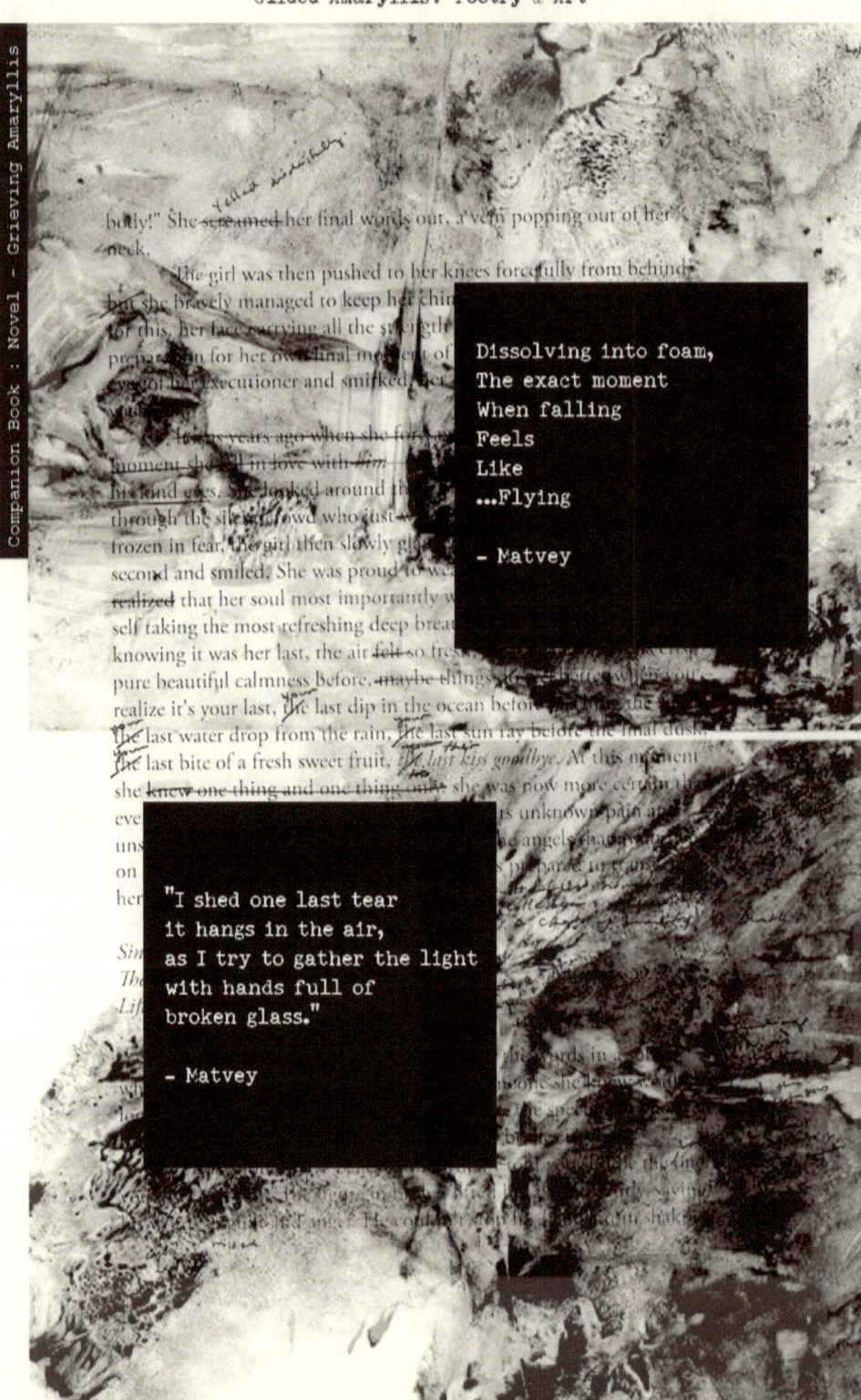

belly!" She screamed her final words out, a vein popping out of her neck.

The girl was then pushed to her knees forcefully from behind, but she bravely managed to keep her chin up for this, her face carrying all the strength in preparation for her own final moment of her executioner and smirked, her

It was years ago when she fell in love with *him* moment she fell in love with *him* his kind eyes. She looked around the through the silent crowd who just froze in fear. The girl then slowly gl second and smiled. She was proud to we realized that her soul most importantly w self taking the most refreshing deep brea knowing it was her last, the air felt so fres pure beautiful calmness before, maybe things realize it's your last, the last dip in the ocean befor the last water drop from the rain, the last sun ray before the final dusk, the last bite of a fresh sweet fruit, *the last kiss goodbye*. At this moment she knew one thing and one thing only, she was now more certain th eve unknown pain a uns the angels on s prepa her

Sin *The* *Lif*

```
Dissolving into foam,
The exact moment
When falling
Feels
Like
...Flying

- Matvey
```

```
"I shed one last tear
it hangs in the air,
as I try to gather the light
with hands full of
broken glass."

- Matvey
```

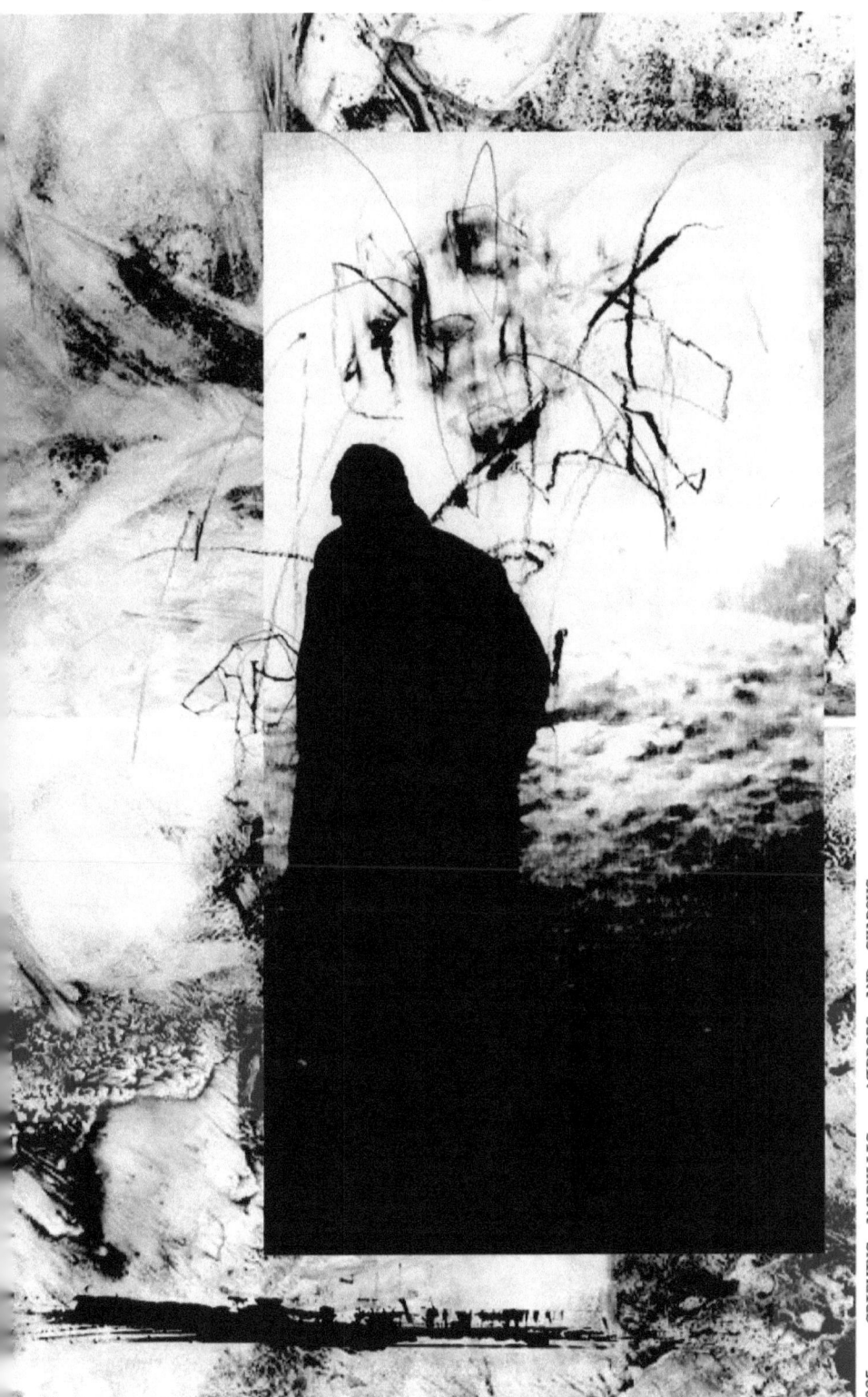

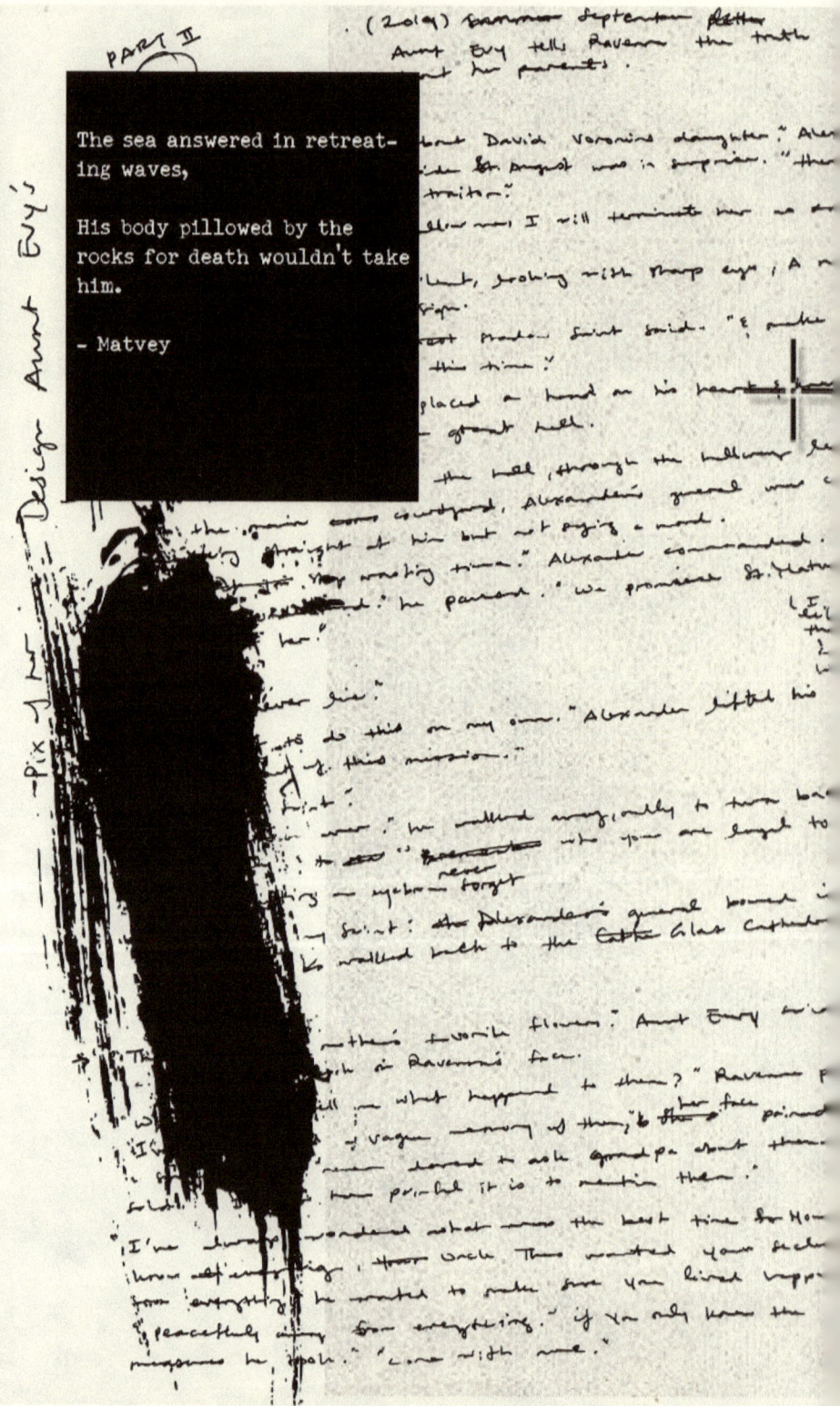

PART II

Fix Art - Design Aunt Evy's

> The sea answered in retreating waves,
>
> His body pillowed by the rocks for death wouldn't take him.
>
> - Matvey

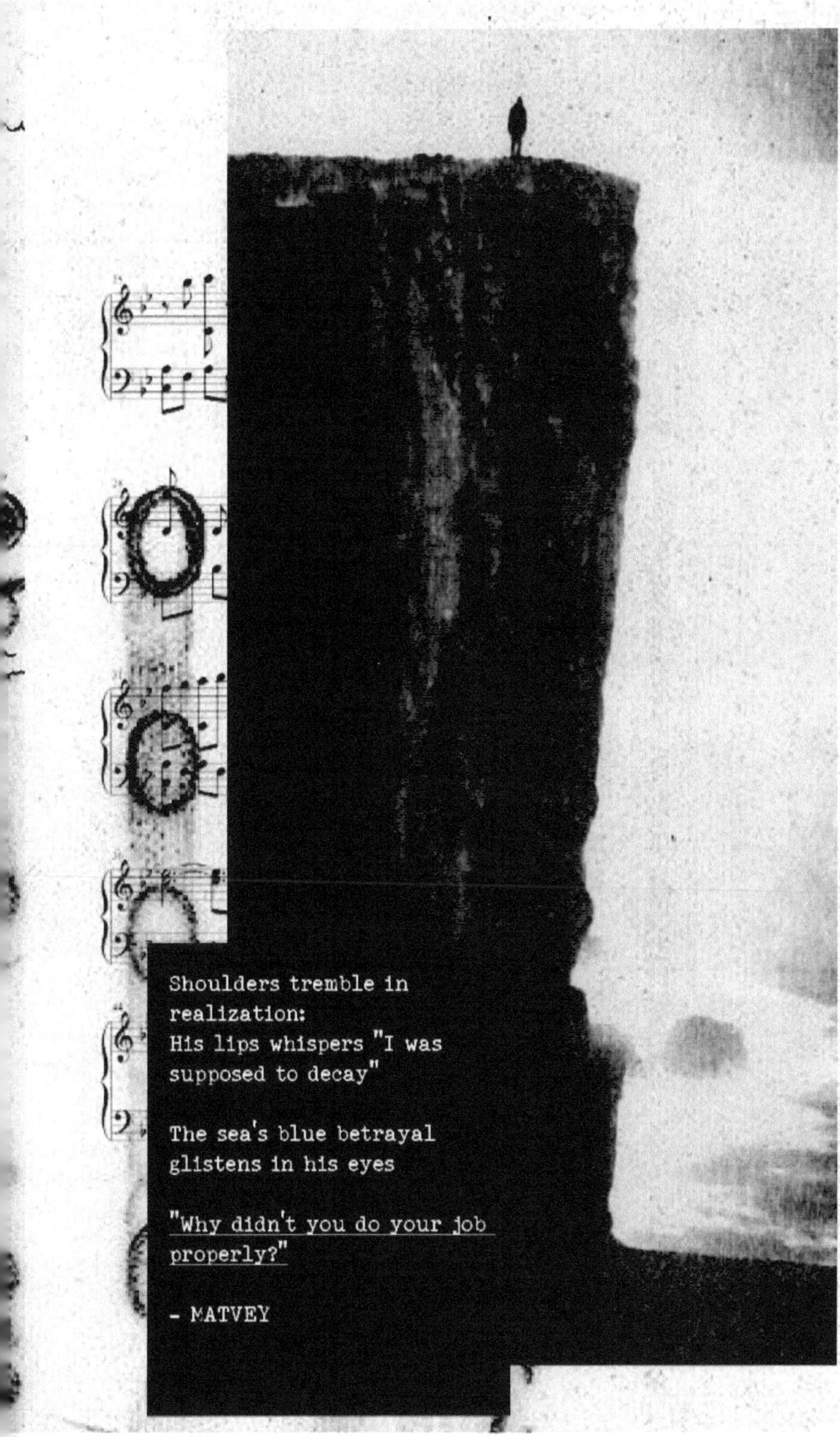

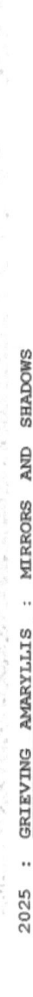

Shoulders tremble in
realization:
His lips whispers "I was
supposed to decay"

The sea's blue betrayal
glistens in his eyes

"Why didn't you do your job
properly?"

- MATVEY

2025 : GRIEVING AMARYLLIS : MIRRORS AND SHADOWS

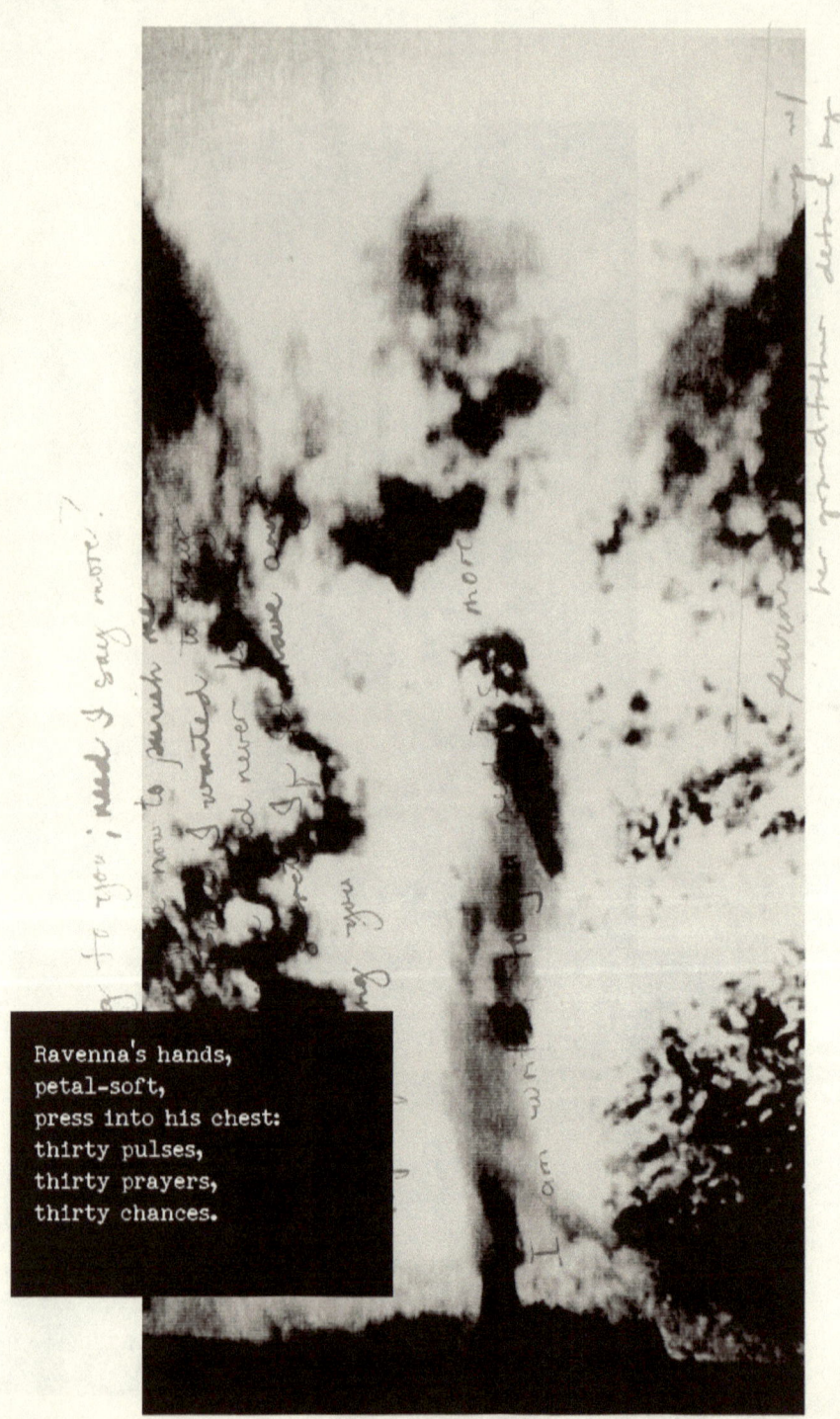

Ravenna's hands,
petal-soft,
press into his chest:
thirty pulses,
thirty prayers,
thirty chances.

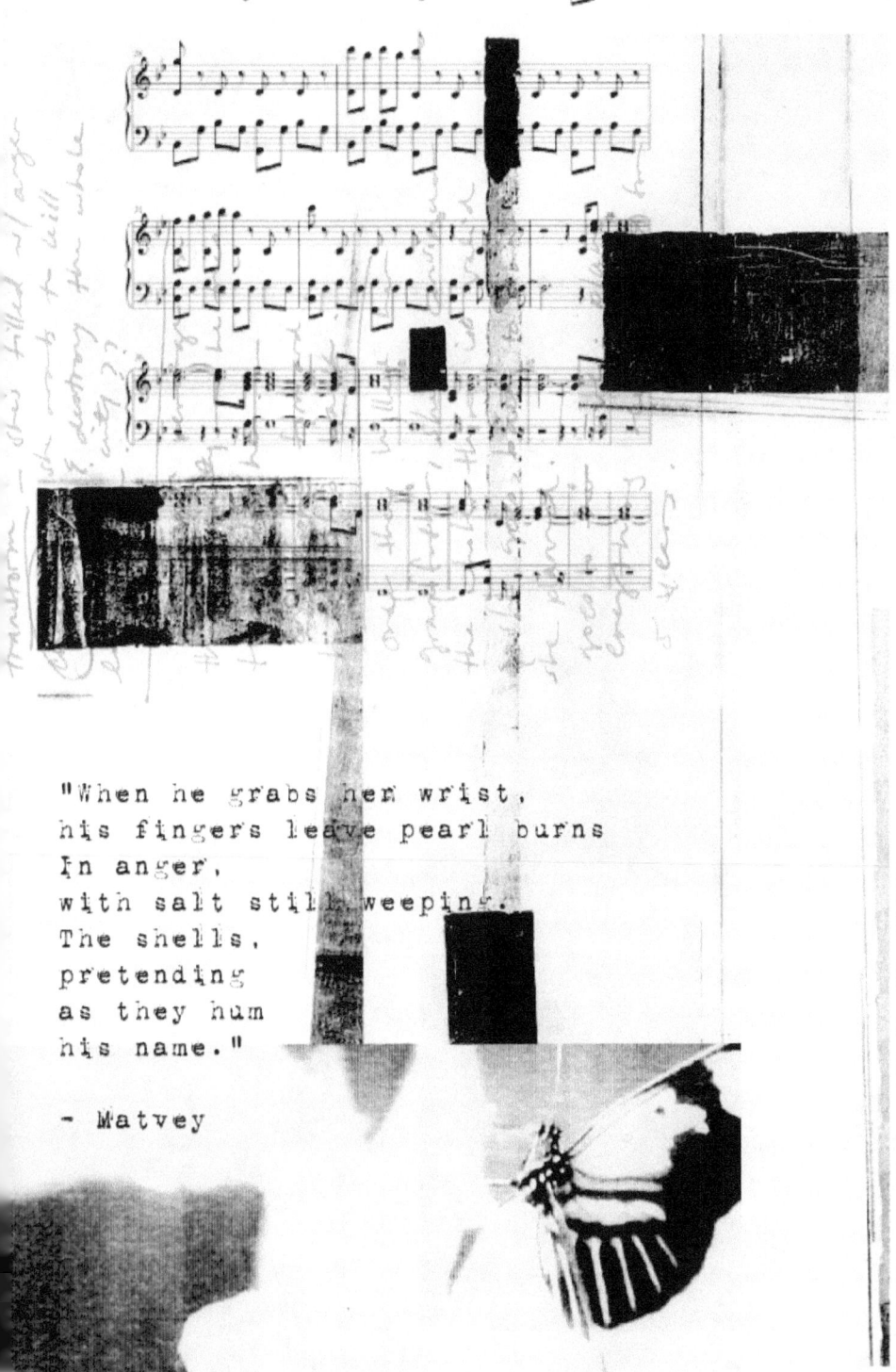

"When he grabs her wrist,
his fingers leave pearl burns
In anger,
with salt still weeping.
The shells,
pretending
as they hum
his name."

- Matvey

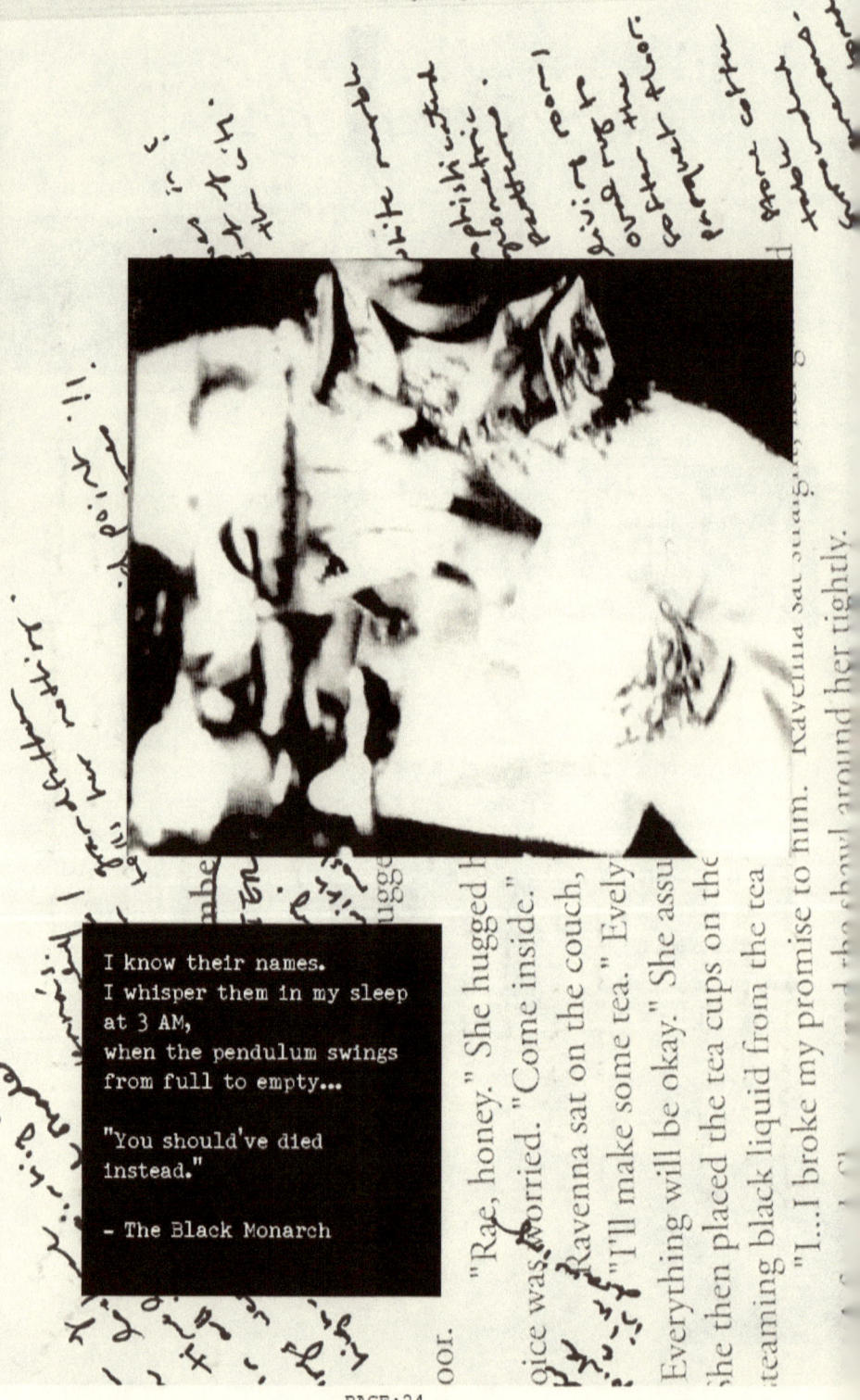

I know their names.
I whisper them in my sleep
at 3 AM,
when the pendulum swings
from full to empty...

"You should've died
instead."

- The Black Monarch

"Rae, honey." She hugged h
gice was worried. "Come inside."
Ravenna sat on the couch,
"I'll make some tea." Evely
Everything will be okay." She assu
she then placed the tea cups on the
teaming black liquid from the tea
"I...I broke my promise to him. Ravenna sat orange to her
the shawl around her tightly.

oor.

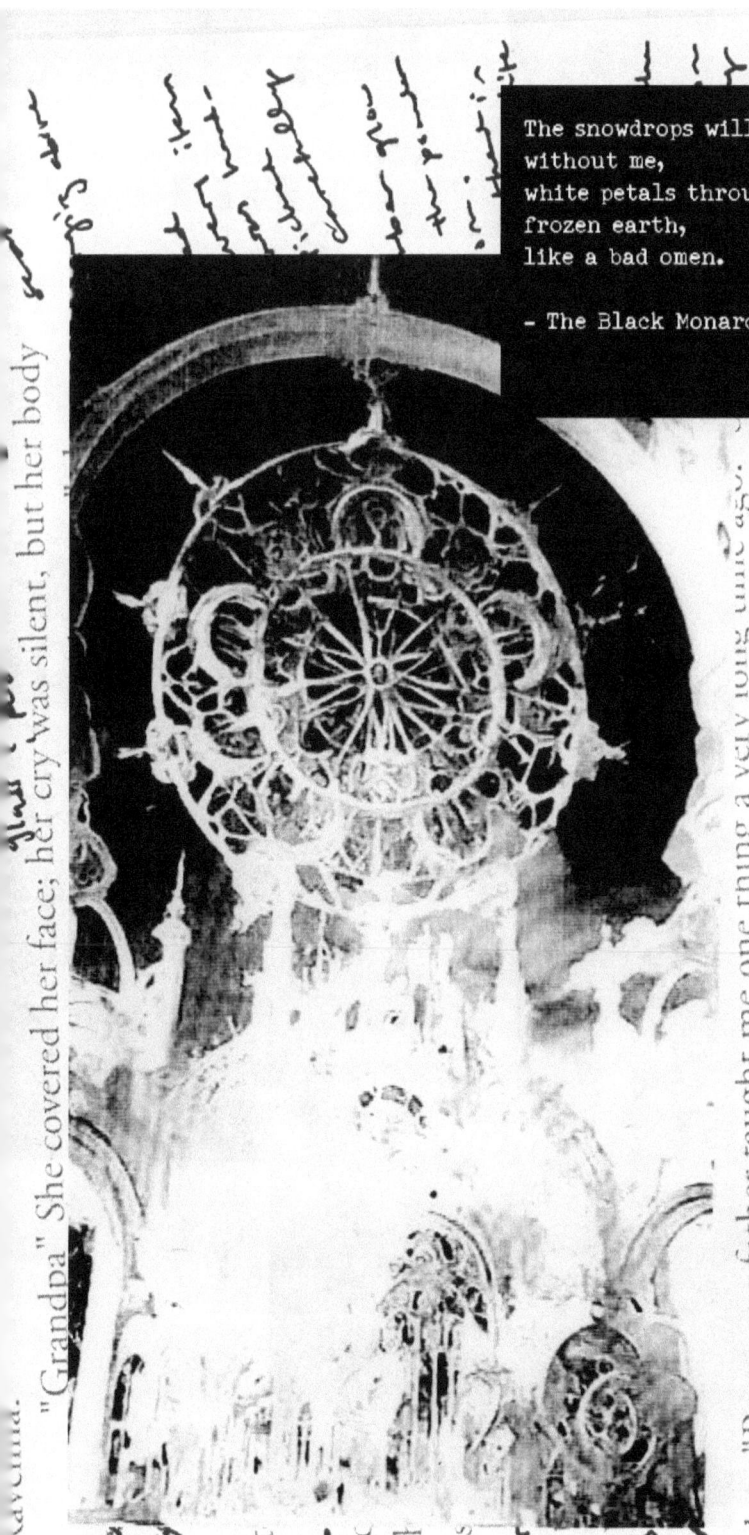

The snowdrops will bloom
without me,
white petals through
frozen earth,
like a bad omen.

- The Black Monarch

"Grandpa." She covered her face; her cry was silent, but her body

her. "Rae, your father taught me one thing a very long time ago."
smiled softly. "He taught me that there are only two types of people
this world." She looked at Ravenna firmly and held her hand. "Peo
blame everyone and everything for their misfortune and just give t
and begged her. "And those who fight

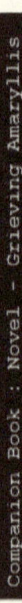

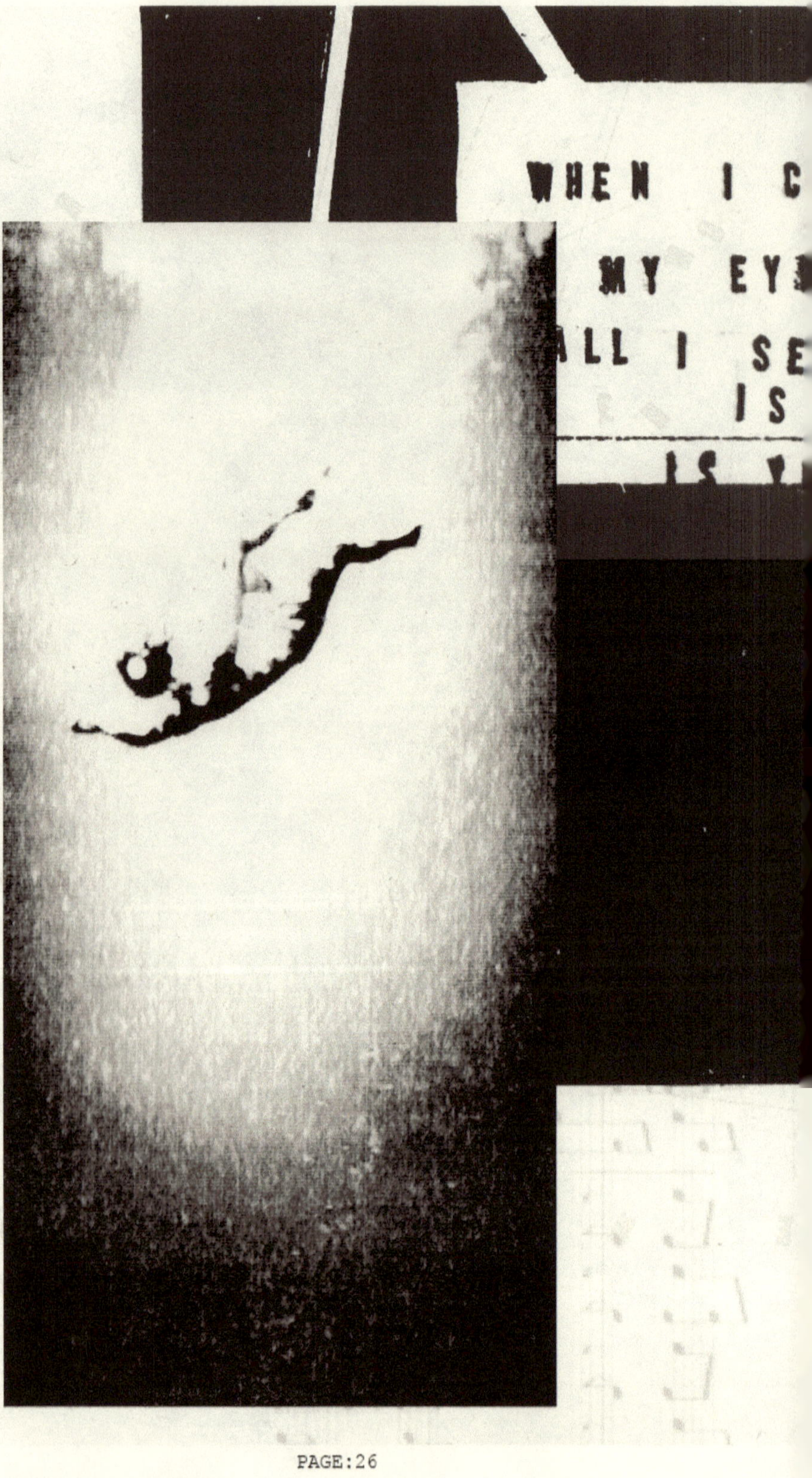

WHEN I C

MY EY

LL I SE

IS

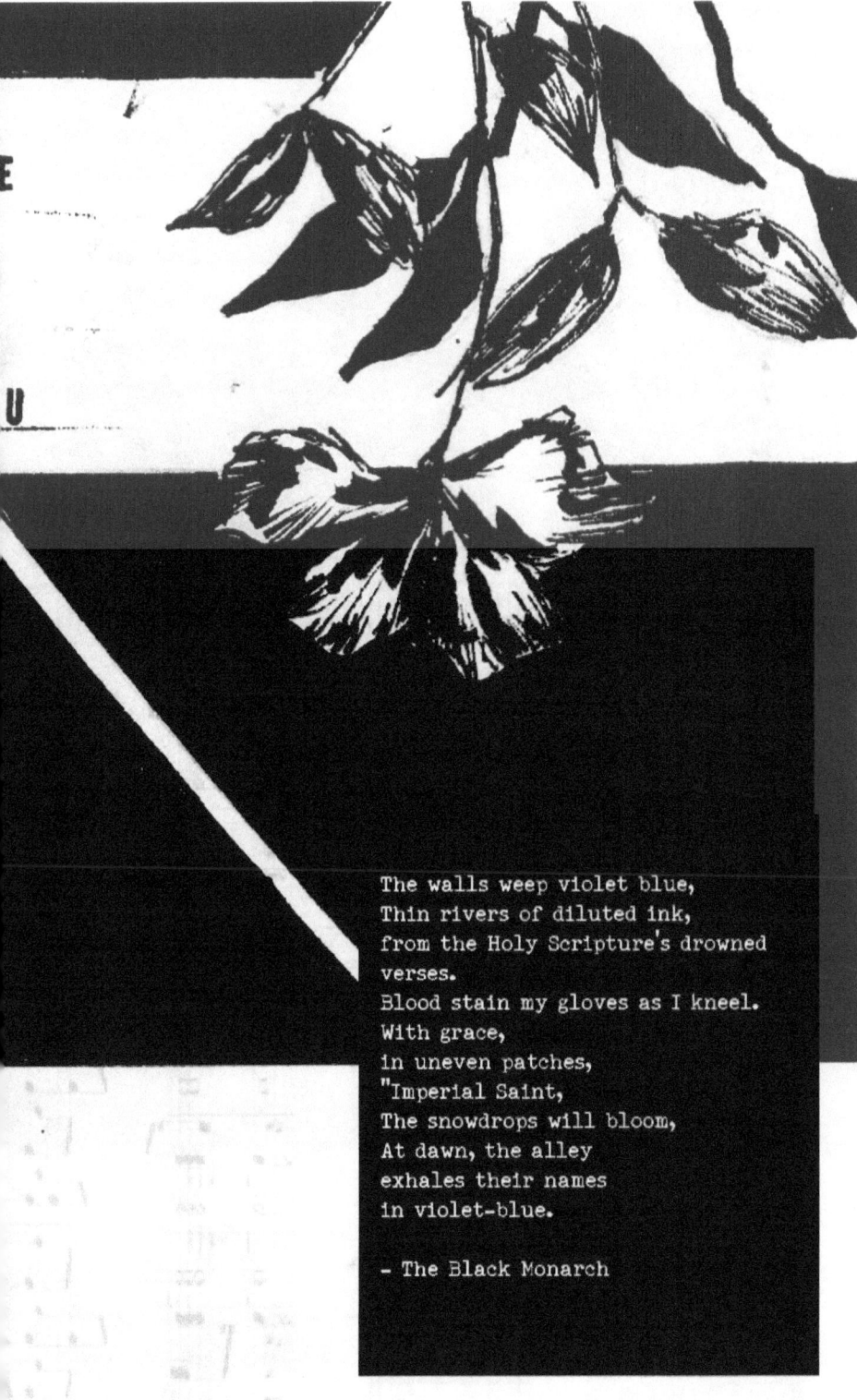

The walls weep violet blue,
Thin rivers of diluted ink,
from the Holy Scripture's drowned
verses.
Blood stain my gloves as I kneel.
With grace,
in uneven patches,
"Imperial Saint,
The snowdrops will bloom,
At dawn, the alley
exhales their names
in violet-blue.

- The Black Monarch

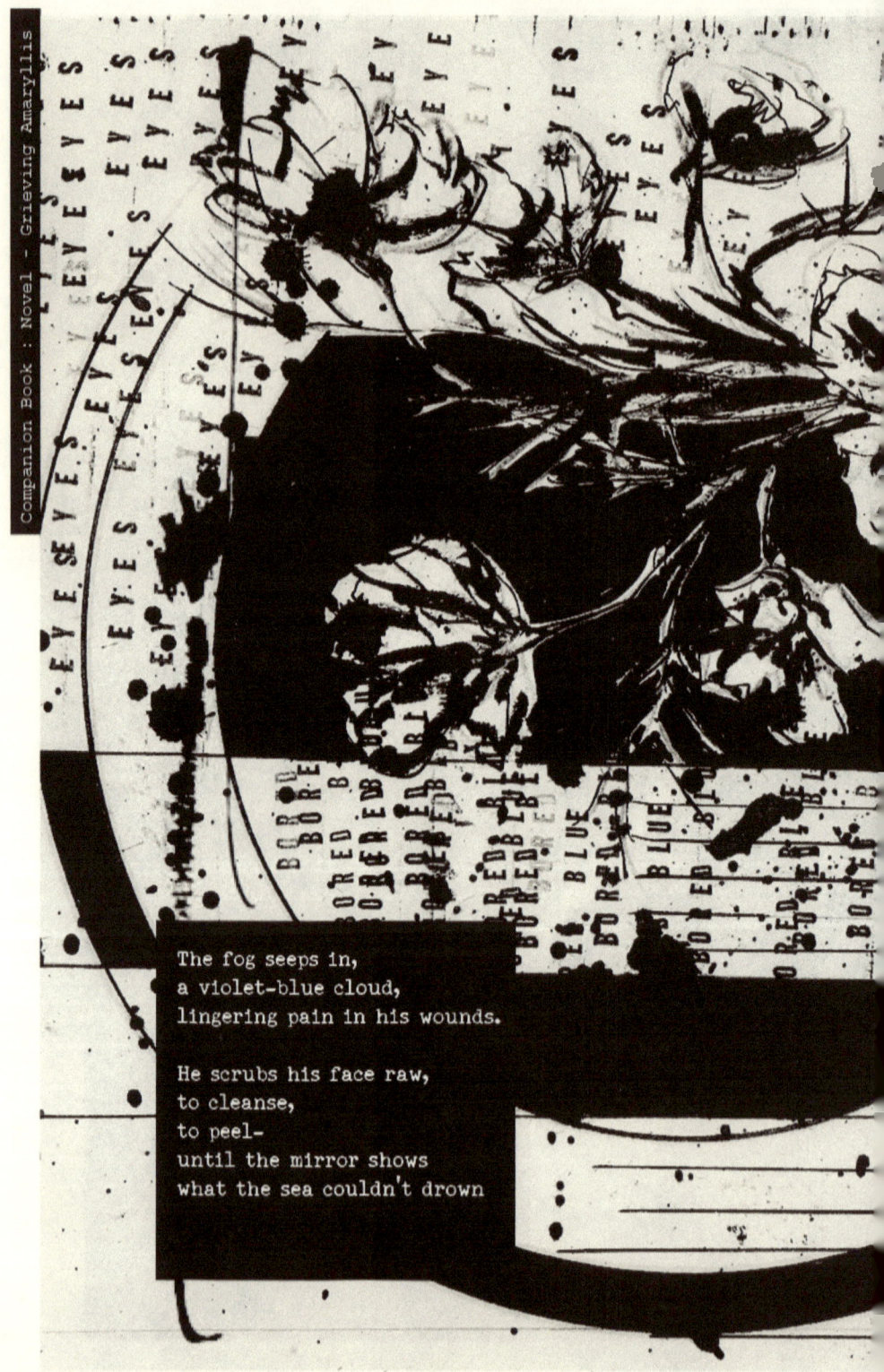

The fog seeps in,
a violet-blue cloud,
lingering pain in his wounds.

He scrubs his face raw,
to cleanse,
to peel—
until the mirror shows
what the sea couldn't drown

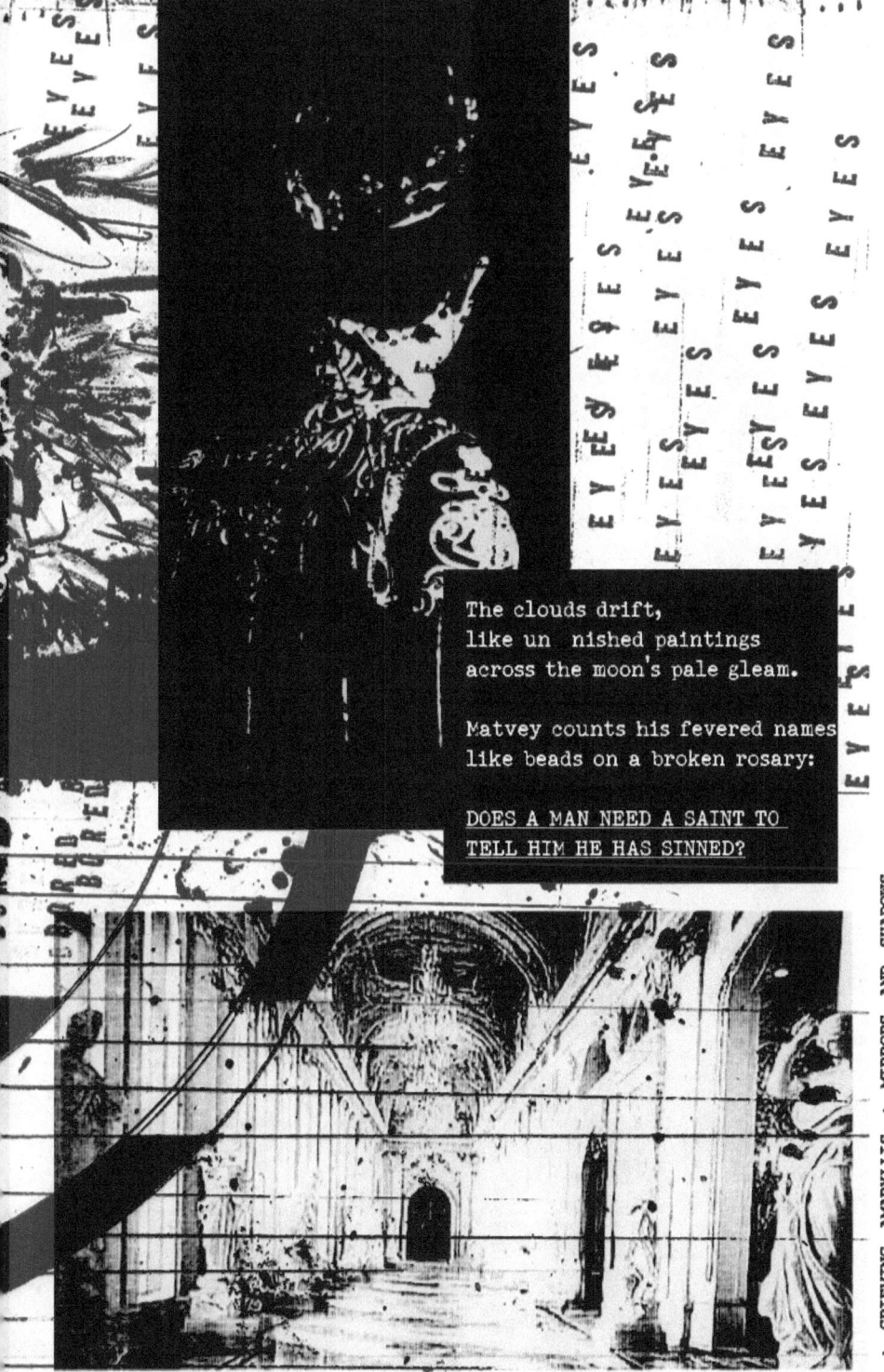

The clouds drift,
like un nished paintings
across the moon's pale gleam.

Matvey counts his fevered names
like beads on a broken rosary:

DOES A MAN NEED A SAINT TO
TELL HIM HE HAS SINNED?

2025 : GRIEVING AMARYLLIS : MIRRORS AND SHADOWS

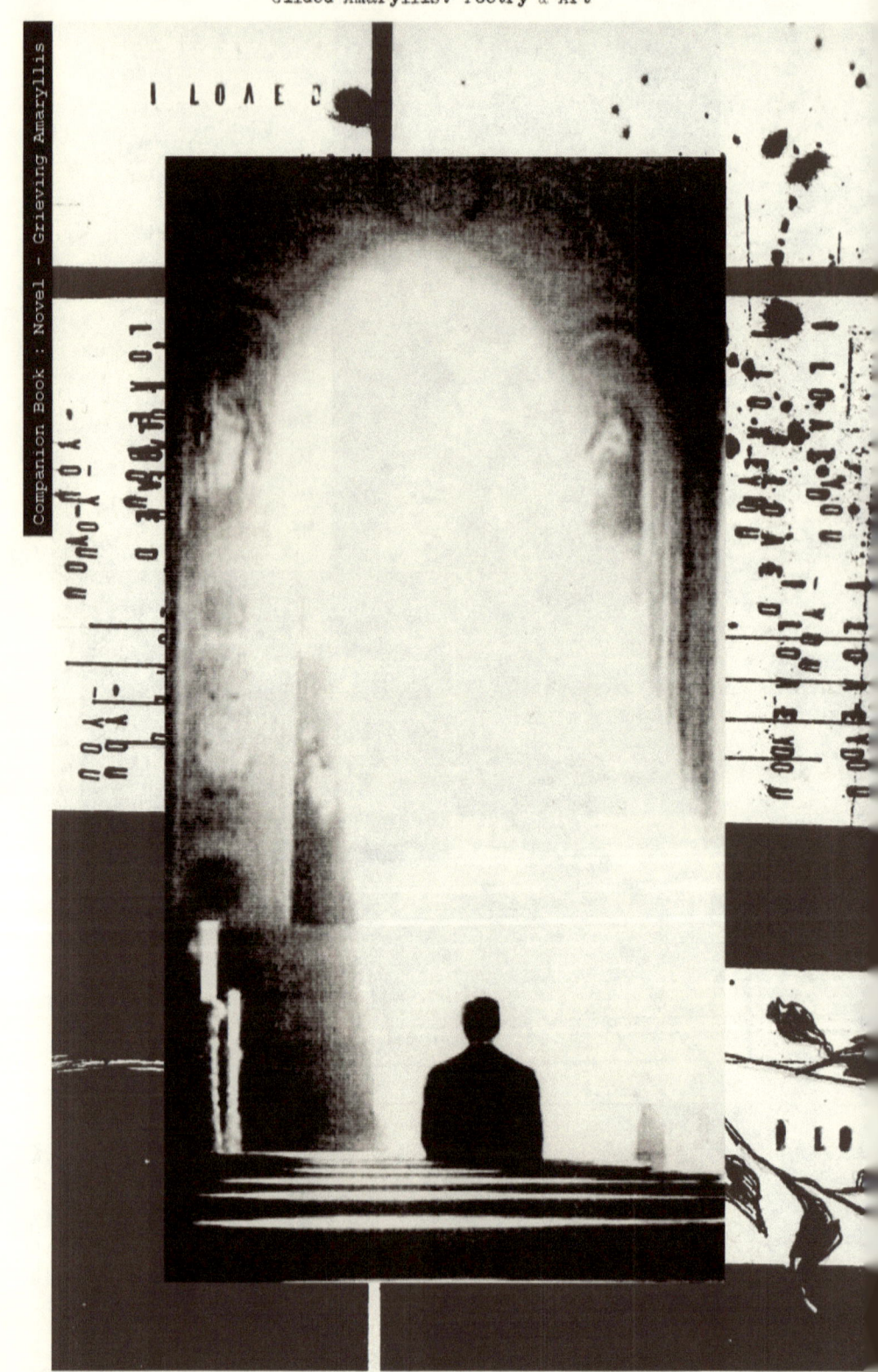

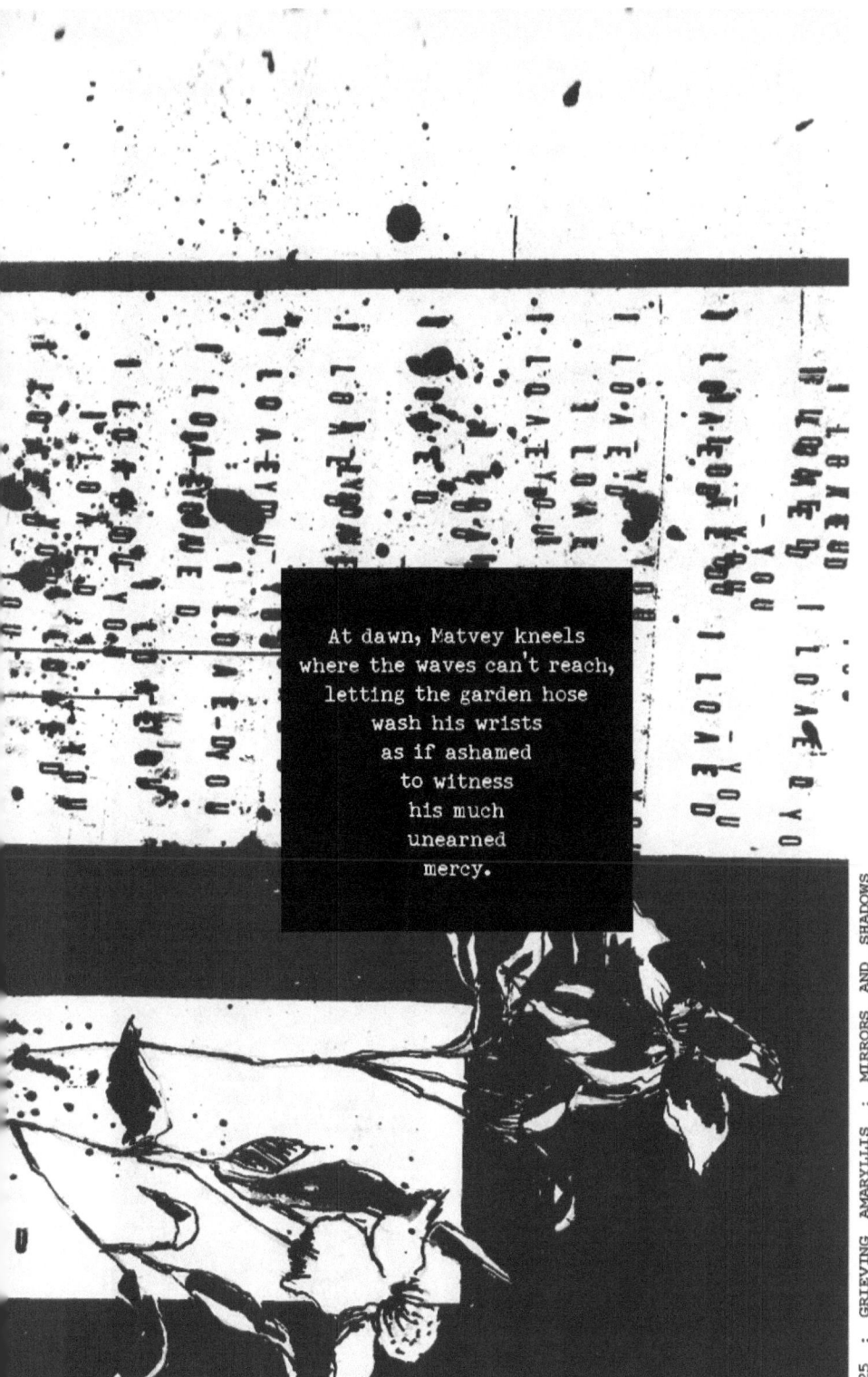

At dawn, Matvey kneels
where the waves can't reach,
letting the garden hose
wash his wrists
as if ashamed
to witness
his much
unearned
mercy.

Have you ever tried standing on a skyscraper? Half of your feet touching nothing but air? You look down and wonder, what's the point of it all? What if you never existed in the rst place?

The ones who love you - who claim to love you, whatever "love" means - will mourn you, for a few days if you're lucky, then they'll move on. Everyone moves on, everyone forgets. You've seen it happen before; the concept of death has stared at you countless times, promising to catch up someday.

The people you know talk about how much they care about those who die, but it's always too late. Everyone will eventually morph into a memory of dust, everything.

You look for something inside you, some kind of reason to live. You used to have a couple at some point, but now, for the life of you, you can't come up with a single thing. You search for some kind of feeling, an emotion, something, anything...

Everything.

Around you, a thunderstorm of biblical proportion ashes and cracks ll the entire sky. The air carries a hint of a burnt electric smell, a nebulous moonlight glimmers over distant buildings. The city in front of you tries its best to deceive you with its beauty and soft red lights, fading in and out from the top of structures.

Complete silence.

Melancholy overcomes you. It's not the rst time. You remember someone saying, "Those who jump are already dead before their bodies even hit the bottom." Their voices were judgmental, indifferent, and condescending. Your breathing somehow gets heavier, and you ask yourself a simple ques- tion: "Is it braver to jump and end it all, or live another day with this unbearable feeling of emptiness?" You look down, and the thought starts lingering deeper and deeper

in your bones, in your skin, burning in your veins. You shut your
eyes and take your nal deep breath, lifting your arms against the
rustling wind brushing over your body. They are your wings now: to
fall, not to y.

Your eyes open and you suddenly jerk backward. It takes you a
while to realize what you're looking at; a ood of memories ashes
before your eyes. You remember how you once believed that you'd
never seen anything so beautiful in your life. You burst into mad-
dening laughter and reach into your pocket for what you've kept
safe all these years. You look at its color and you feel the ten-
sion lighten from your face. "Things were simpler back then," you
whisper to yourself.

You feel a little dampness on your cheek. You look up at the
electri ed sky, but it's not raining. "How did this happen?" Your
eyebrows draw down and you smile, staring at your wet ngers.

Your eyes shift back to the gure marking random lines on the
skyscraper ahead of you. Your eyes squint, trying to make some
sense of it. "What do these lines mean?" you think mutedly. You can
hear your heartbeat again. You step down and whisper a prayer of
gratitude to God,

"She's alive."

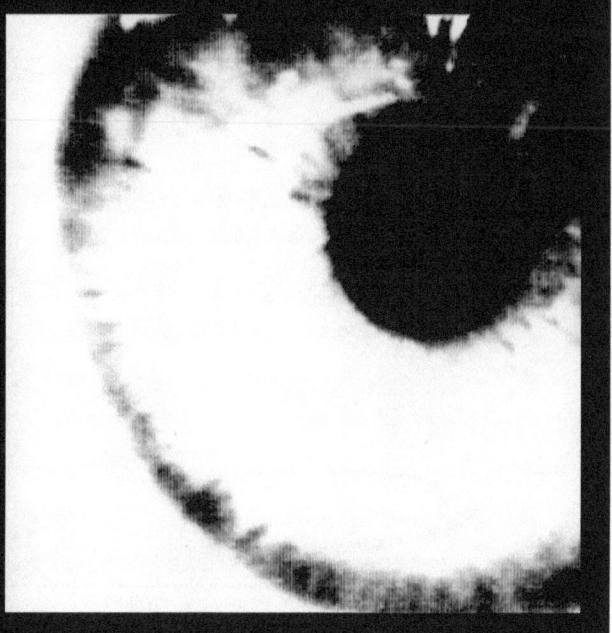

"City Veins"

The map whispers beneath her   ngers,
its inked arteries pulsing
where her touch graze the Glass Temple's key.

Cities are born:
from concrete,
from a child's whisper of
"I want everyone
to be happy."

The Organs of City-A:
The Lungs (Gardens):
Staircases leading nowhere
Books bleeding ink like the riverbanks.

Years later,
Ravenna kneels
in the Temple's aisle,
praying for God's forgiveness,
her green ribbon fragments
was given back to her,
by the love of her life.

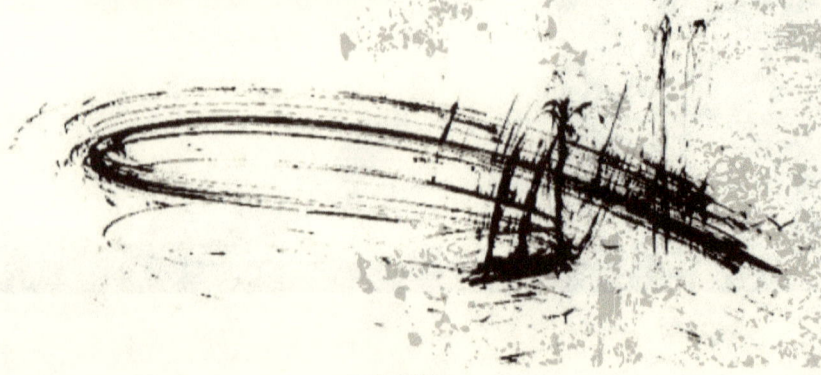

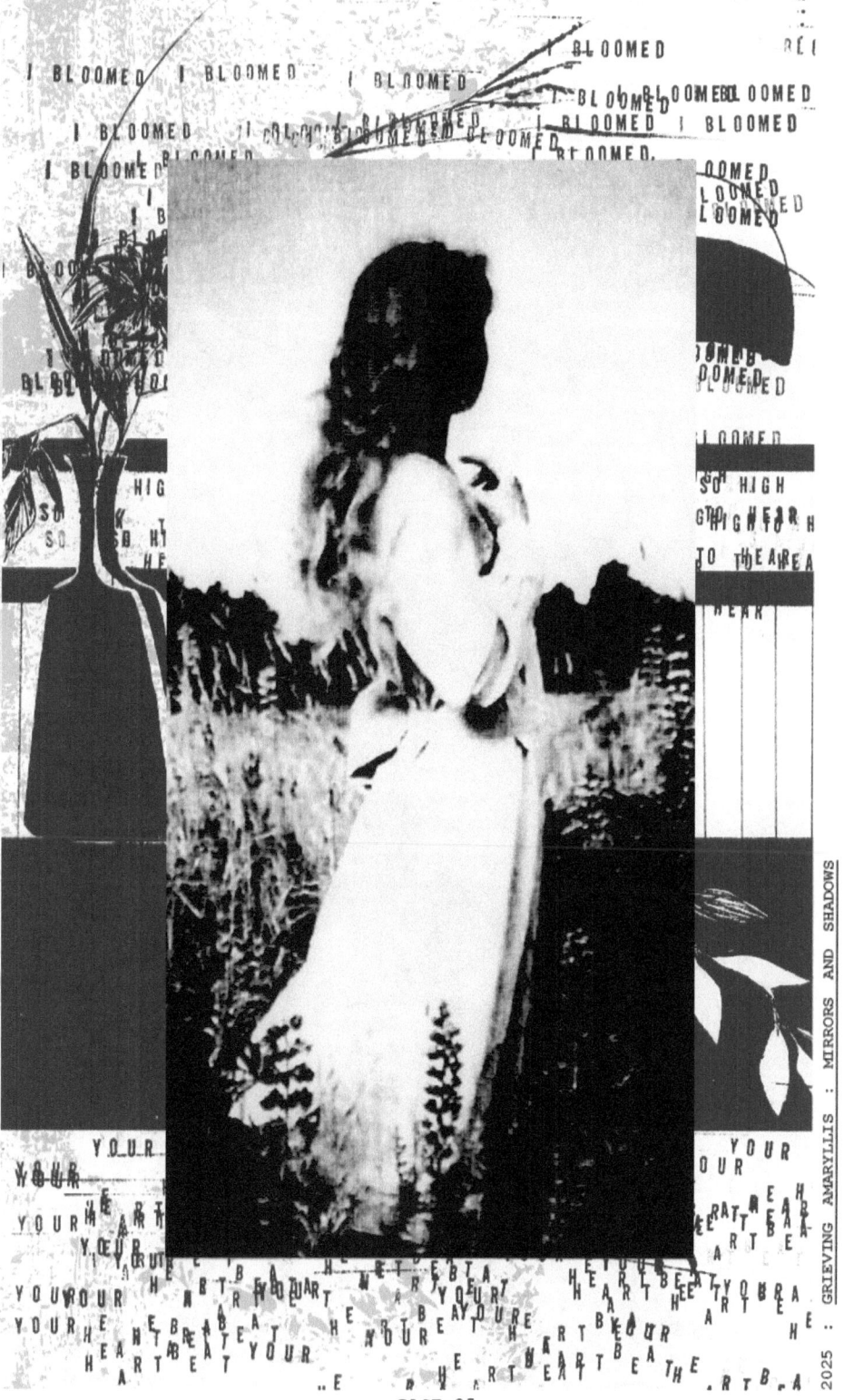

2025 : GRIEVING AMARYLLIS : MIRRORS AND SHADOWS

Companion Book : Novel - Grieving Amaryllis

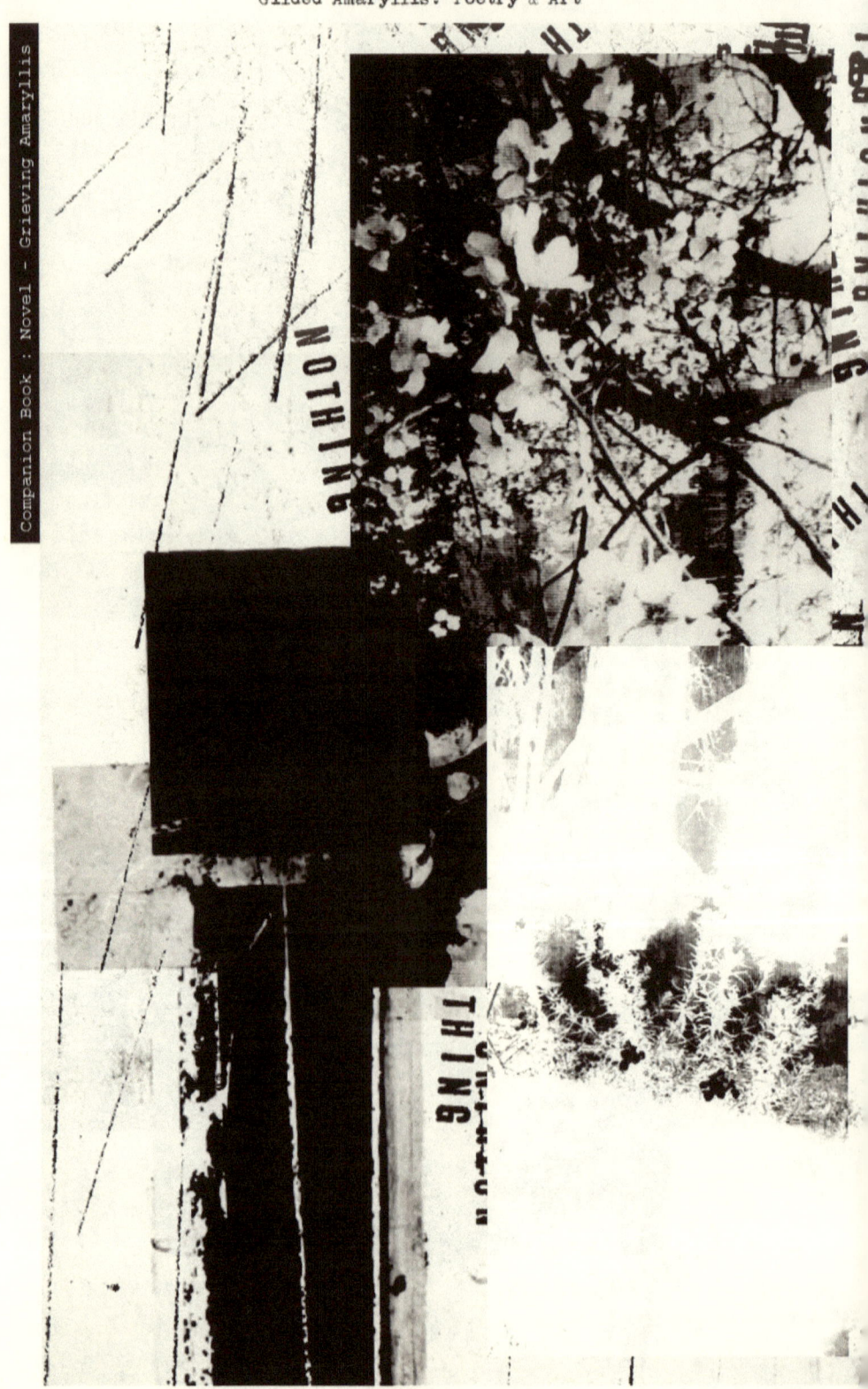

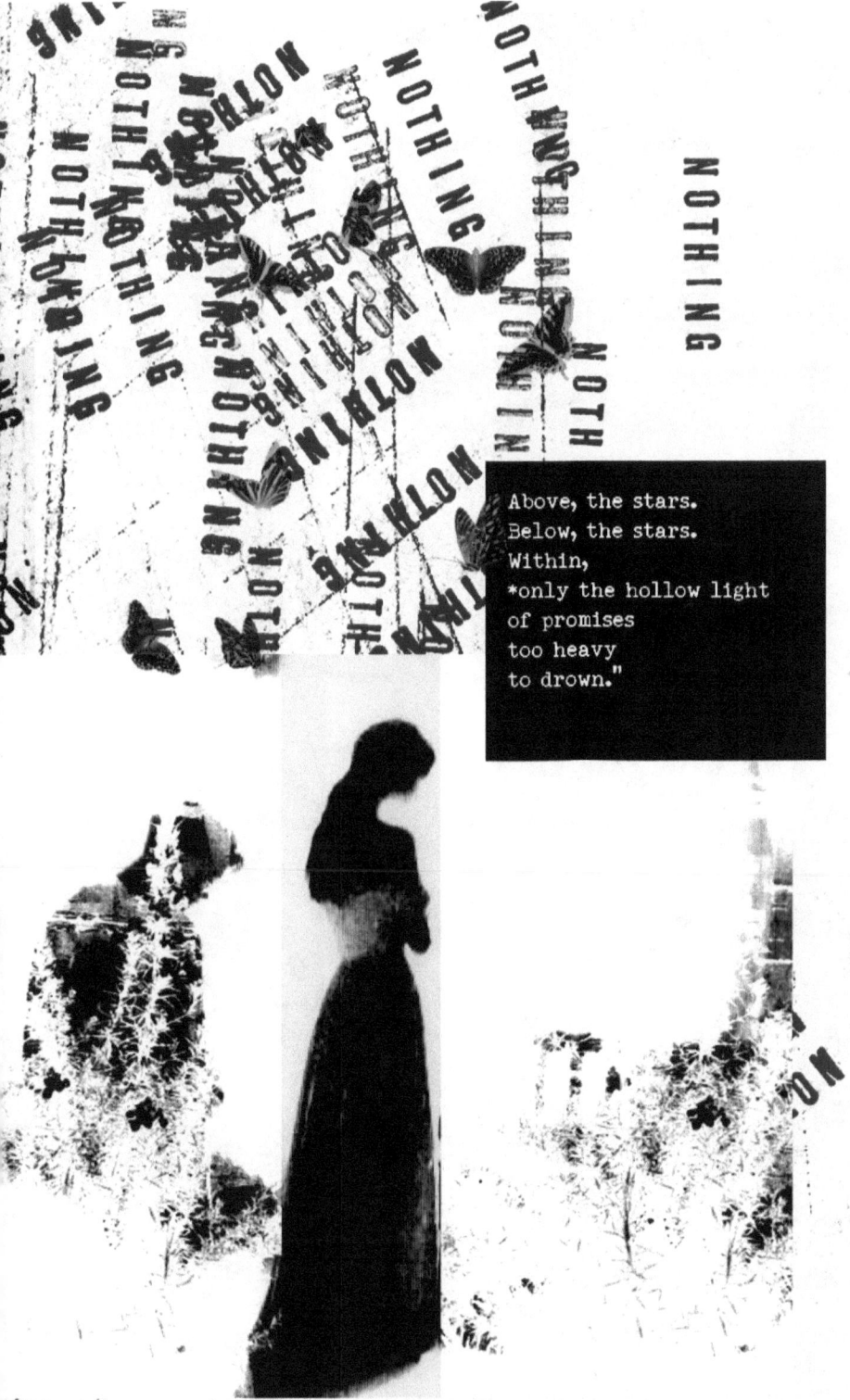

Above, the stars.
Below, the stars.
Within,
*only the hollow light
of promises
too heavy
to drown."

2025 : GRIEVING AMARYLLIS : MIRRORS AND SHADOWS

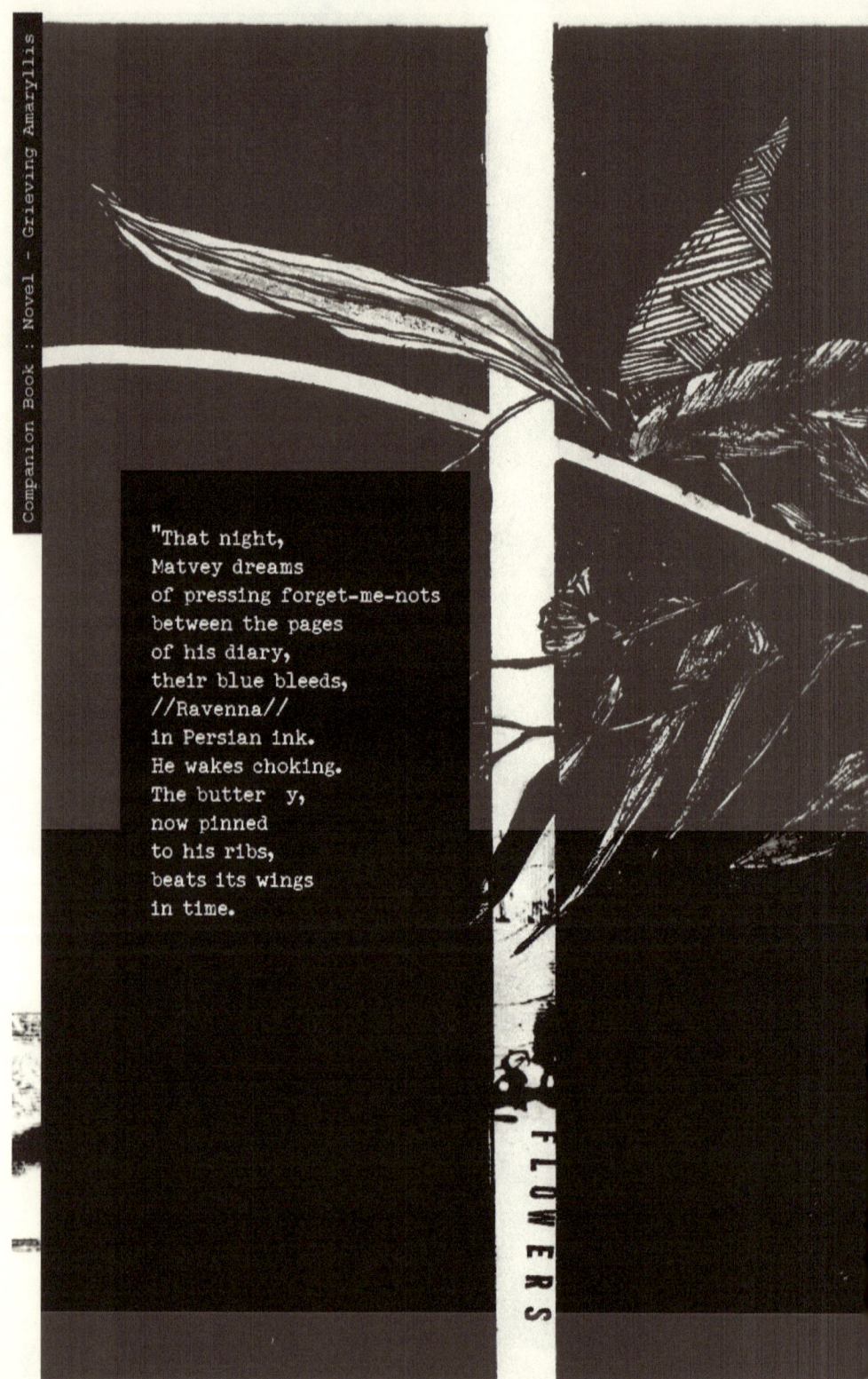

"That night,
Matvey dreams
of pressing forget-me-nots
between the pages
of his diary,
their blue bleeds,
//Ravenna//
in Persian ink.
He wakes choking.
The butter y,
now pinned
to his ribs,
beats its wings
in time.

FLOWERS

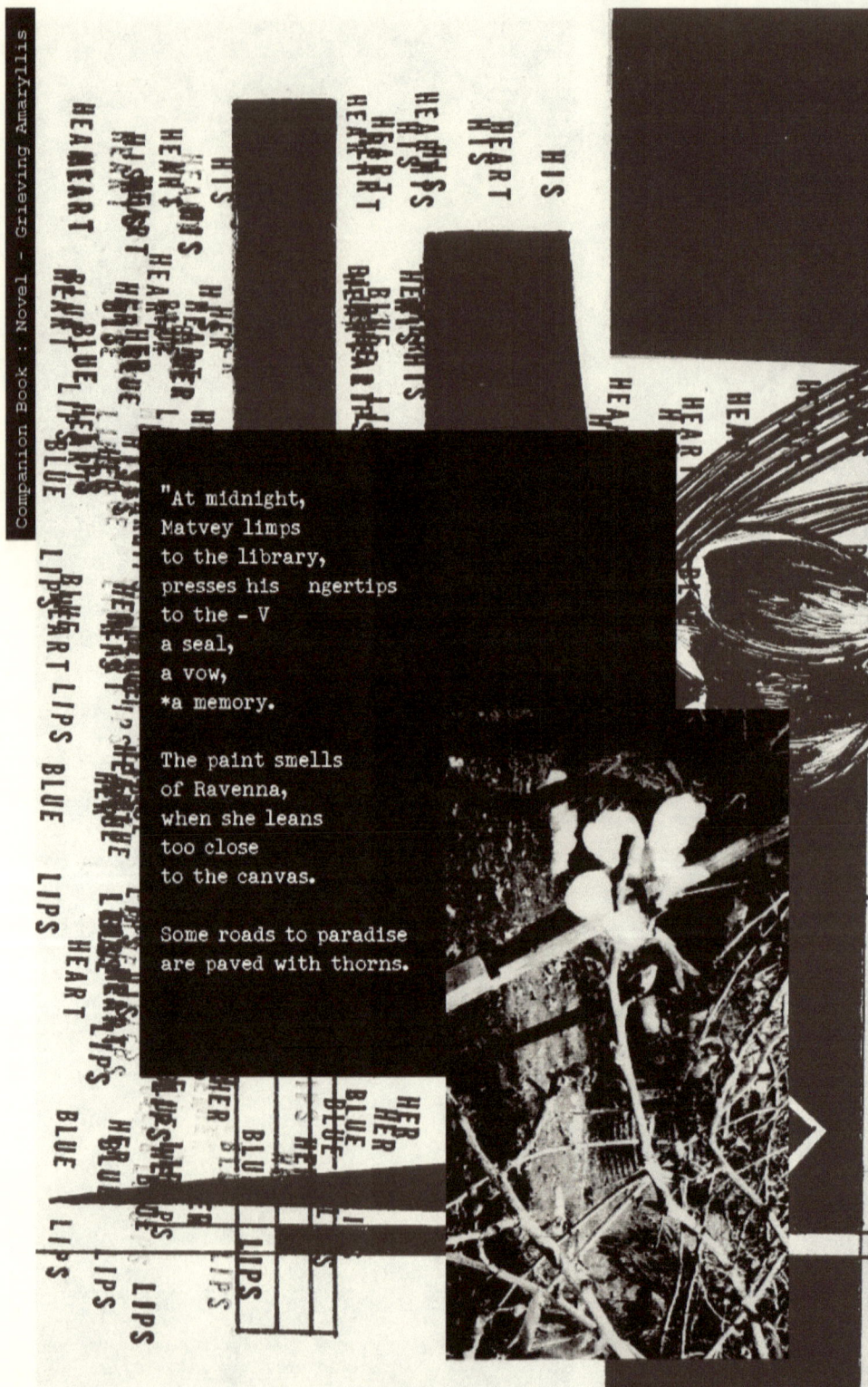

"At midnight,
Matvey limps
to the library,
presses his ngertips
to the - V
a seal,
a vow,
*a memory.

The paint smells
of Ravenna,
when she leans
too close
to the canvas.

Some roads to paradise
are paved with thorns.

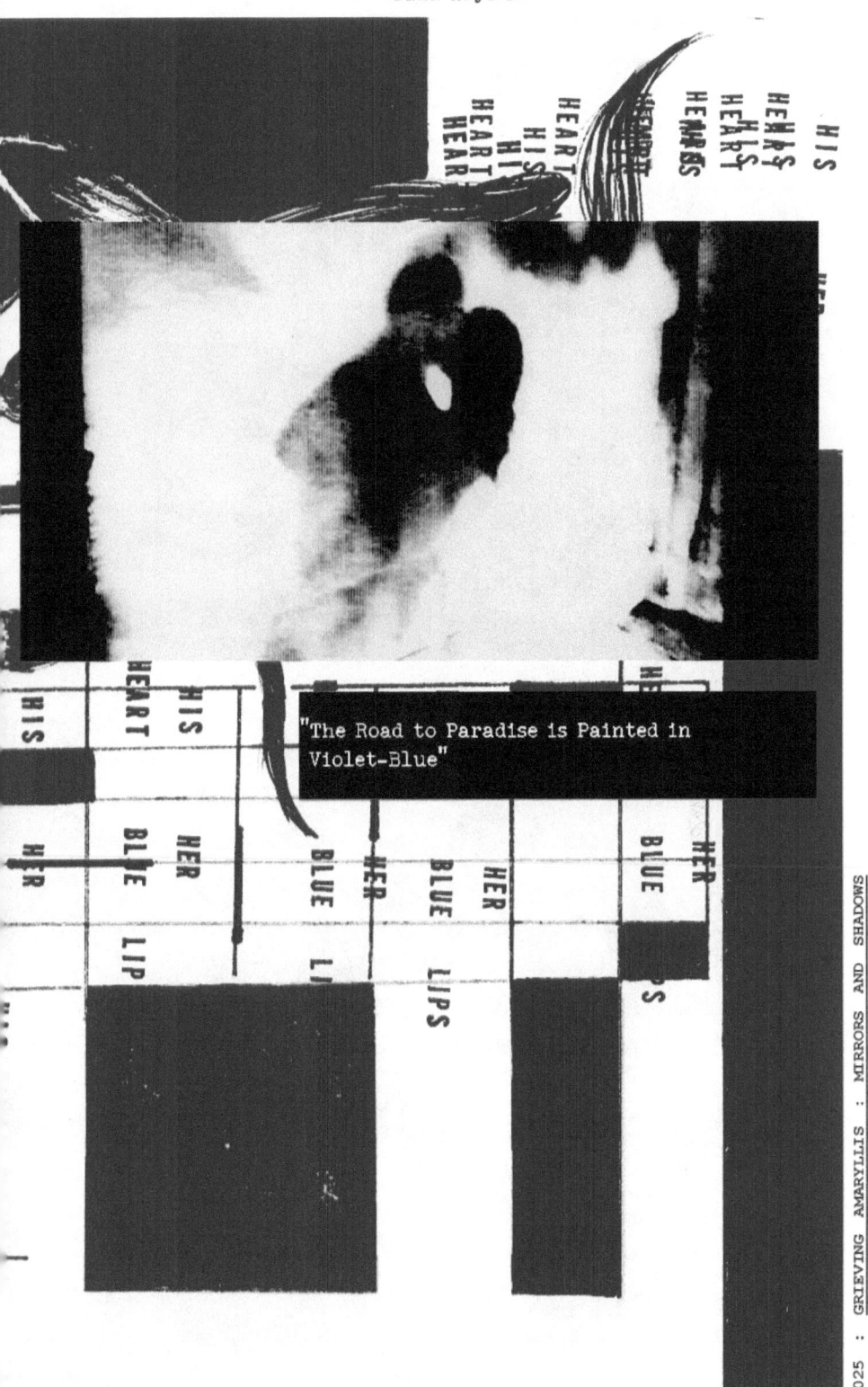

"The Road to Paradise is Painted in Violet-Blue"

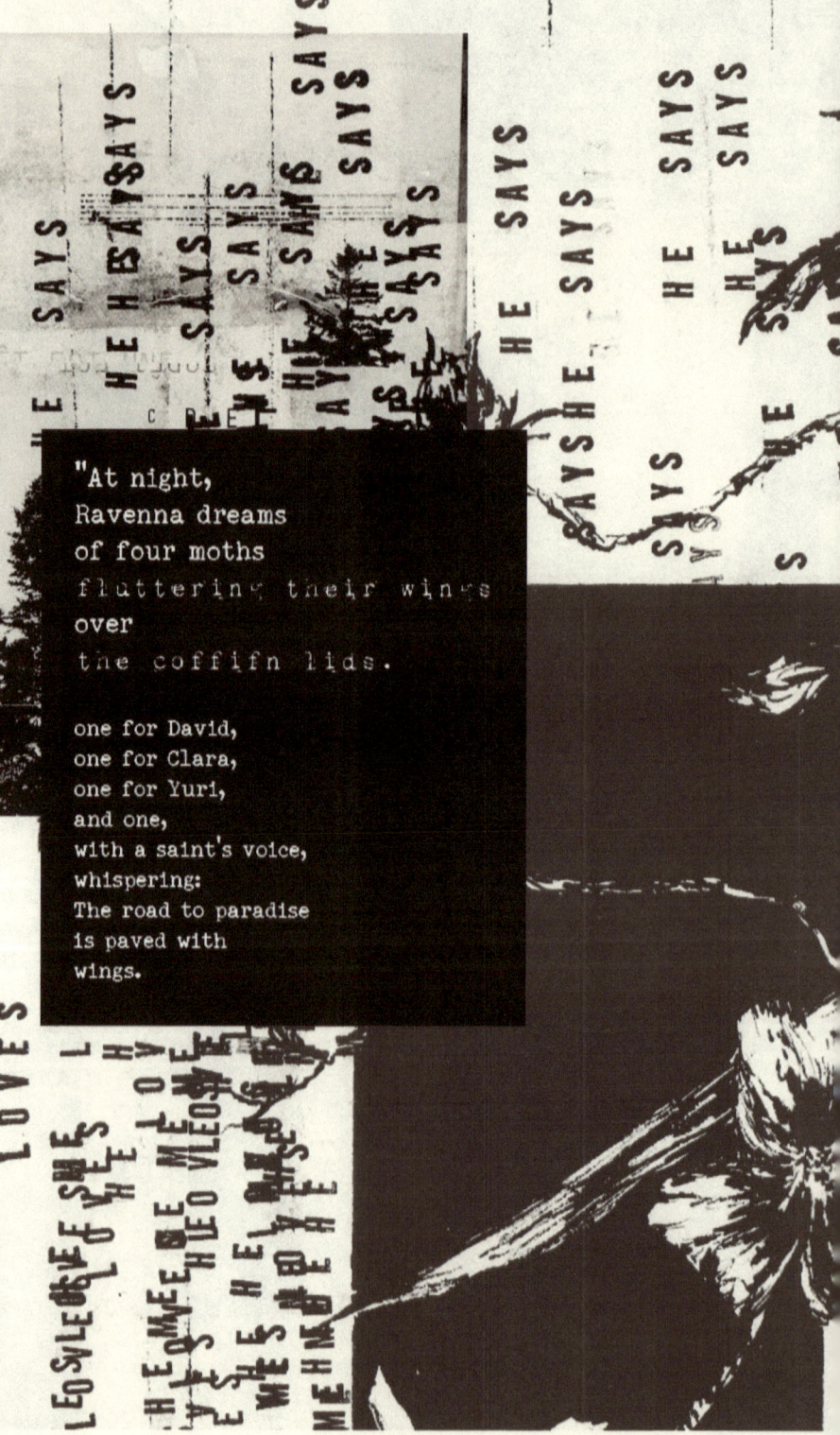

"At night,
Ravenna dreams
of four moths
fluttering their wings
over
the coffifn lids.

one for David,
one for Clara,
one for Yuri,
and one,
with a saint's voice,
whispering:
The road to paradise
is paved with
wings.

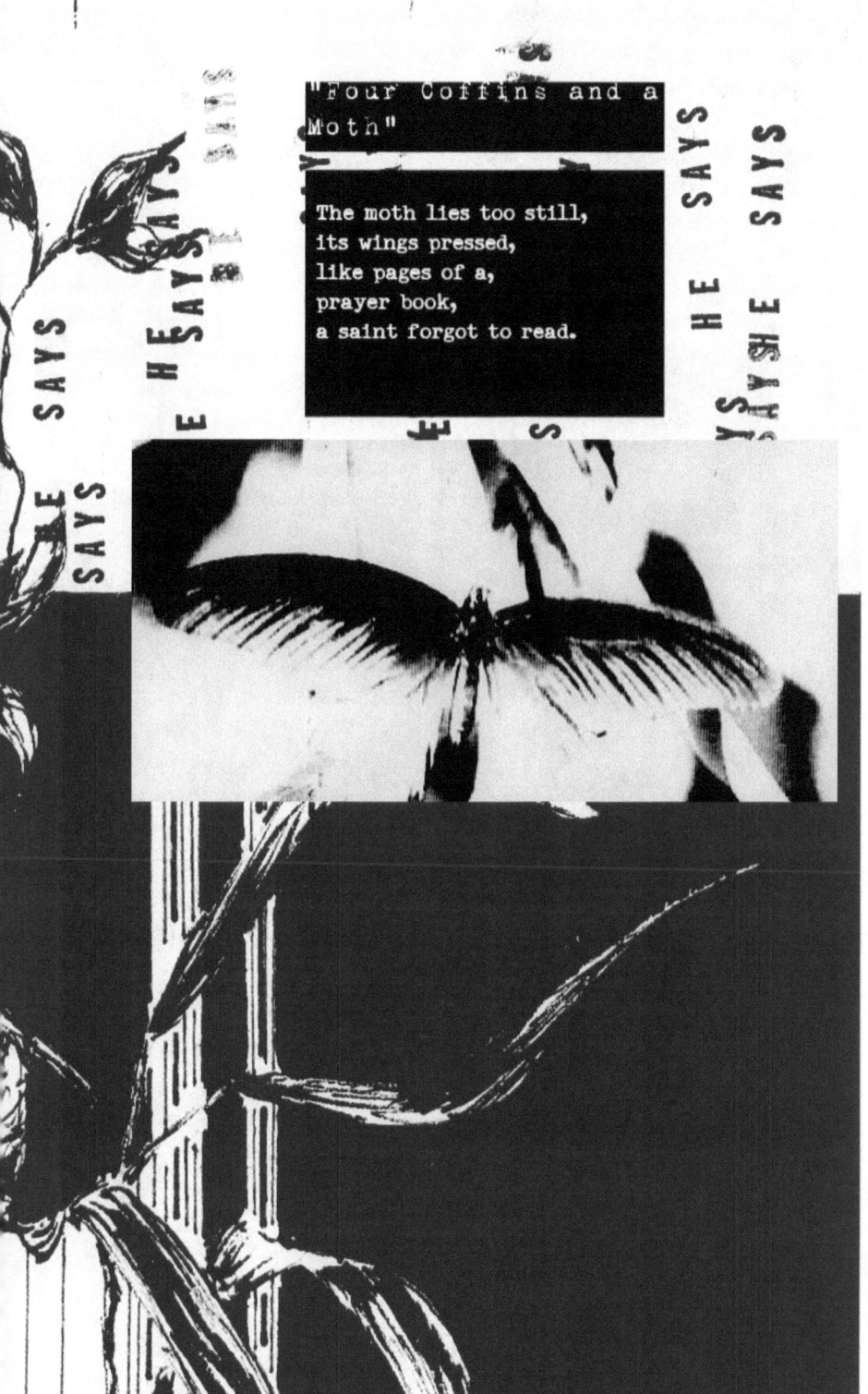

"Four Coffins and a Moth"

The moth lies too still,
its wings pressed,
like pages of a,
prayer book,
a saint forgot to read.

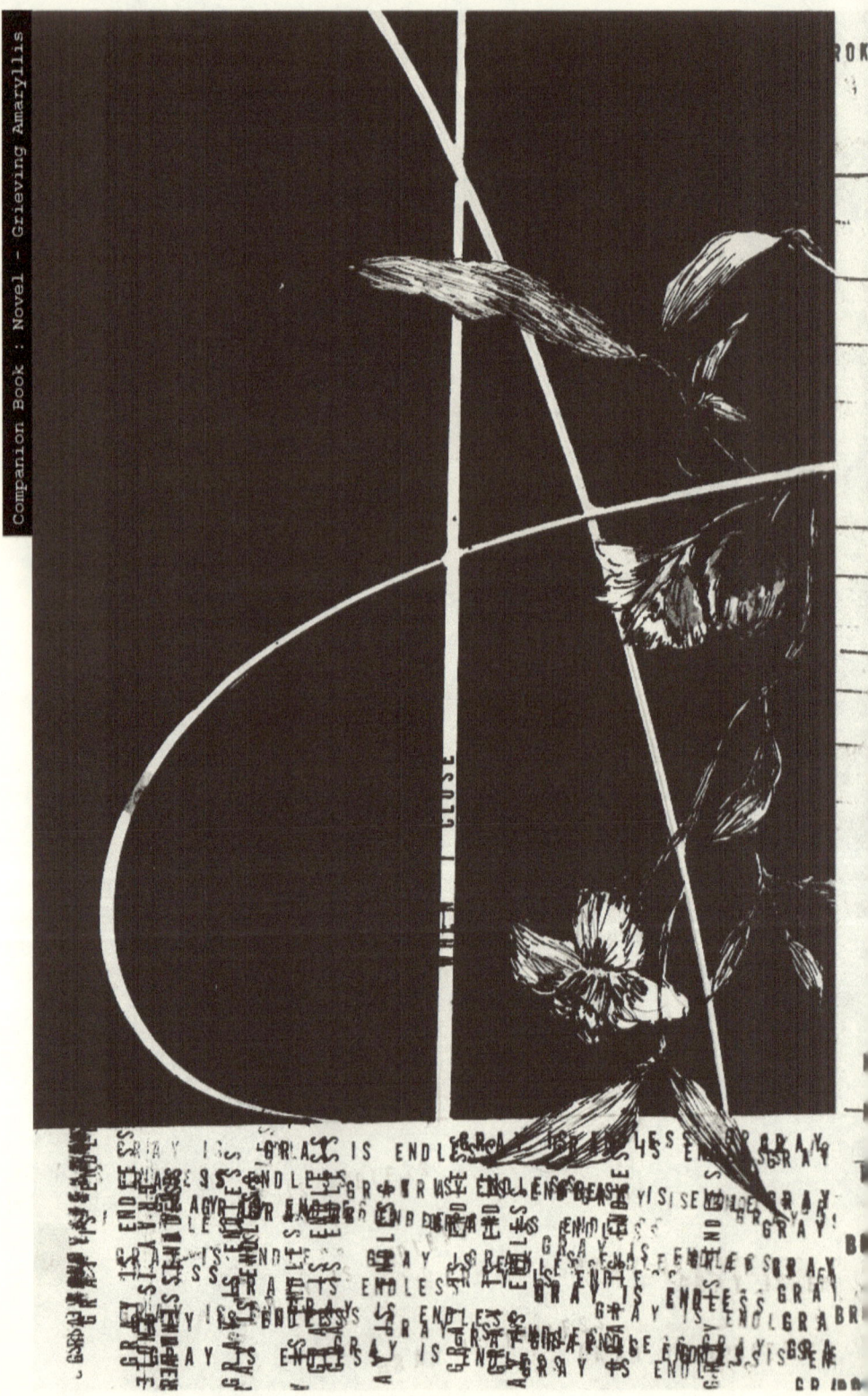

BROKEN BROKEN BROKEN BROKEN BROKEN BROKEN BROKEN BROKEN

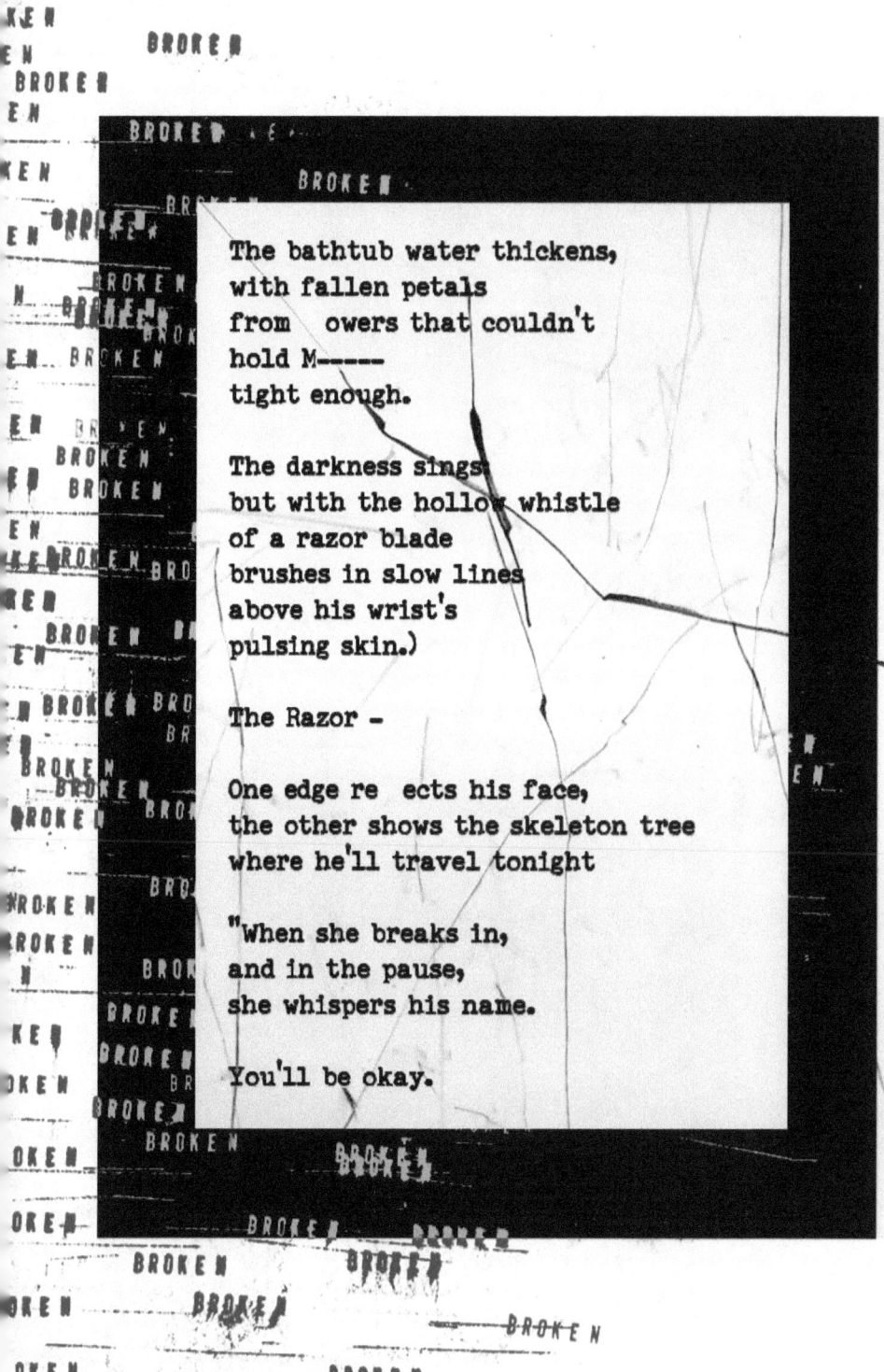

The bathtub water thickens,
with fallen petals
from owers that couldn't
hold M------
tight enough.

The darkness sings,
but with the hollow whistle
of a razor blade
brushes in slow lines
above his wrist's
pulsing skin.)

The Razor -

One edge re ects his face,
the other shows the skeleton tree
where he'll travel tonight

"When she breaks in,
and in the pause,
she whispers his name.

You'll be okay.

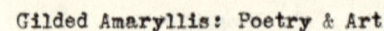

Dana Krystle

Pages 60-65 from the novel :
Excerpt -
Piano scene.

[Spring, 2018] - Amaryllis

"The road I take to the nirvana is paved with Amaryllis."

He played the piano at a slow pace, one note at a time. Petals of almond blossoms touched the windowpanes like white snow. The keys, black and white, responded to his fingers like the locked-in magic of waiting—a symphony of a dream-like world.

"That was beautiful," Ravenna walked into the room. "I didn't know you could play the piano."

Matvey stopped playing abruptly. He lifted his fingers and stared at his hands, flexing them open and shut, as if it hurt just to play the keynotes.

Ravenna came closer and caressed his hand; he had fresh bruises and red marks on his knuckles.

"It's nothing," he pulled them away and brushed his untamed, now longer, hair away from his face.

"Can you play more?" She sat beside him on the piano bench. "It sounded melancholic, and a little bittersweet," her eyes begging him to continue.

"I haven't played in a long time," Matvey smiled and placed his fingers over the keys, just close enough to touch them without pressing a sound. "It doesn't have a name," he paused for a while, his eyes fixed on the ocean ahead, its faint waves glittering in the red-orange dusk.

"How about you name it?" he looked at Ravenna playfully, his eyes softer than the first time they met, his smile sweeter.

"Amaryllis," she said as soon as she saw the flowers placed on a nearby vase, being kissed by the rose and amber sun rays, their colors changing hues in the golden afternoon.

Matvey straightened his back and took a deep breath. Placing his hands on the keys, he turned to glance shortly at Ravenna and began to play the notes softly, the tune wistful and anguished.

Matvey improvised a melody of his past and his present, his pain, and his forlorn attempts to end everything.

The more he played, the more he heard the screams of people from his past, begging him not to follow his destiny. For years he had tried to convince himself that he was on the right path, that he was doing what he

60

was meant to do—a devotion to his faith, a service to the divine will.

Emotions rushed through his body, his heart beating with torment, agonized by the fog inside his head—chaotic and confusing. He wanted all the noise to decay and disappear; he needed to break free from all the guilt, all the blood that stained his hands. He had craved clarity his entire life, and for a very long time, he did what he was told to do: to follow orders and not be selfish, to do what's best for the divinity, no questions asked.

He froze for a split second when Ravenna rested her head gently on his shoulder, but then quickly continued to play. A sudden jolt of terror ran through him. He had never questioned his valor, but this was different. This time he had something to lose. In a moment they could hurt her, they could take her away, and his new universe would crash into a thousand pieces. The sea ahead would turn into a wasteland, the calm sky above into a tempest, and the lofty clouds over him into thunderstorms.

He could lose her, forever. Matvey stopped playing, the thoughts jarring in his head louder and louder. His heart was on the verge of exploding. The ocean waves outside were too deafening to endure any longer. The silence was harsh and turbulent; everything turned into a cacophony of painful noise.

He stopped playing.

"That sounded a bit abrupt; doesn't it have an ending?" Ravenna lifted her head away from his shoulder, her eyes shifting at the keys, imagining that maybe by looking, she could finish the notes in her head.

Matvey was staring blankly at the piano keys, his brows crossed and in distress. "The cliff, the house, the flowers, you..." His voice broke. He stared at Ravenna, his eyes red and misted with tears.

"Matvey?" She called his name. "Is everything okay?" Her voice faded as she faced him; he had never looked so defeated.

"No." He leaned in and kissed her, her lips tender as the ripest petal.

Ravenna felt a tear on her cheek as she kissed him back.

2025 :: GRIEVING AMARYLLIS :: MIRRORS AND SHADOWS

(Amaryllis) - Music Sheet

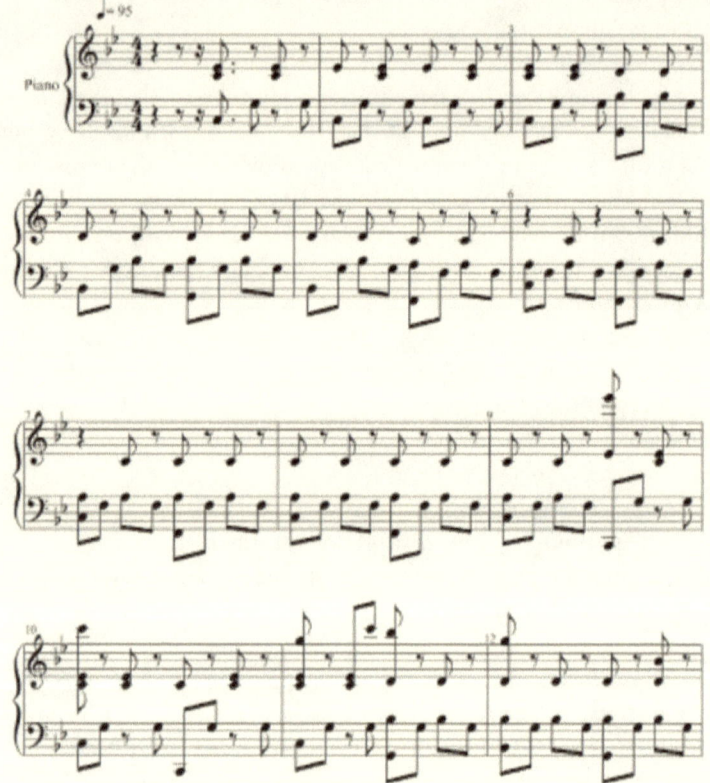

Dana Krystle

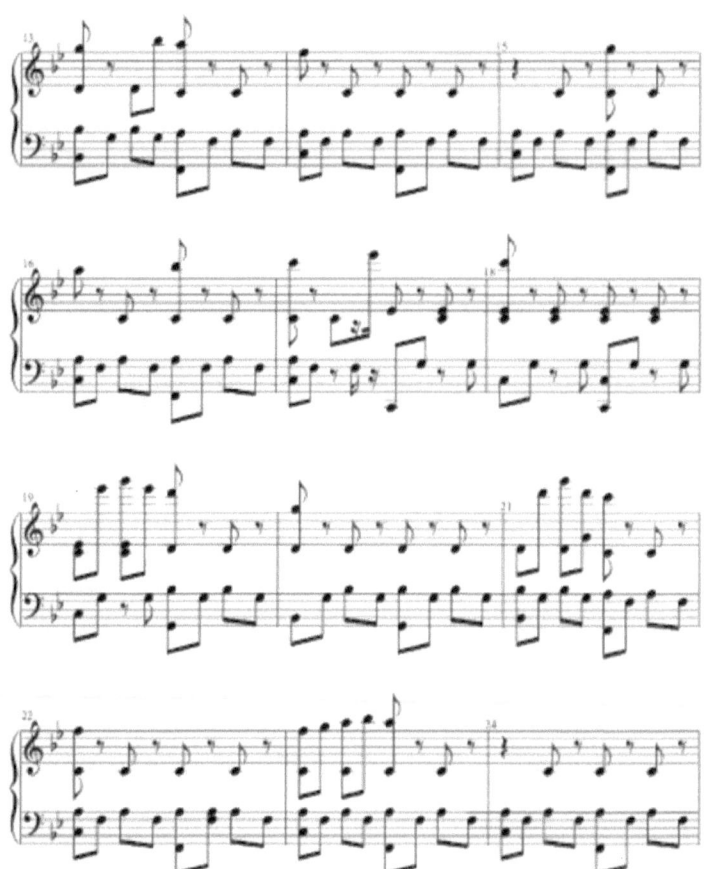

2025 : GRIEVING AMARYLLIS : MIRRORS AND SHADOWS

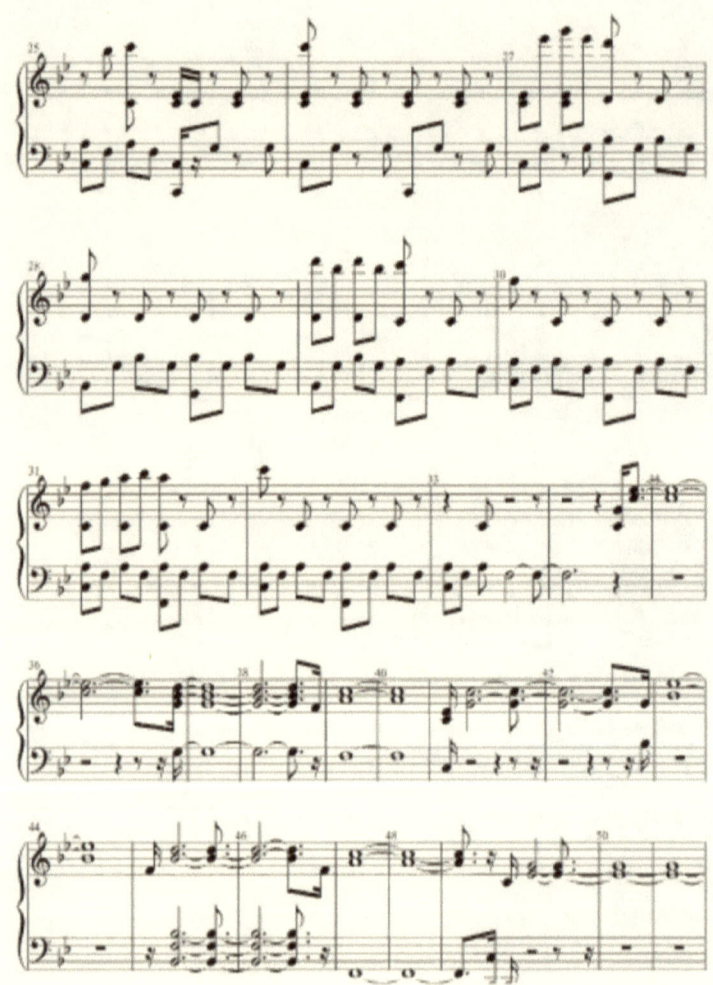

64

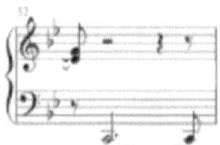

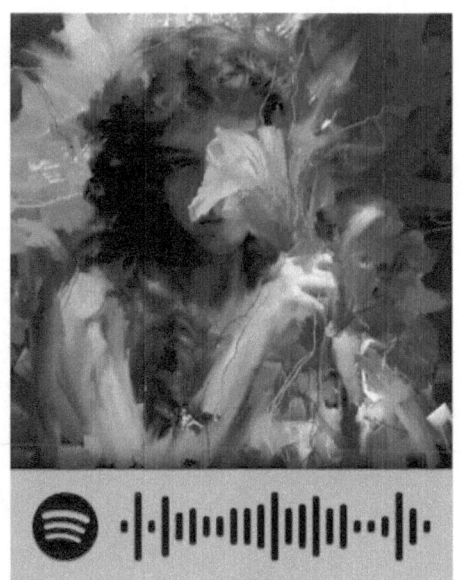

Scan this image on Spotify to hear the song - Amaryllis

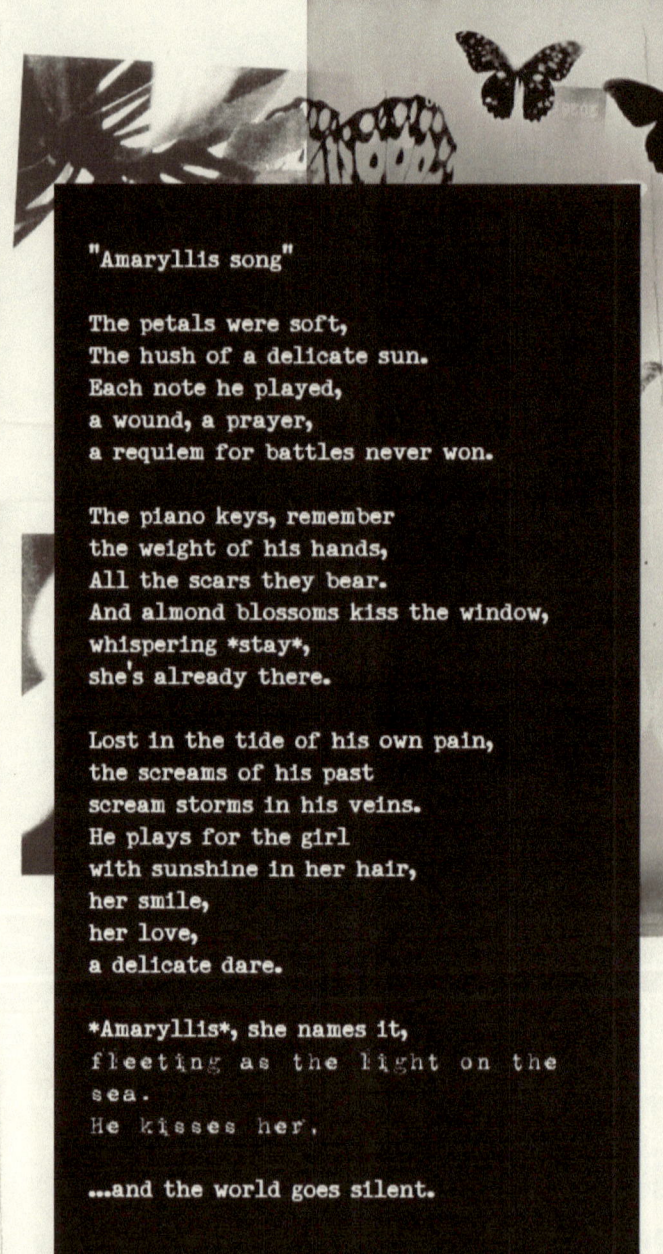

"Amaryllis song"

The petals were soft,
The hush of a delicate sun.
Each note he played,
a wound, a prayer,
a requiem for battles never won.

The piano keys, remember
the weight of his hands,
All the scars they bear.
And almond blossoms kiss the window,
whispering *stay*,
she's already there.

Lost in the tide of his own pain,
the screams of his past
scream storms in his veins.
He plays for the girl
with sunshine in her hair,
her smile,
her love,
a delicate dare.

Amaryllis, she names it,
fleeting as the light on the
sea.
He kisses her,

...and the world goes silent.

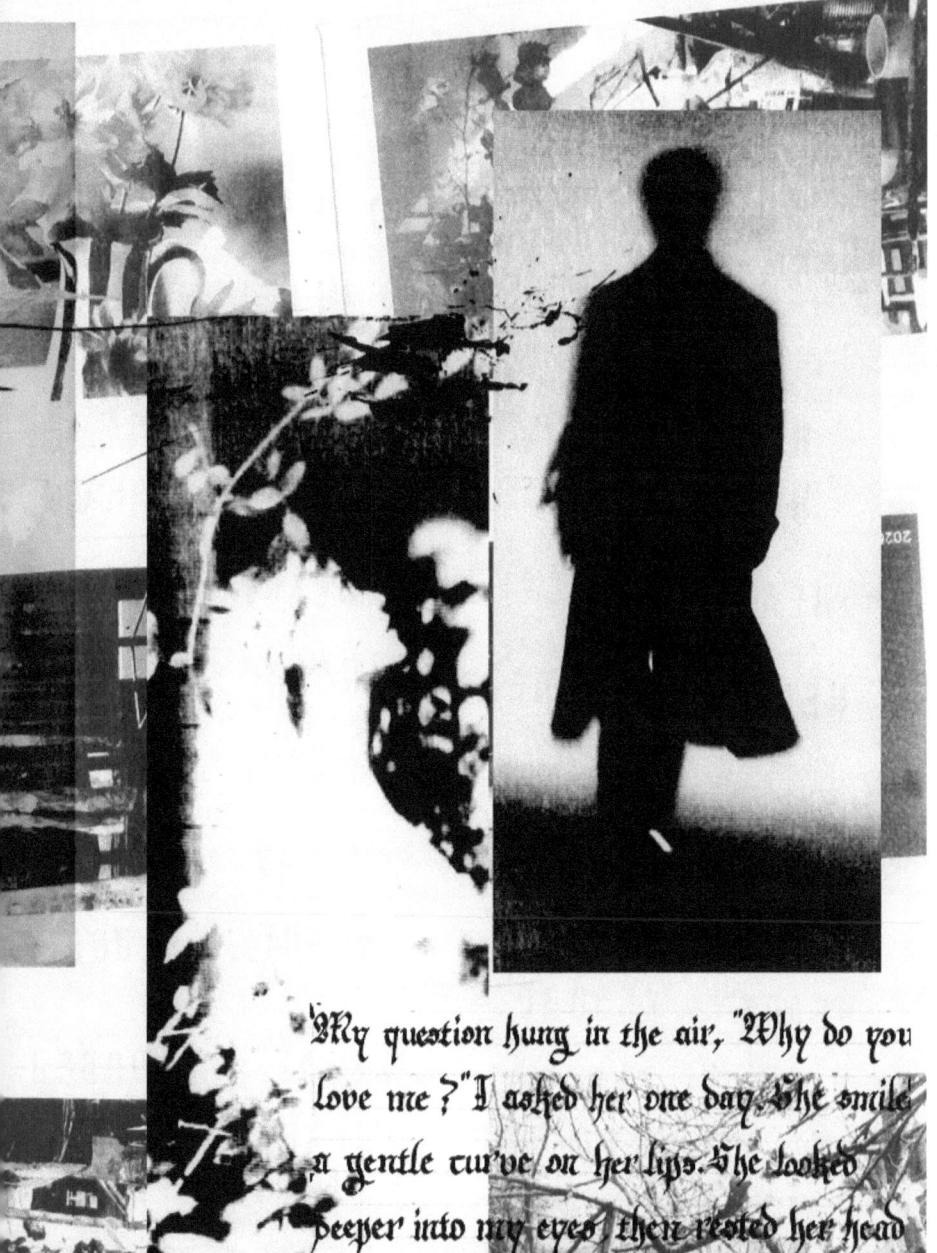

My question hung in the air, "Why do you love me?" I asked her one day. She smile a gentle curve on her lips. She looked deeper into my eyes, then rested her head on my shoulders. My heart gave a lurch at the touch of her skin. I closed my eyes, and in the sudden quiet

HEART FLOODED

HEART FLOODED

HEART HEART FLOODED HEART FLO

HEART

HEART HEART FLOODED HEART

HEART HEART FLOODED

HEART FLOODED

ART FLOODED HEART FLOODED

HEART HEART FLOODED

HEART FLOODED

HEART HEART FLOODED HEART

HEART FLOODED

HEART FLOODED HEART FLOODED

HEART FLOODED HEART FLOODED

HEART FLOODED HEART FLOODED

HEART FLOODED HEART FLOODED

HEART FLOODED HEART FLOODED
HEART FLOODED
HEART FLOODED

HEART FLOODED HEART FLOODED

HEART FLOODED HEART FLOODED

HEART FLOODED

HEART FLOODED HEART FLOODED

HEART FLOODED HEART FLOODED
HEART FLOODED

HEART FLOODED HEART

HEART

HEA

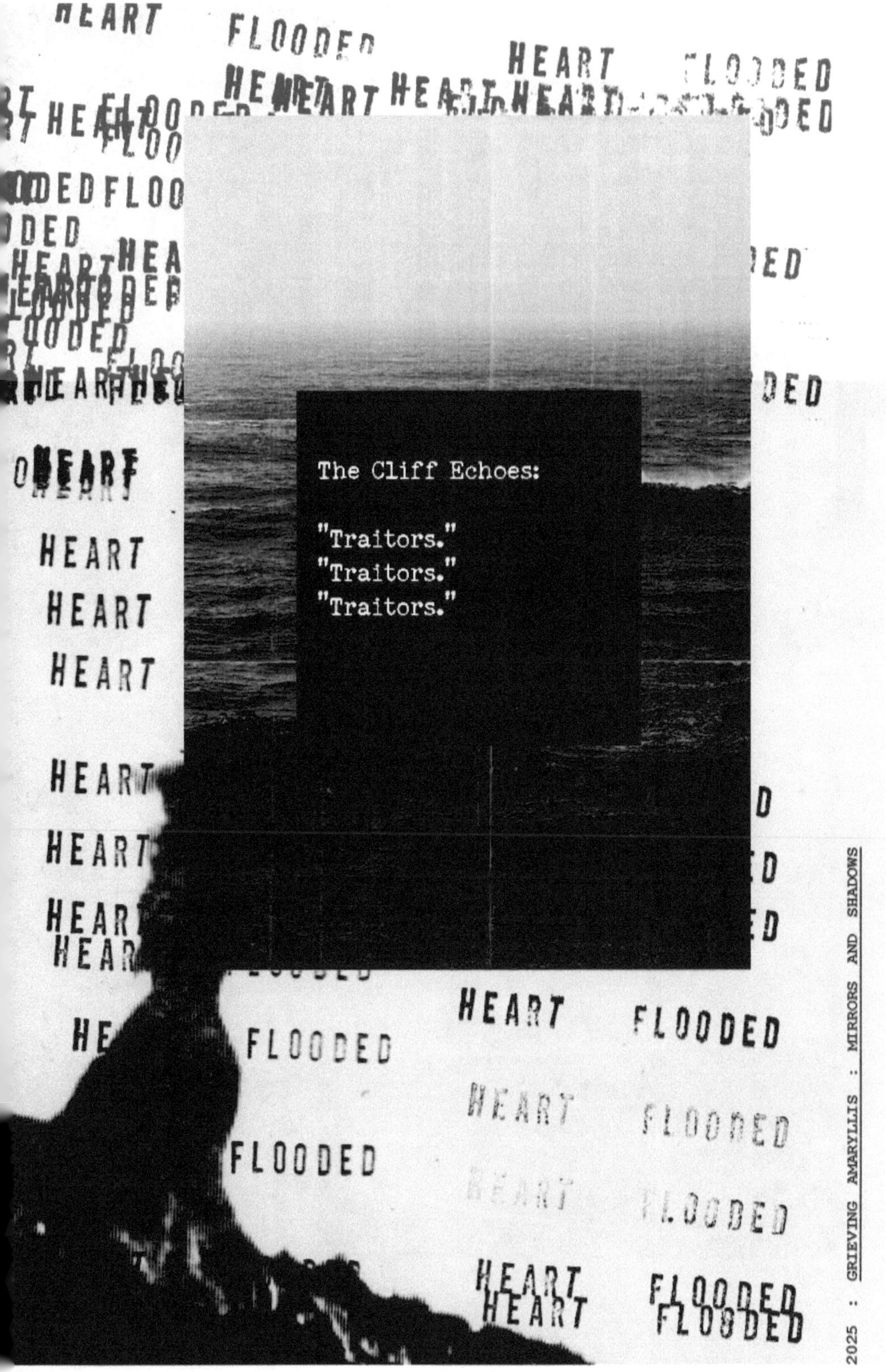

HEART FLOODED HEART FLOODED HEART HEART HEART HEART FLOODED THEART FLOO DED FLOO ODED FLOO DED HEART HEA DED HEART EAT DED FLOODED RZ FLOO R HEAR DED DED

OHEART

HEART

HEART

HEART

HEART

HEART

HEART

HEART

HE

The Cliff Echoes:

"Traitors."
"Traitors."
"Traitors."

HEART FLOODED FLOODED HEART FLOODED FLOODED HEART FLOODED FLOODED HEART FLOODED HEART FLOODED

2025 : GRIEVING AMARYLLIS : MIRRORS AND SHADOWS

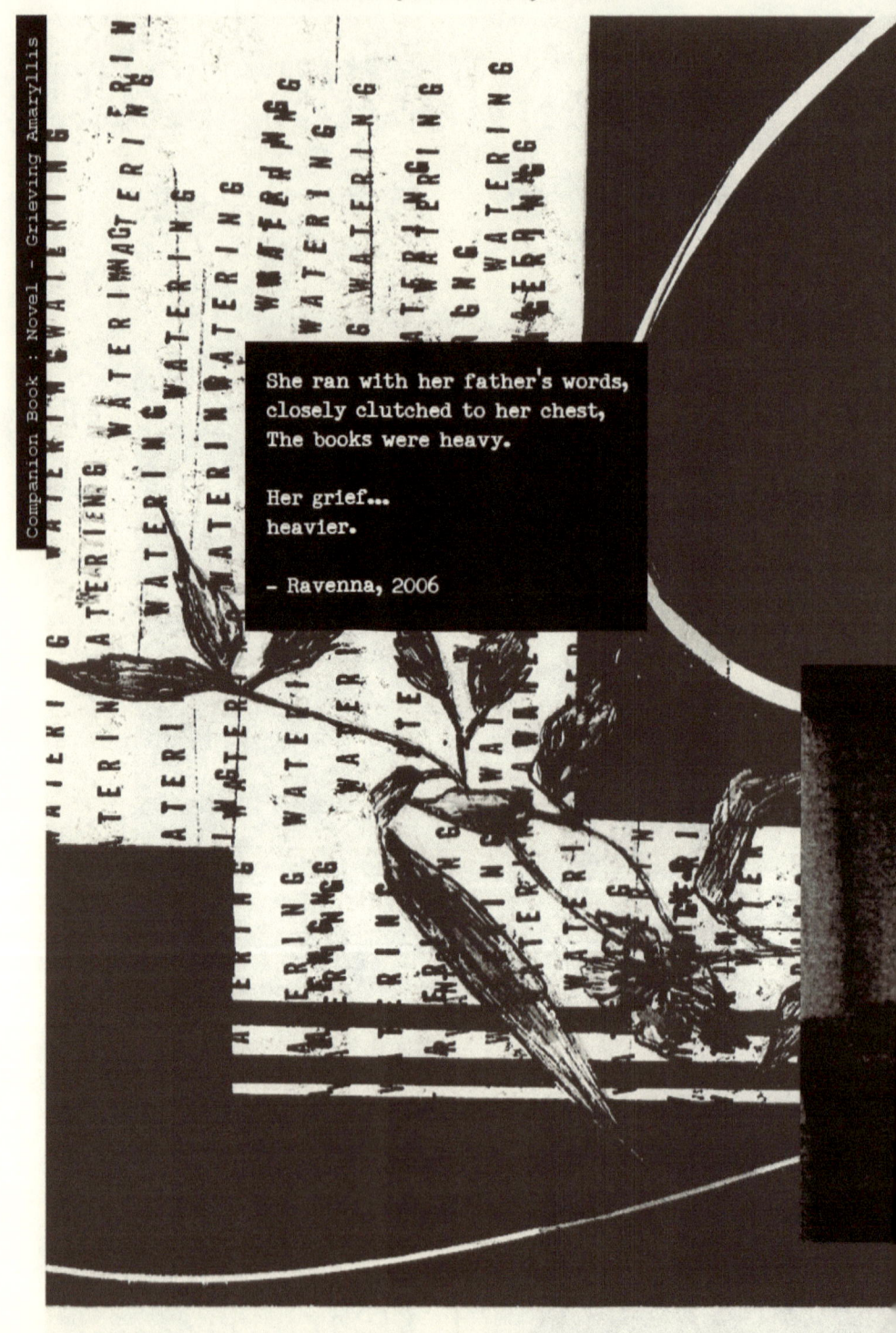

Companion Book : Novel - Grieving Amaryllis

She ran with her father's words,
closely clutched to her chest,
The books were heavy.

Her grief...
heavier.

- Ravenna, 2006

DEAR PLANTS

(Some promises are fading.
Some lovers are only ash in
waiting.)

2025 : GRIEVING AMARYLLIS : MIRRORS AND SHADOWS

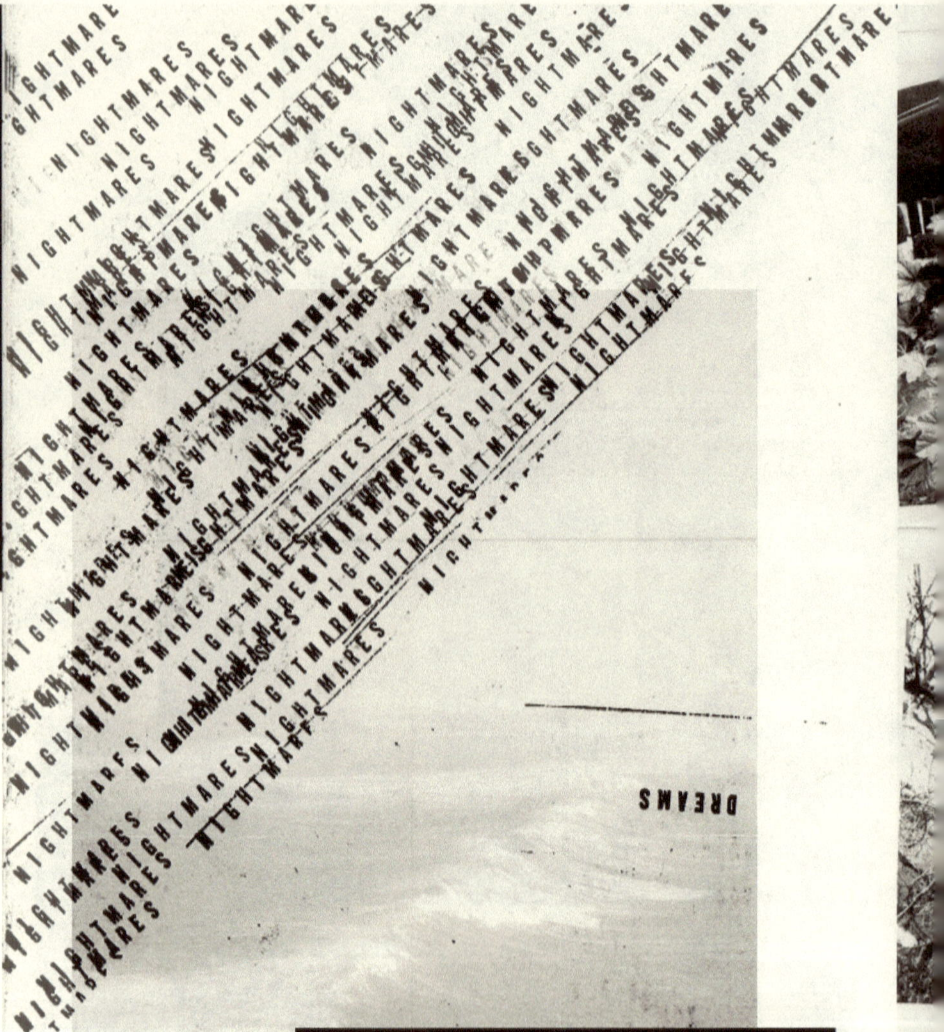

NIGHTMARES

DREAMS

Pages swell like dying lungs,
ink bleeding where her father once
pressed his   ngers to a favorite line.

Grandfather's arms are cold as stone,
his silence louder,
of cof ns on gravel,
doors that shut.

The chrysanthemum,
dissolves in the mud.

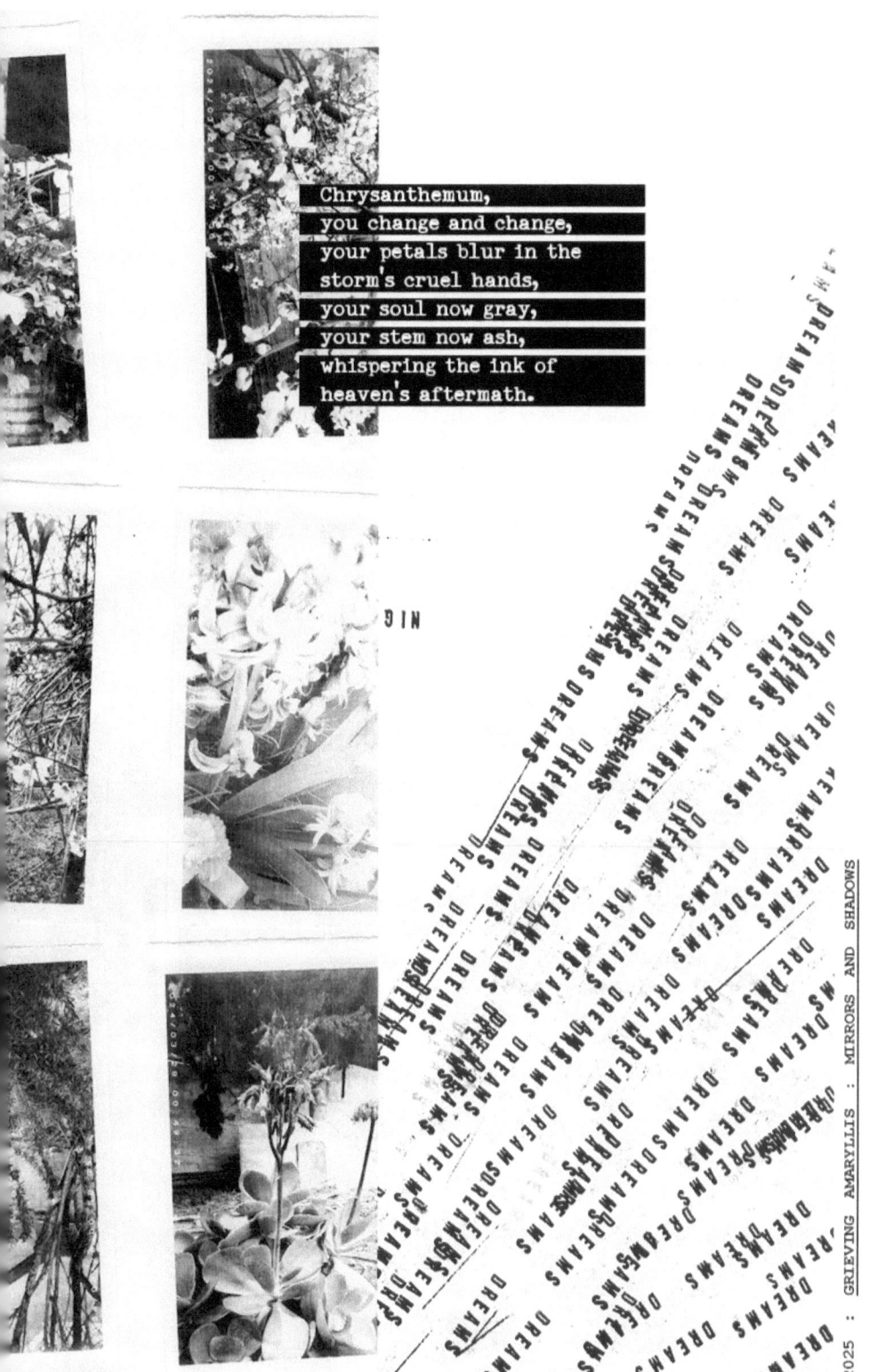

Chrysanthemum,
you change and change,
your petals blur in the
storm's cruel hands,
your soul now gray,
your stem now ash,
whispering the ink of
heaven's aftermath.

2025 : GRIEVING AMARYLLIS : MIRRORS AND SHADOWS

Will my moon still kiss the bright star?

(He doesn't ask who'll hold the match when the
embers rise.
when the house becomes a pyre for all her
painted skies.)

The workshop hums with ghosts of chisels,
with half-formed faces in the stone.
Niccolo's hammer counts the seconds,
some saints deserve to die.

Matvey's pulse screams *leave*,
but the sculpture of Ravenna
(serene in false death, marble eyelids half-shut)
holds him hostage.

Theodore's ngers trace the apocalypse
hung neat above his drafting table.

her brush strokes violent as prophecy:
*See how the stars fall like snow.
See how the sea turns to glass.*

"Burn it all," the old man says,
and the words taste like bitter poison.
"Even the garden?"
"Especially the garden."

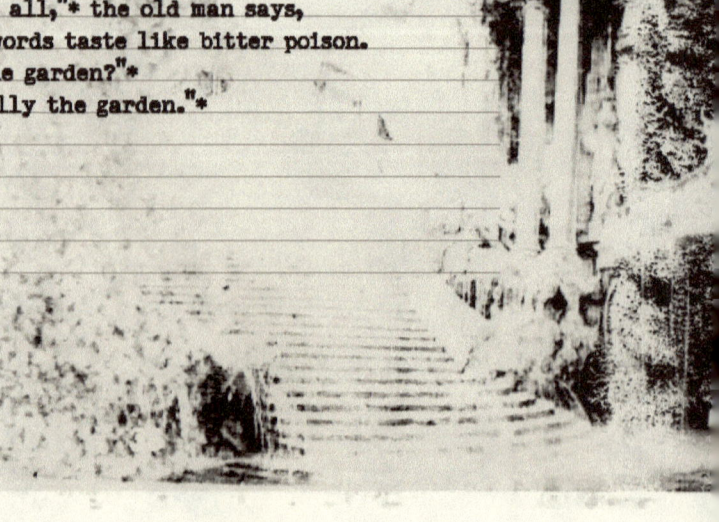

Outside, the tide pretends to sleep.
Niccolo's shadow stretches long
across the gravel's too long, too sharp,
a blade's silhouette where a man should stand.

Matvey watches Ravenna's painting bleed
its golds to black, its blues to rust.

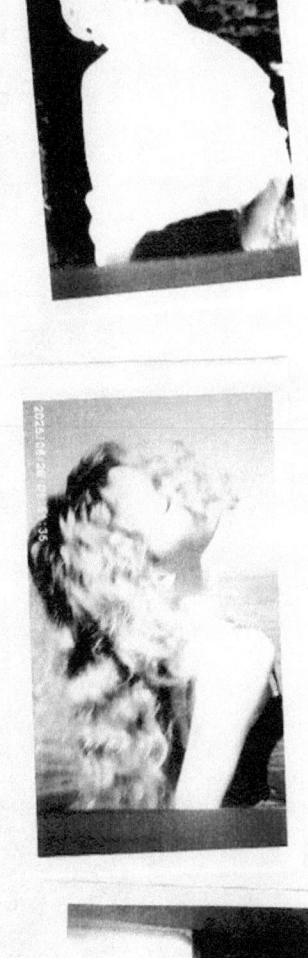
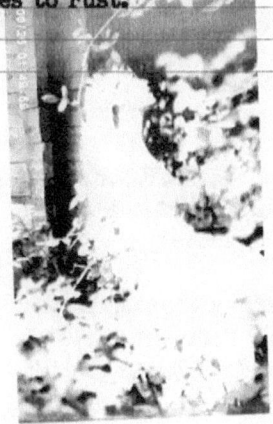
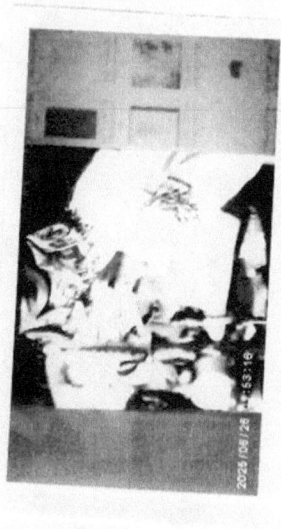
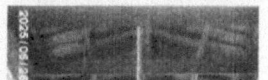

"On a journey, ill-"
heart was burning.

Morning walks were brief prayers-
emerald-green in his pocket,
salt on his lips,
hope of love that can last.

Then:
rotors shred the sky.
Boots on the cliff stairs.
The old sculptor's body
pouring crimson thread
onto gravel.

(Matvey counts the wounds-
Ten? Fifteen? The Glass Temple's bullets
overkill their victims.)

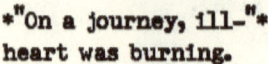

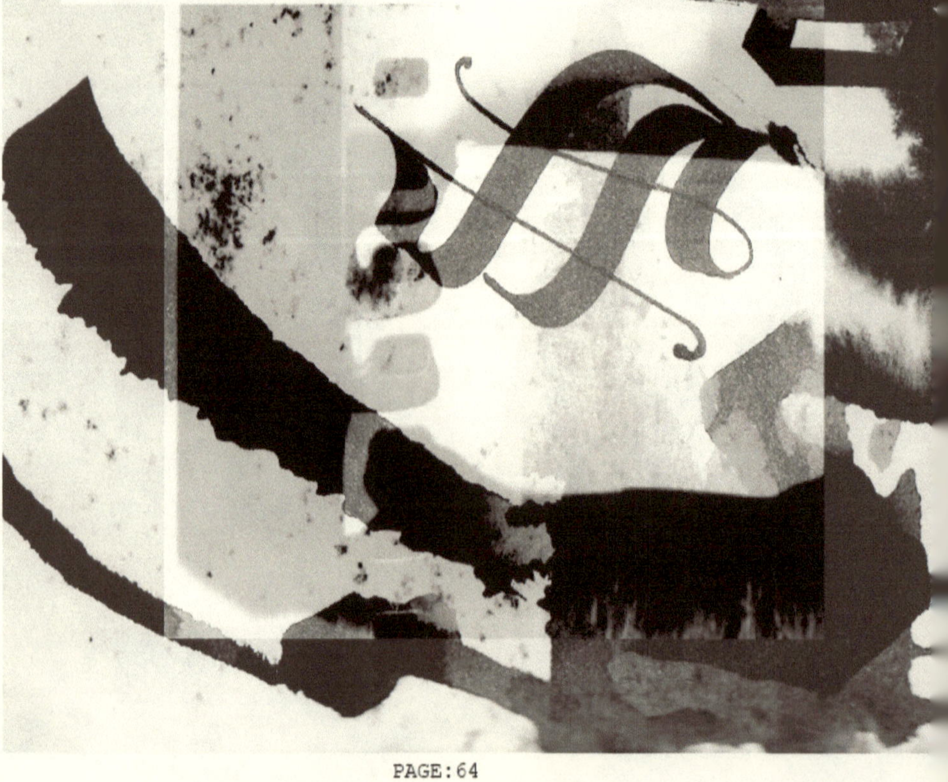

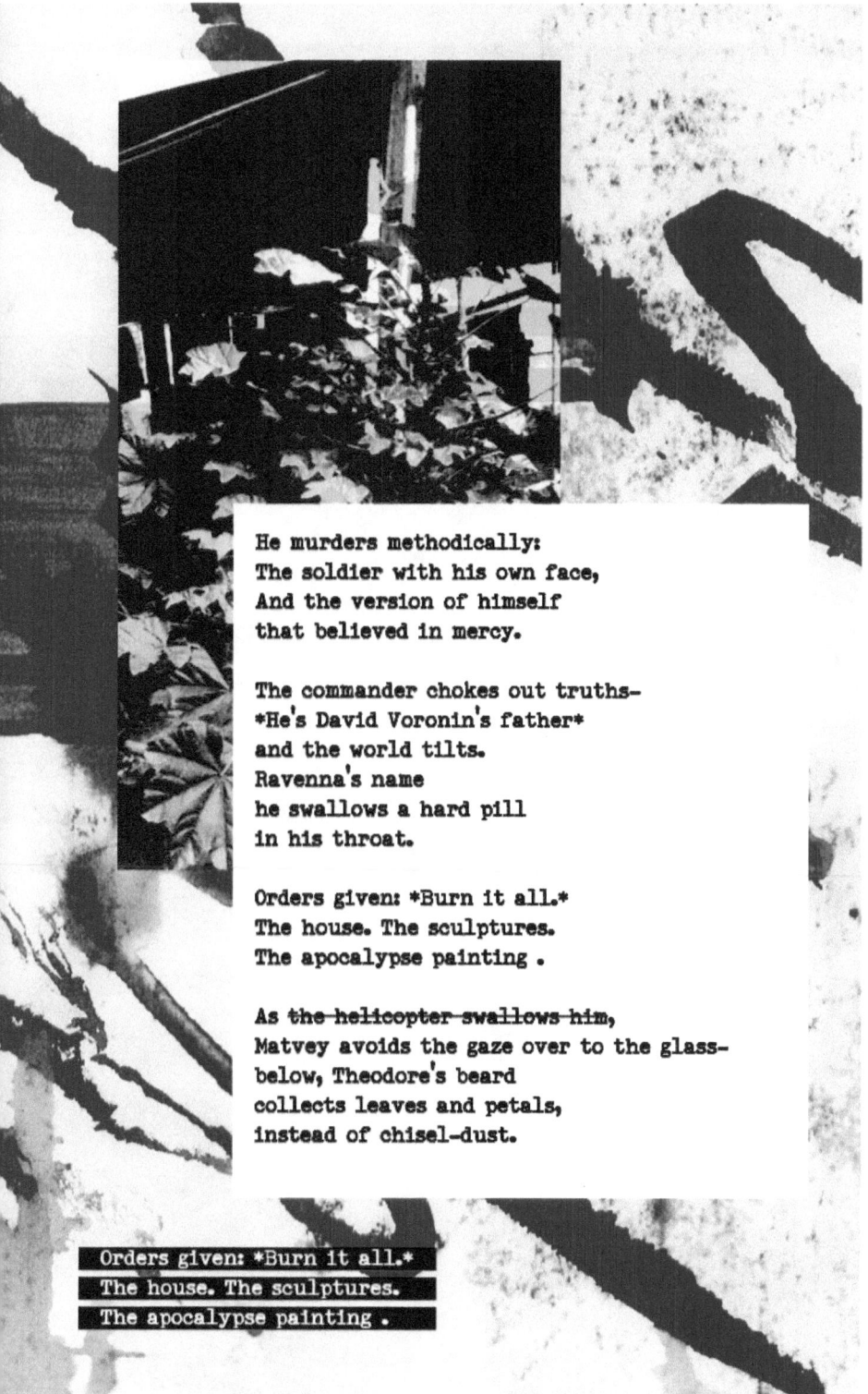

He murders methodically:
The soldier with his own face,
And the version of himself
that believed in mercy.

The commander chokes out truths-
He's David Voronin's father
and the world tilts.
Ravenna's name
he swallows a hard pill
in his throat.

Orders given: *Burn it all.*
The house. The sculptures.
The apocalypse painting .

As the helicopter swallows him,
Matvey avoids the gaze over to the glass-
below, Theodore's beard
collects leaves and petals,
instead of chisel-dust.

Orders given: *Burn it all.*
The house. The sculptures.
The apocalypse painting .

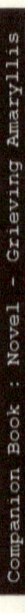

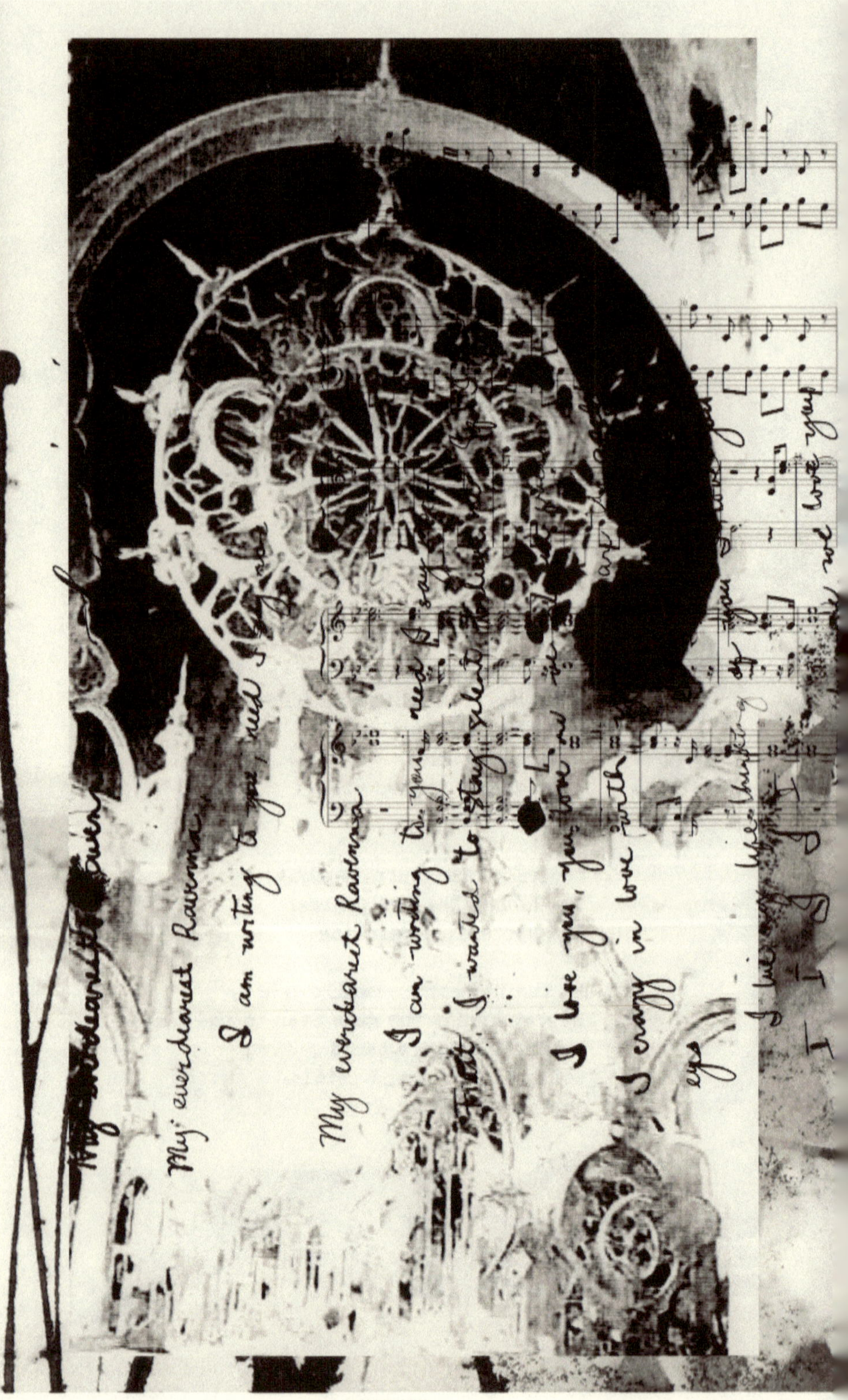

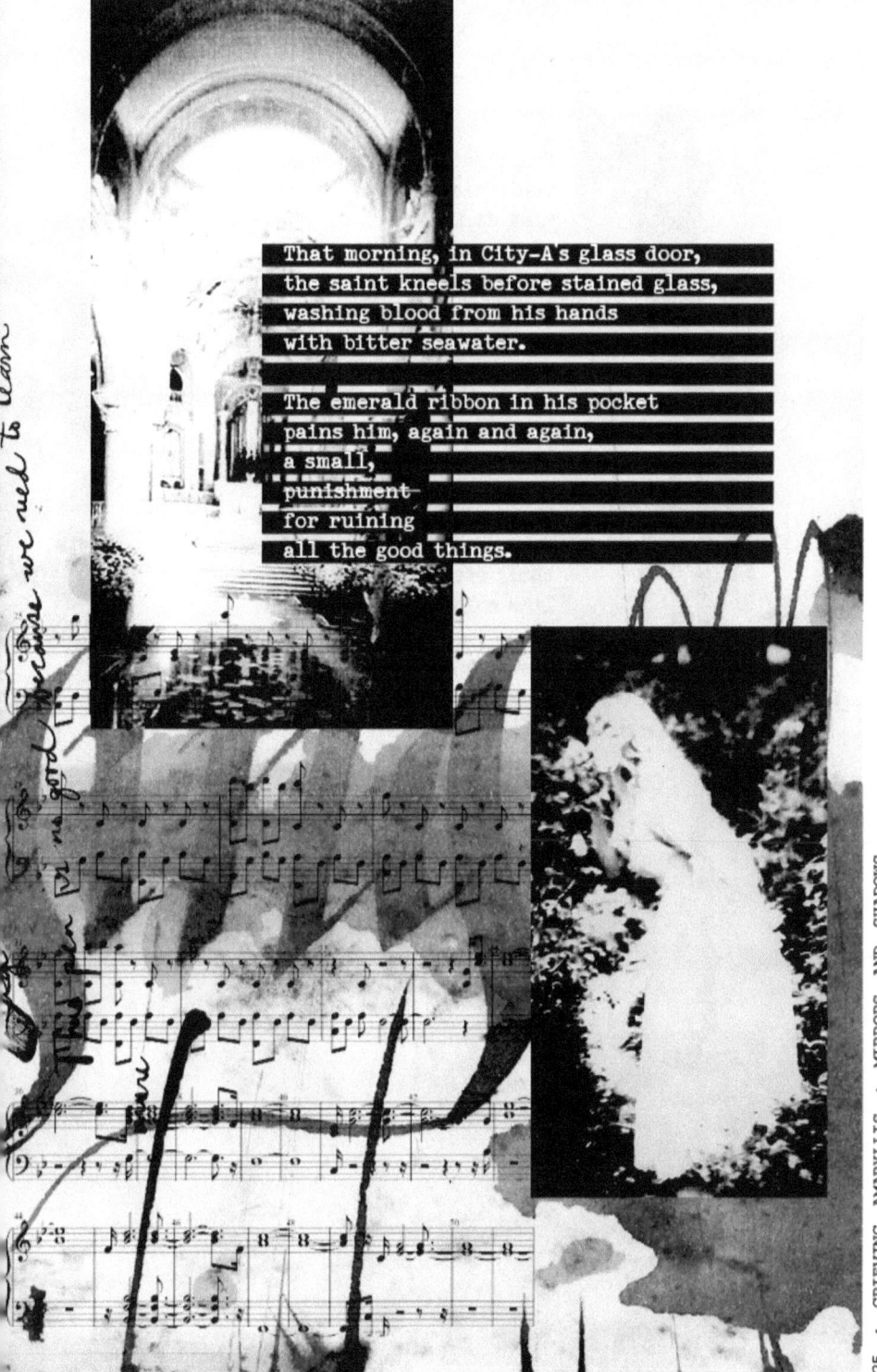

That morning, in City-A's glass door,
the saint kneels before stained glass,
washing blood from his hands
with bitter seawater.

The emerald ribbon in his pocket
pains him, again and again,
a small,
punishment
for ruining
all the good things.

2025 : GRIEVING AMARYLLIS : MIRRORS AND SHADOWS

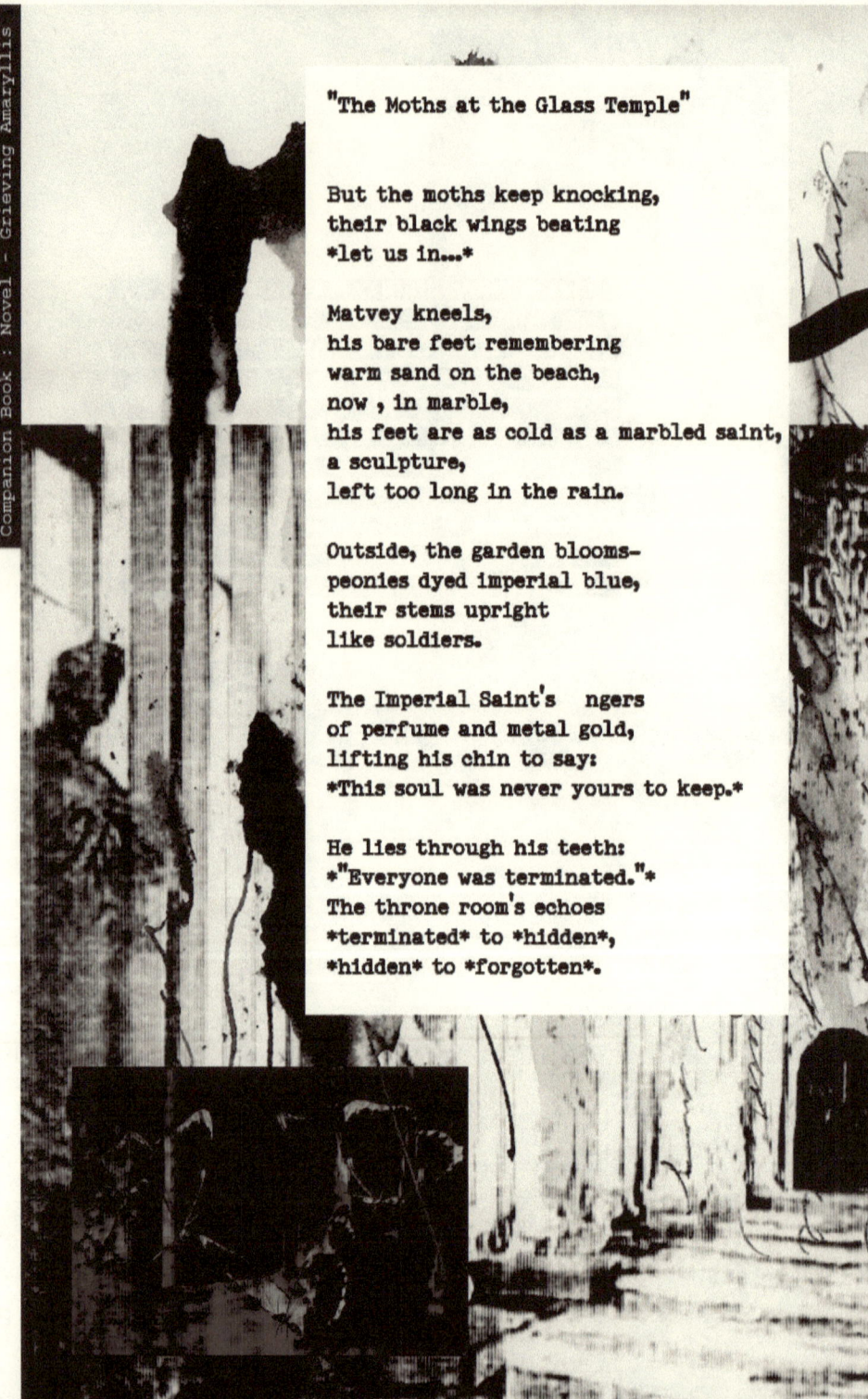

"The Moths at the Glass Temple"

But the moths keep knocking,
their black wings beating
let us in...

Matvey kneels,
his bare feet remembering
warm sand on the beach,
now , in marble,
his feet are as cold as a marbled saint,
a sculpture,
left too long in the rain.

Outside, the garden blooms-
peonies dyed imperial blue,
their stems upright
like soldiers.

The Imperial Saint's   ngers
of perfume and metal gold,
lifting his chin to say:
This soul was never yours to keep.

He lies through his teeth:
"Everyone was terminated."
The throne room's echoes
terminated to *hidden*,
hidden to *forgotten*.

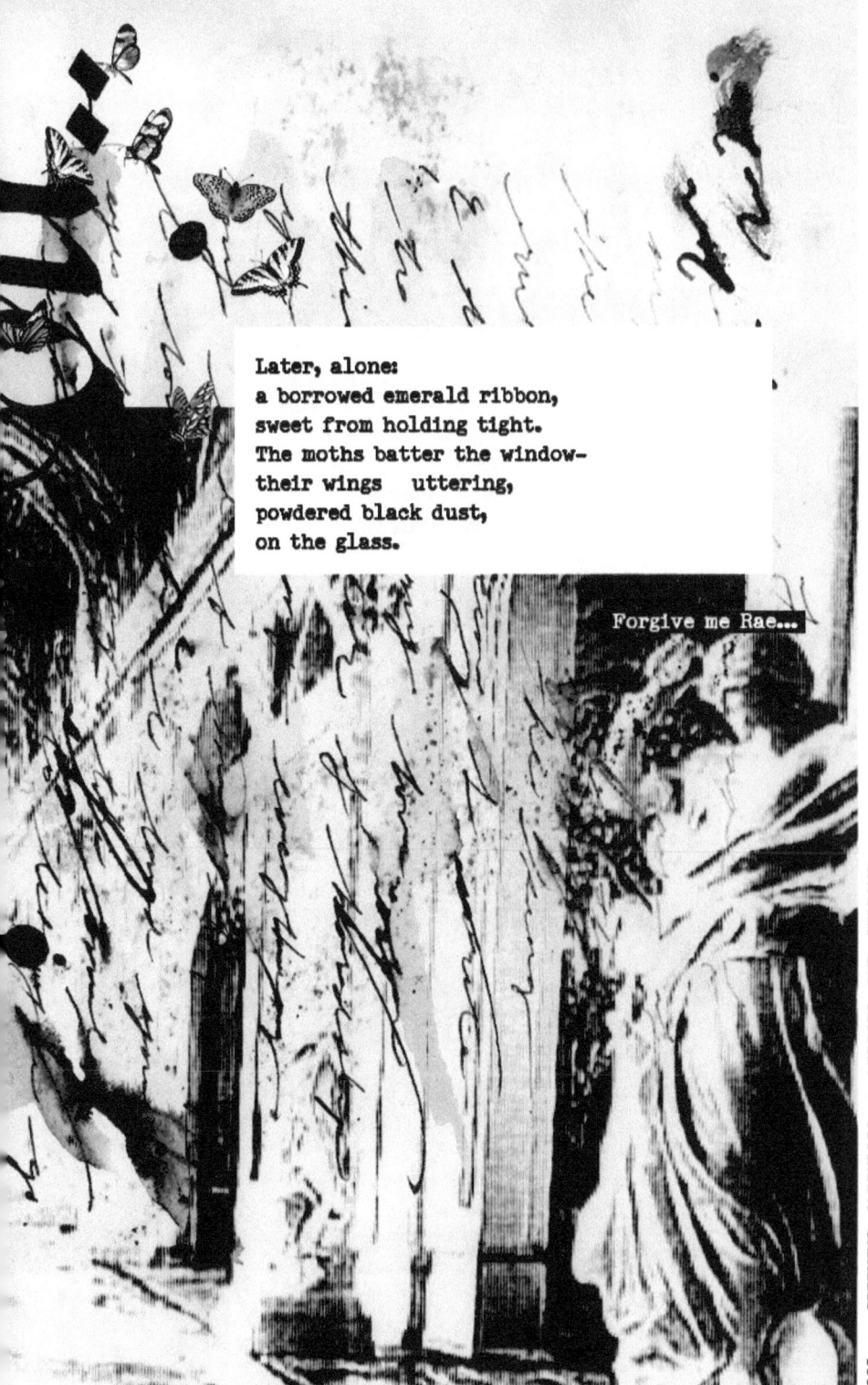

Later, alone:
a borrowed emerald ribbon,
sweet from holding tight.
The moths batter the window-
their wings   uttering,
powdered black dust,
on the glass.

Forgive me Rae...

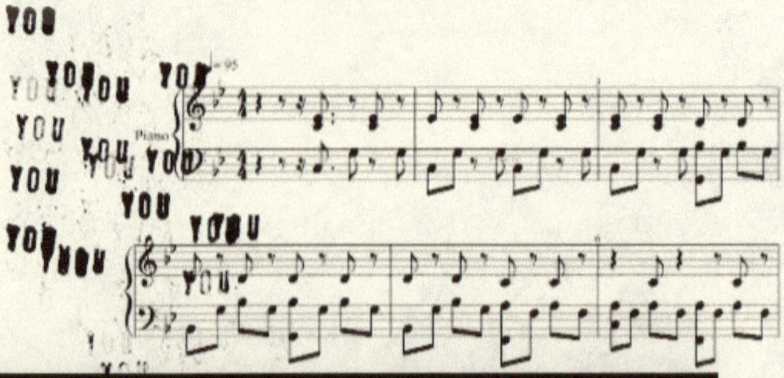

YOU
YOU YOU YOU
YOU YOU
YOU YOU YOU
YOU YOU
YOU YOU YOU

// Morning had been hydrangea-blue,

Smoke smudged the horizon,
a helicopter's blade slicing the sky

She finds him among the flowers.
bullet wounds blooming crimson .

She cries, and cries, and cries.

His gardening gloves
clutching dry soil,
Death was just
another thing to tend.

The house burns.

Amaryllis
a faint sound playing in the heat,
ivory keys
stones like bones.
She claws at the door,
the fire pushes back.
a furnace-breath,
her desperate skin learned
how easily flesh burns.

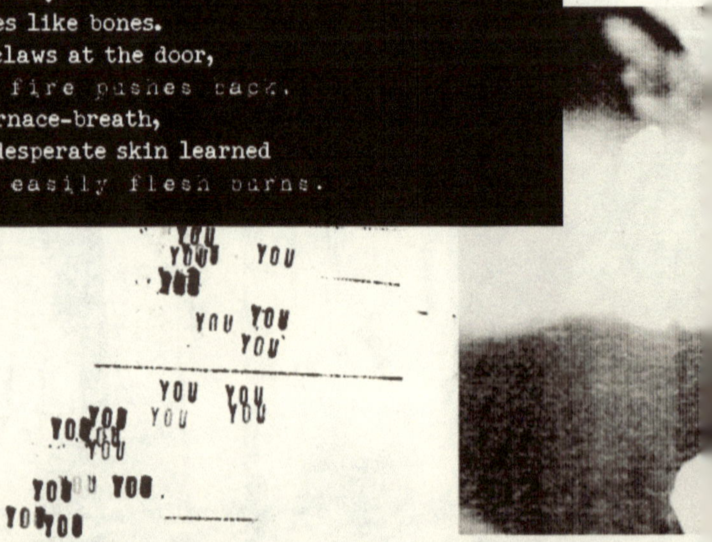

YOU
YOU YOU
YOU
YOU YOU
YOU
YOU YOU
YOU YOU
YOU YOU
YOU YOU
YOU
YOU YOU .
YOU YOU

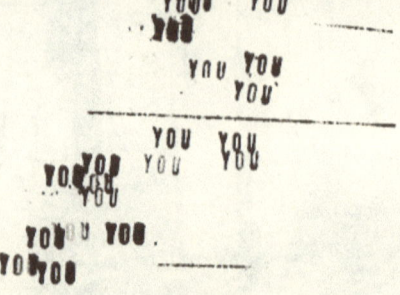

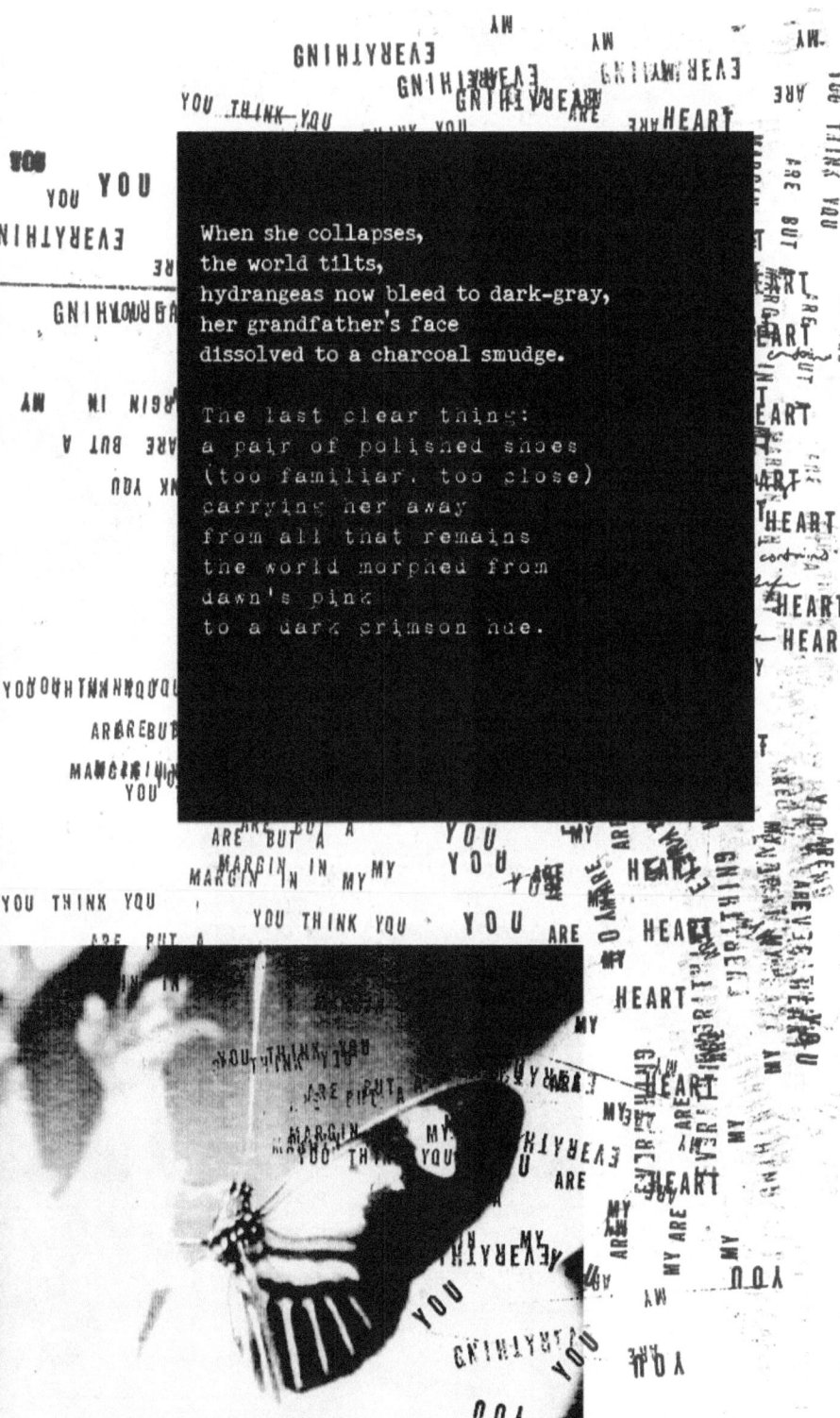

When she collapses,
the world tilts,
hydrangeas now bleed to dark-gray,
her grandfather's face
dissolved to a charcoal smudge.

The last clear thing:
a pair of polished shoes
(too familiar, too close)
carrying her away
from all that remains
the world morphed from
dawn's pink
to a dark crimson hue.

2025 : GRIEVING AMARYLLIS : MIRRORS AND SHADOWS

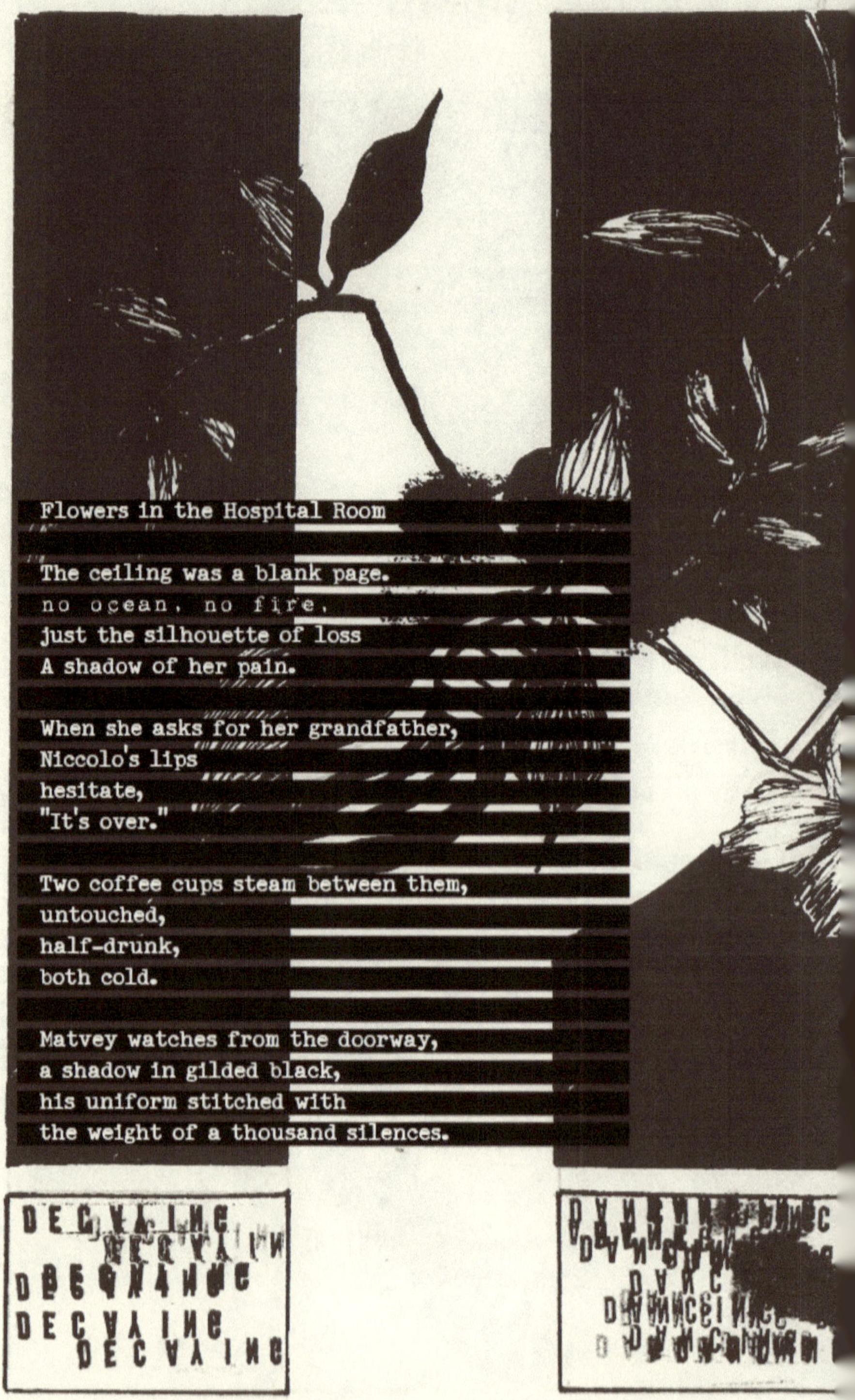

Flowers in the Hospital Room

The ceiling was a blank page.
no ocean, no fire,
just the silhouette of loss
A shadow of her pain.

When she asks for her grandfather,
Niccolo's lips
hesitate,
"It's over."

Two coffee cups steam between them,
untouched,
half-drunk,
both cold.

Matvey watches from the doorway,
a shadow in gilded black,
his uniform stitched with
the weight of a thousand silences.

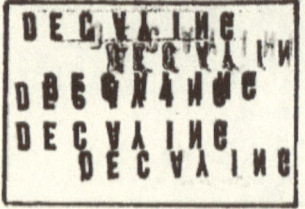

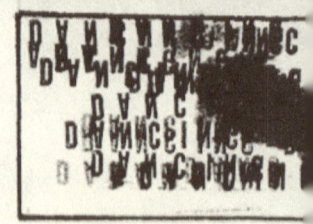

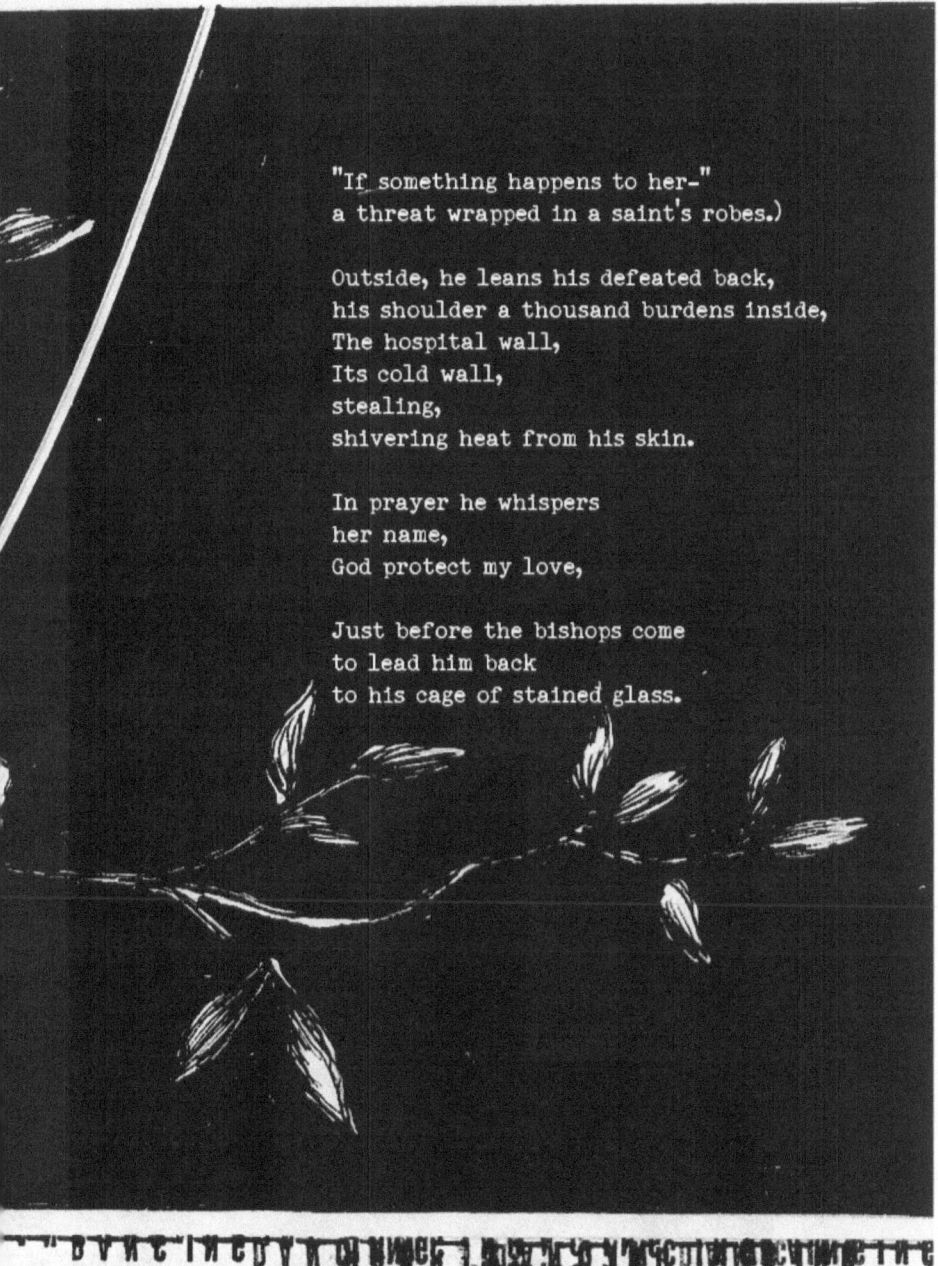

"If something happens to her-"
a threat wrapped in a saint's robes.)

Outside, he leans his defeated back,
his shoulder a thousand burdens inside,
The hospital wall,
Its cold wall,
stealing,
shivering heat from his skin.

In prayer he whispers
her name,
God protect my love,

Just before the bishops come
to lead him back
to his cage of stained glass.

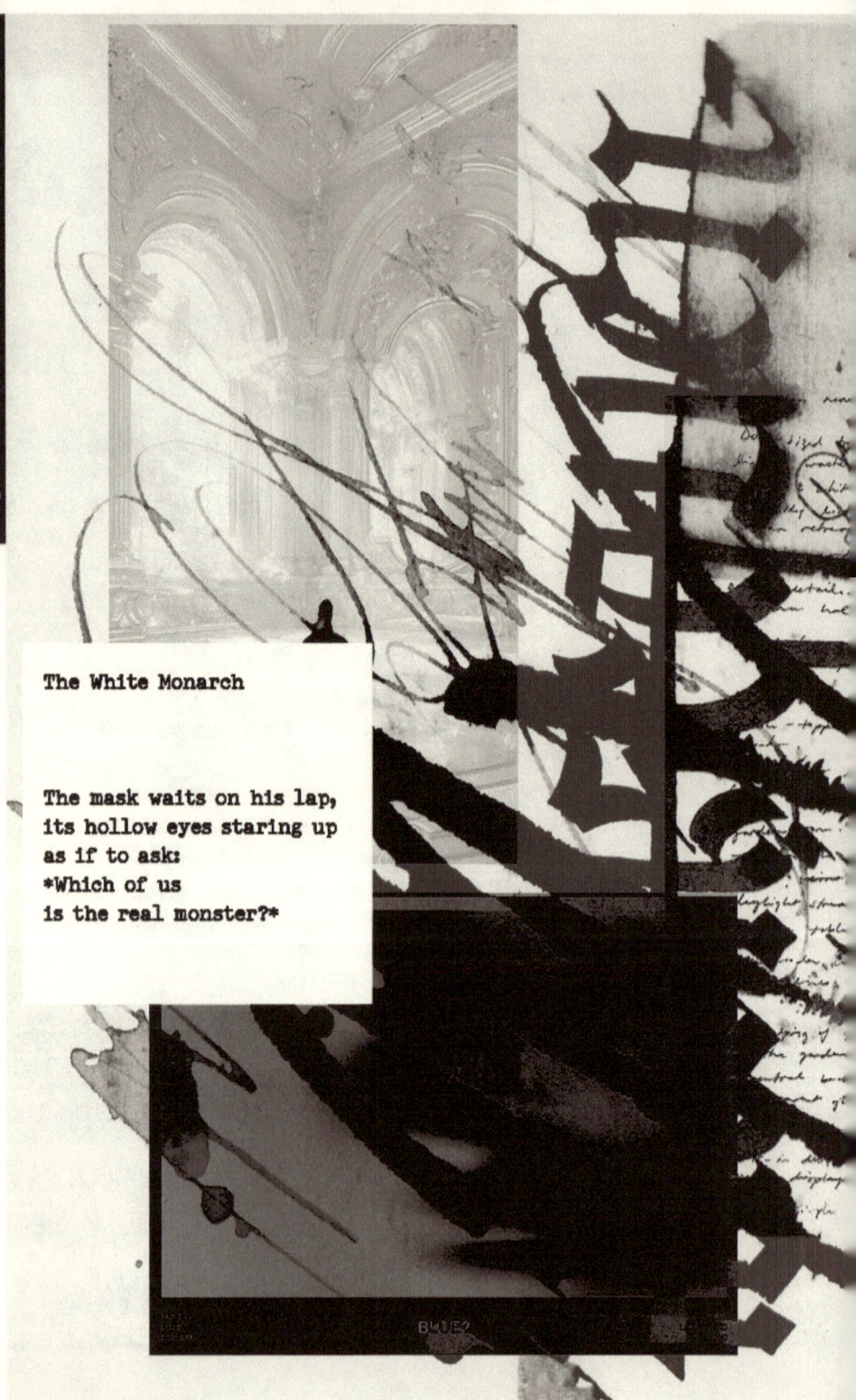

The White Monarch

The mask waits on his lap,
its hollow eyes staring up
as if to ask:
*Which of us
is the real monster?*

*Which of us
is the real monster?*

2025 : GRIEVING AMARYLLIS : MIRRORS AND SHADOWS

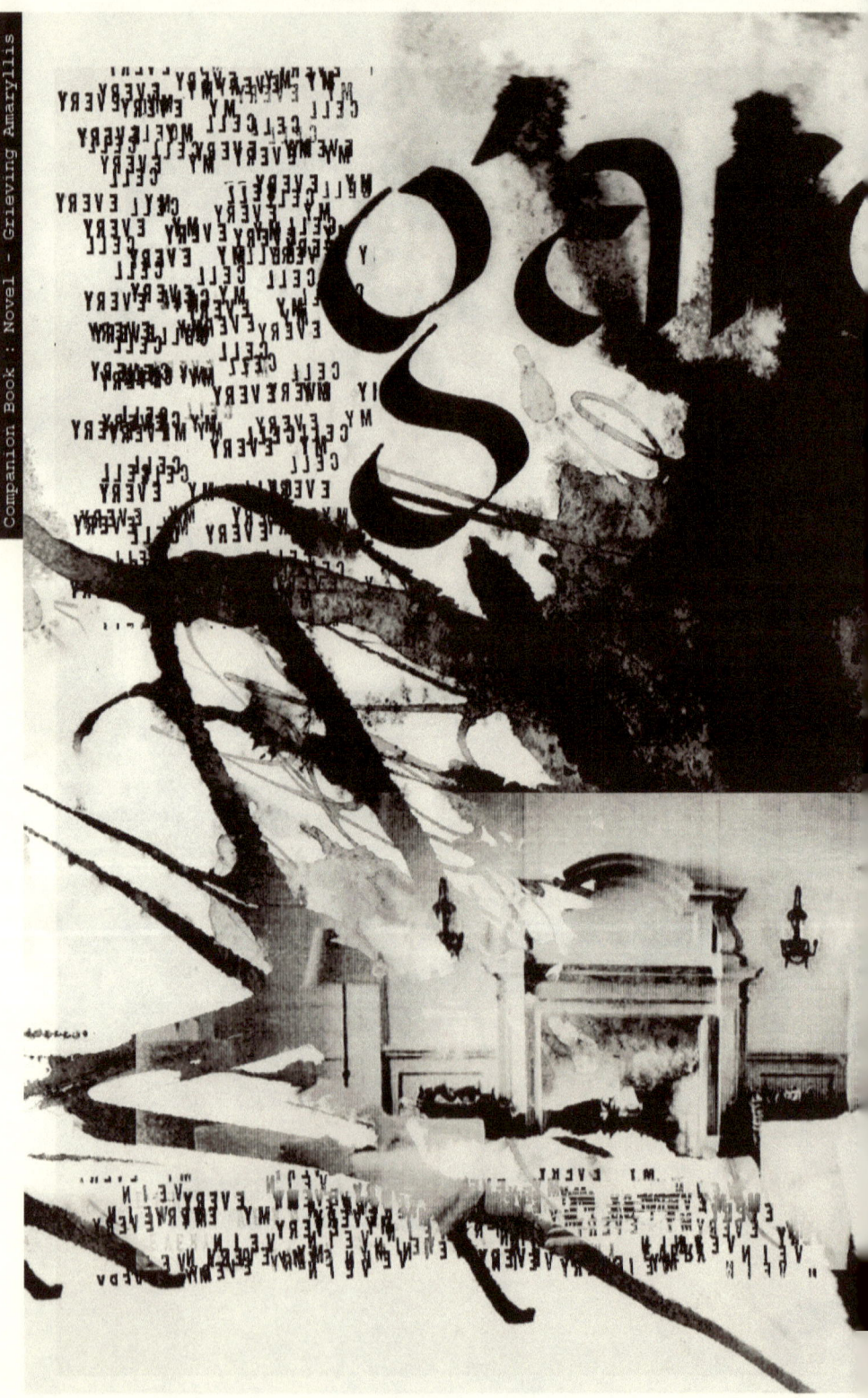

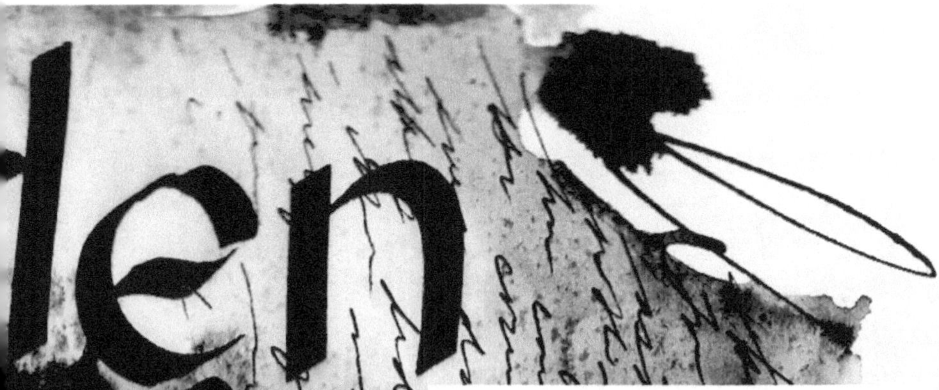

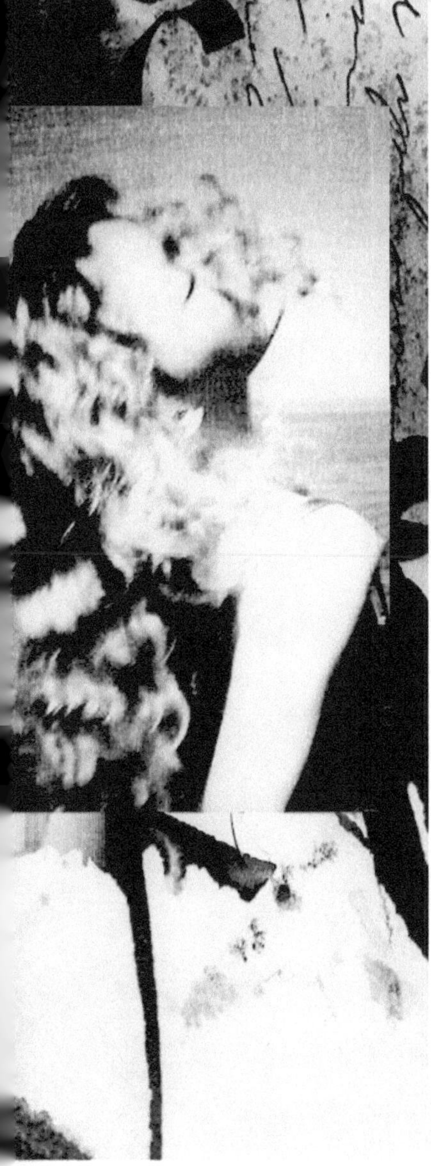

"Canis Minor"

The snow was falling
between brothers.

Two boys whispering
between scripture lines,
their eyes reflecting
the Sky's Eden-
roses painfully red,
foliage too green,
a paradise vivid
over bones.

Alexander stands
at the window where
they once looked,
over late dark nights
over bright glass,
counting constellations.

Matvey's confession hangs
"I wanted to marry her."

saint and *traitor*,
brother and *blood*.

Some vows are made
to be broken.
Some saints,
are made to fight.
Alexander's words.

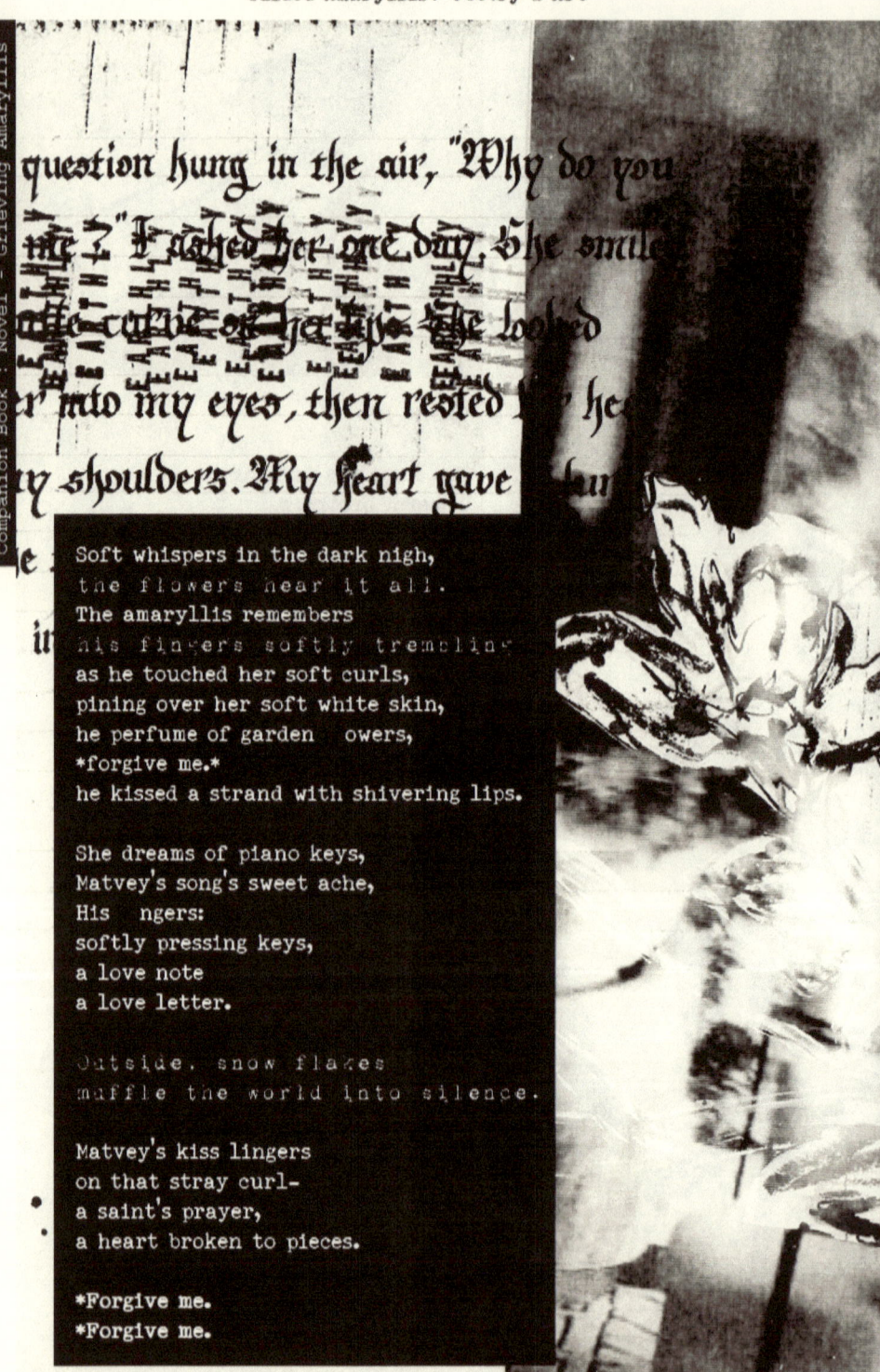

question hung in the air, "Why do you
me ?" I asked her one day. She smiled
the curve of her lips. She looked
r into my eyes, then rested her he
y shoulders. My heart gave

Soft whispers in the dark nigh,
the flowers hear it all.
The amaryllis remembers
his fingers softly trembling
as he touched her soft curls,
pining over her soft white skin,
he perfume of garden owers,
forgive me.
he kissed a strand with shivering lips.

She dreams of piano keys,
Matvey's song's sweet ache,
His ngers:
softly pressing keys,
a love note
a love letter.

Outside, snow flakes
muffle the world into silence.

Matvey's kiss lingers
on that stray curl—
a saint's prayer,
a heart broken to pieces.

*Forgive me.
*Forgive me.

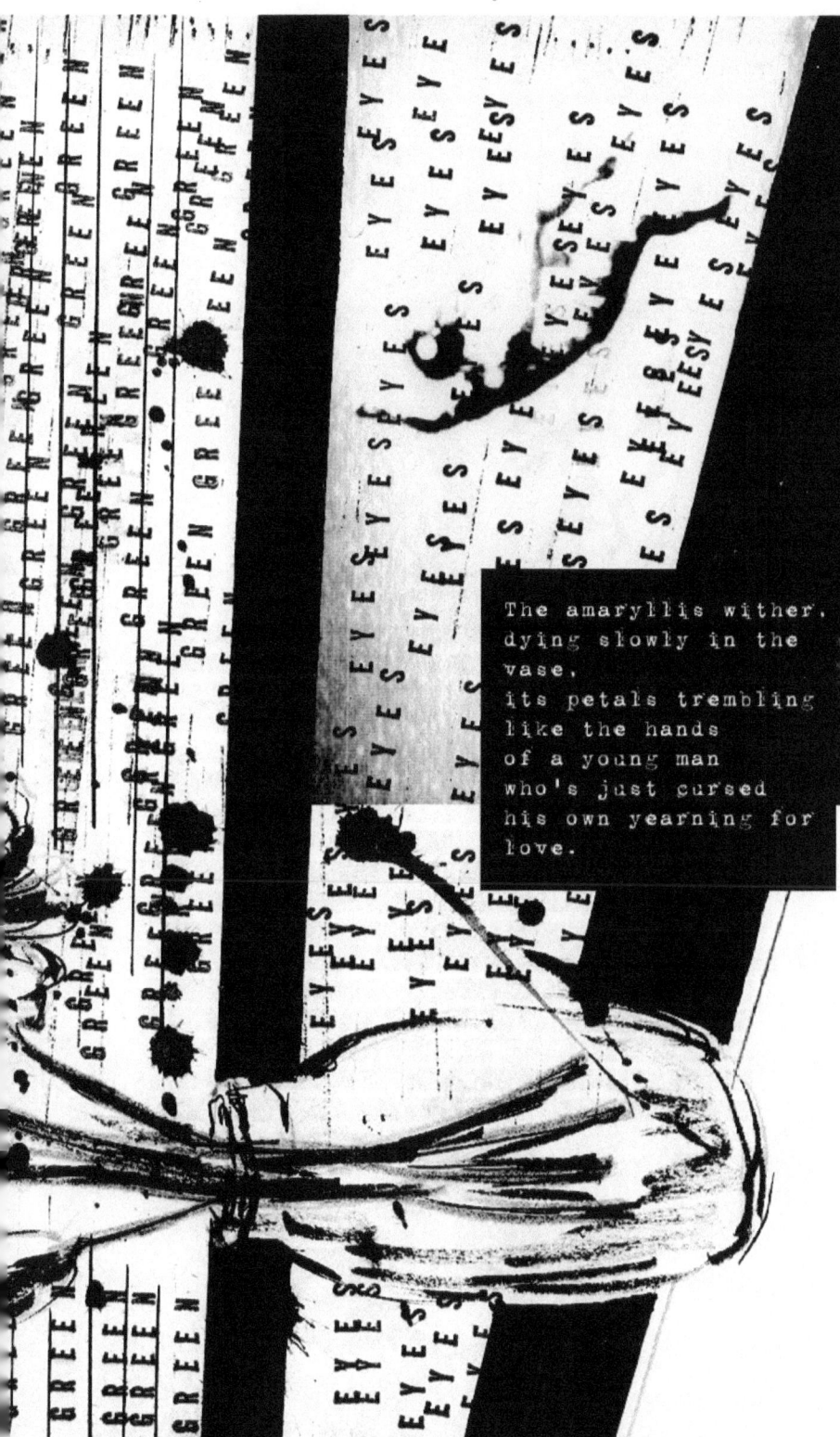

The amaryllis wither,
dying slowly in the
vase,
its petals trembling
like the hands
of a young man
who's just cursed
his own yearning for
love.

2025 : GRIEVING AMARYLLIS : MIRRORS AND SHADOWS

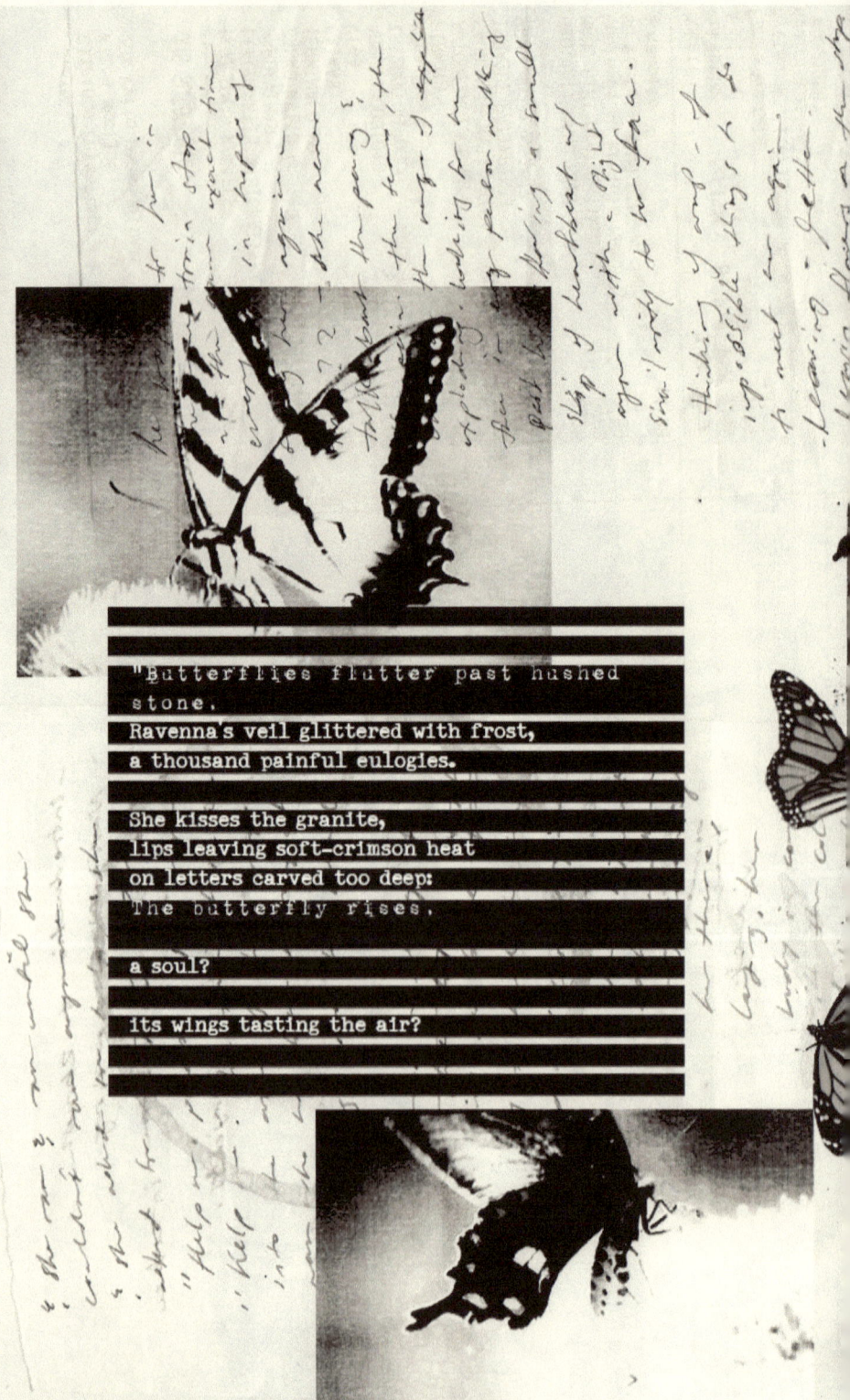

"Butterflies flutter past hushed stone.
Ravenna's veil glittered with frost,
a thousand painful eulogies.

She kisses the granite,
lips leaving soft-crimson heat
on letters carved too deep:
The butterfly rises,

a soul?

its wings tasting the air?

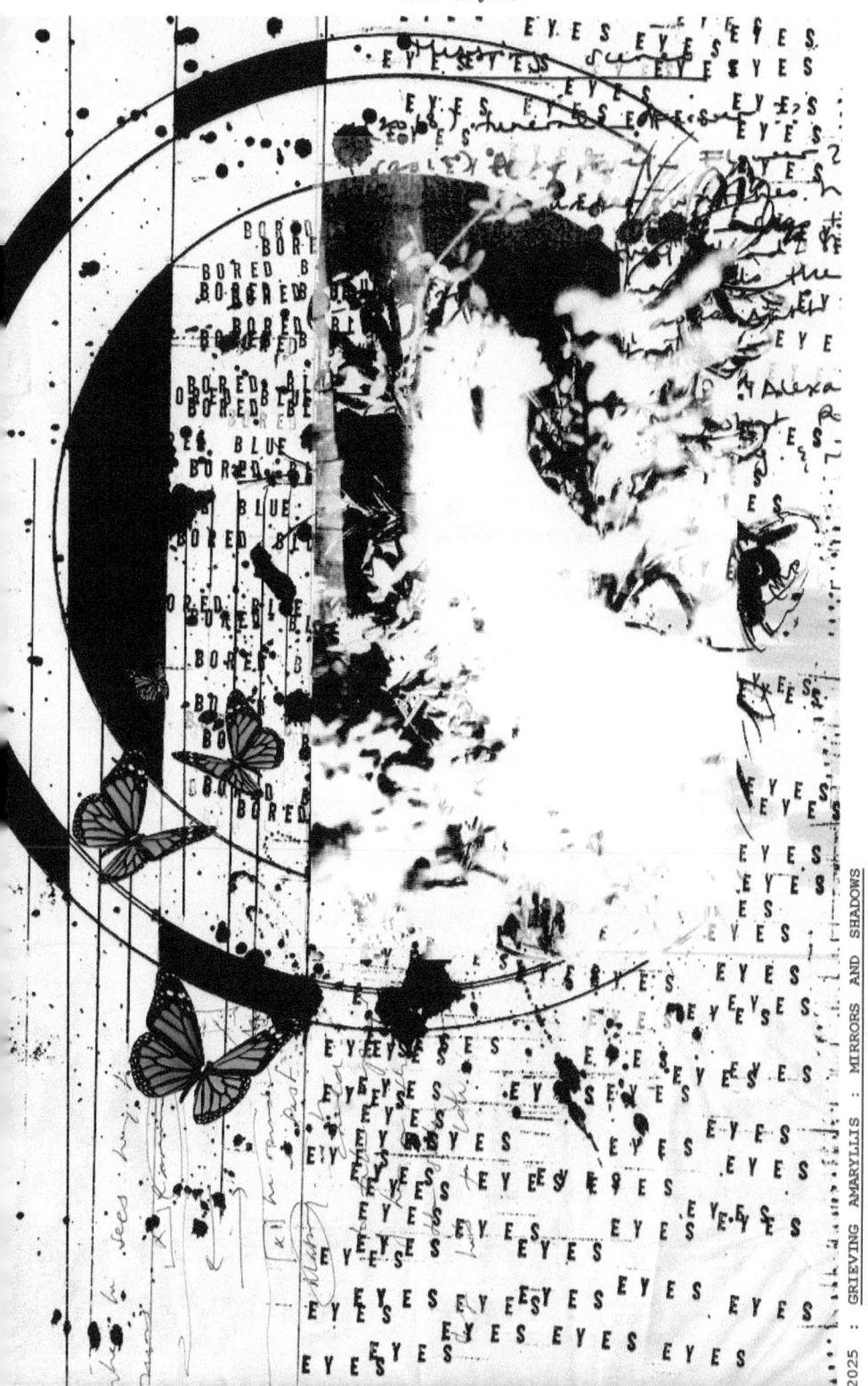

2025 : GRIEVING AMARYLLIS : MIRRORS AND SHADOWS

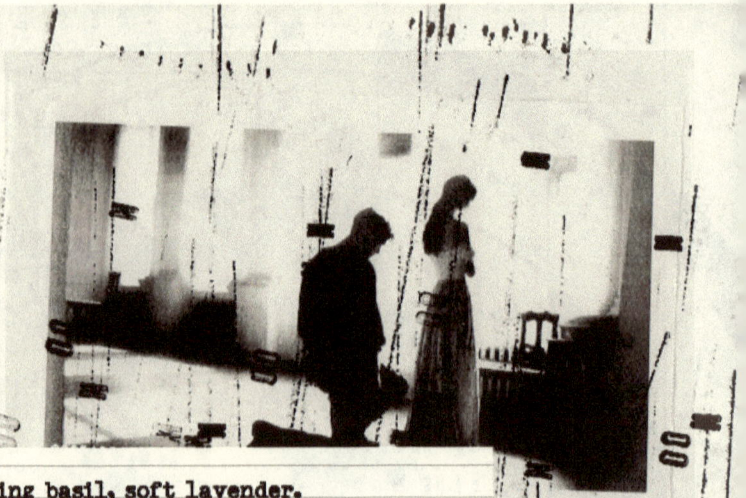

Deceiving basil, soft lavender.

Morning rage   nds Niccolo:
shattered vase, torn books,
a note   uttering
like a white feather
on the scar
of Niccolo's heart.

Anais reads the words aloud,
"Don't come looking for me.
Thank you for everything,
Love, Ravenna..."

Ravenna stood, the night before,
at the river-view window,
counting the steps
to the Glass Temple.

Niccolo's studio waits in silence,
his half- nished sculptures
watching with stone eyes,
as he tears the guest room
apart:
"Why?"
"Why?"
"Why can't she just love me?"

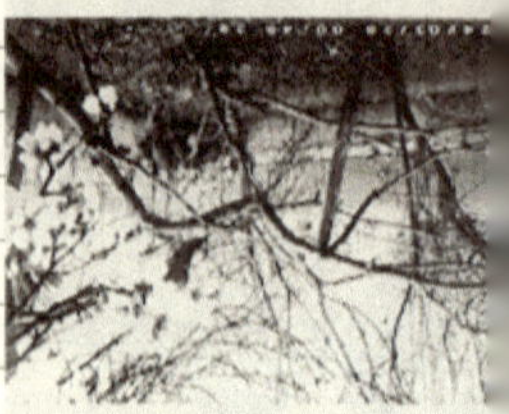

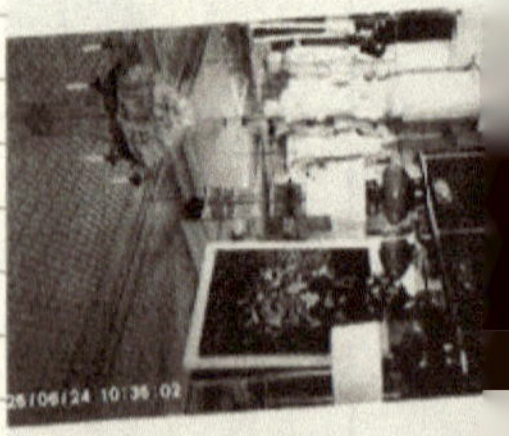

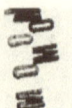
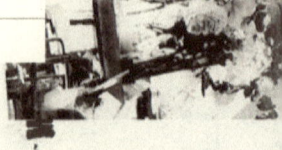

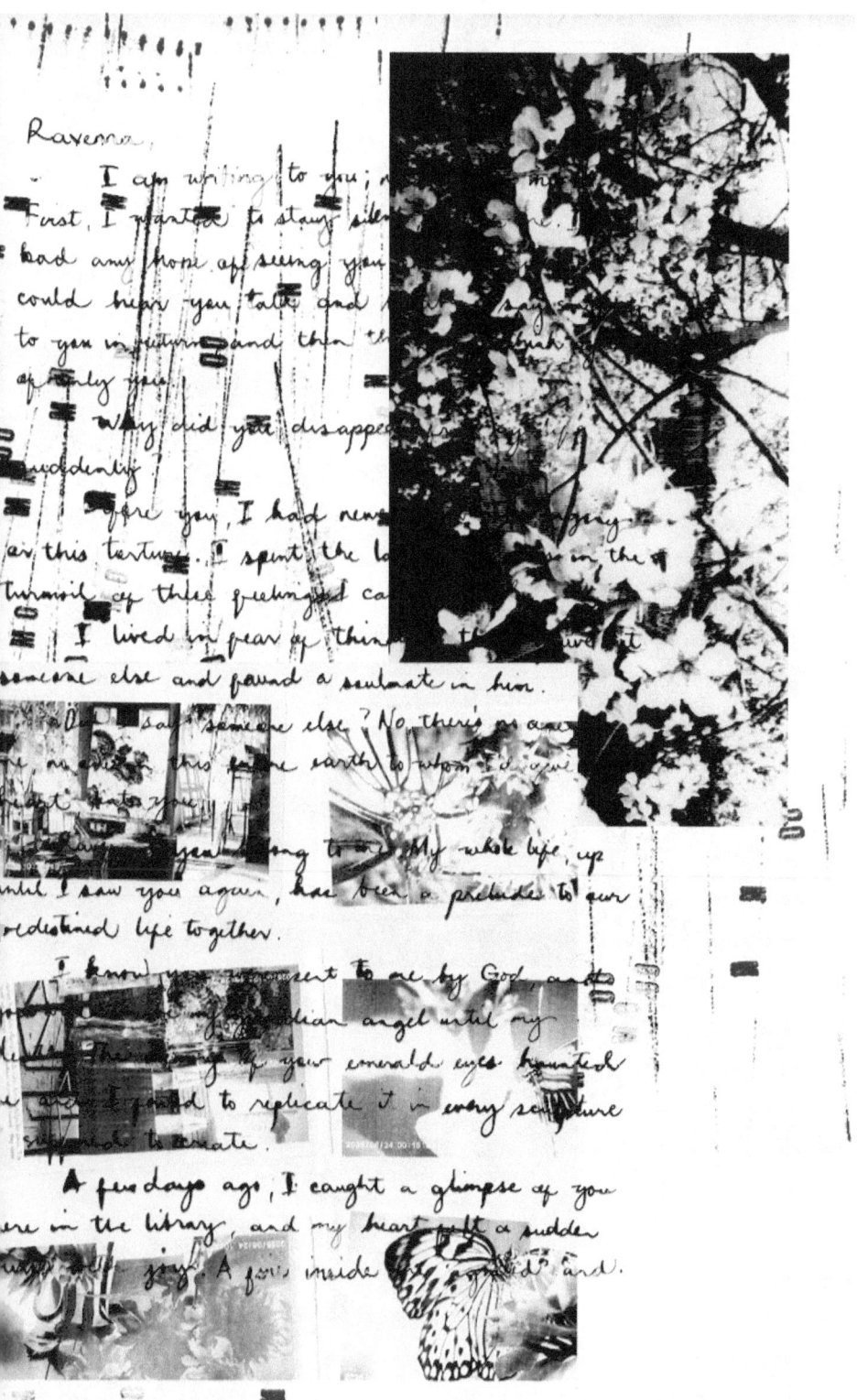

Ravenna,

I am writing to you, ...

First, I wanted to stay sil... ...re. I
had any hope of seeing you ...
could hear you talk and ... say ...
to you in return and then th... ...
of only you...

Why did you disappear so ...
suddenly ...

...fore you, I had nev... ...joy...
as this texture... I spent the l... ...se in the
turmoil of these feelings ... ca...

I lived in fear of thin... ...t
someone else and found a soulmate in him.

...say "someone else"? No, there's no...
...no on... this ... earth to whom I ...ve...
...at... you...

...you ...long t... My whole life, up
until I saw you again, has been a prelude to our
predestined life together.

I know y... ...sent to me by God ...
...my ...an angel until my
...The ...ing of your emerald eyes haunted
...and ...ned to replicate it in every sculpture
...to create.

A few days ago, I caught a glimpse of you
...re in the library, and my heart ...t a sudden
...zi... A fire inside ... ...d and.

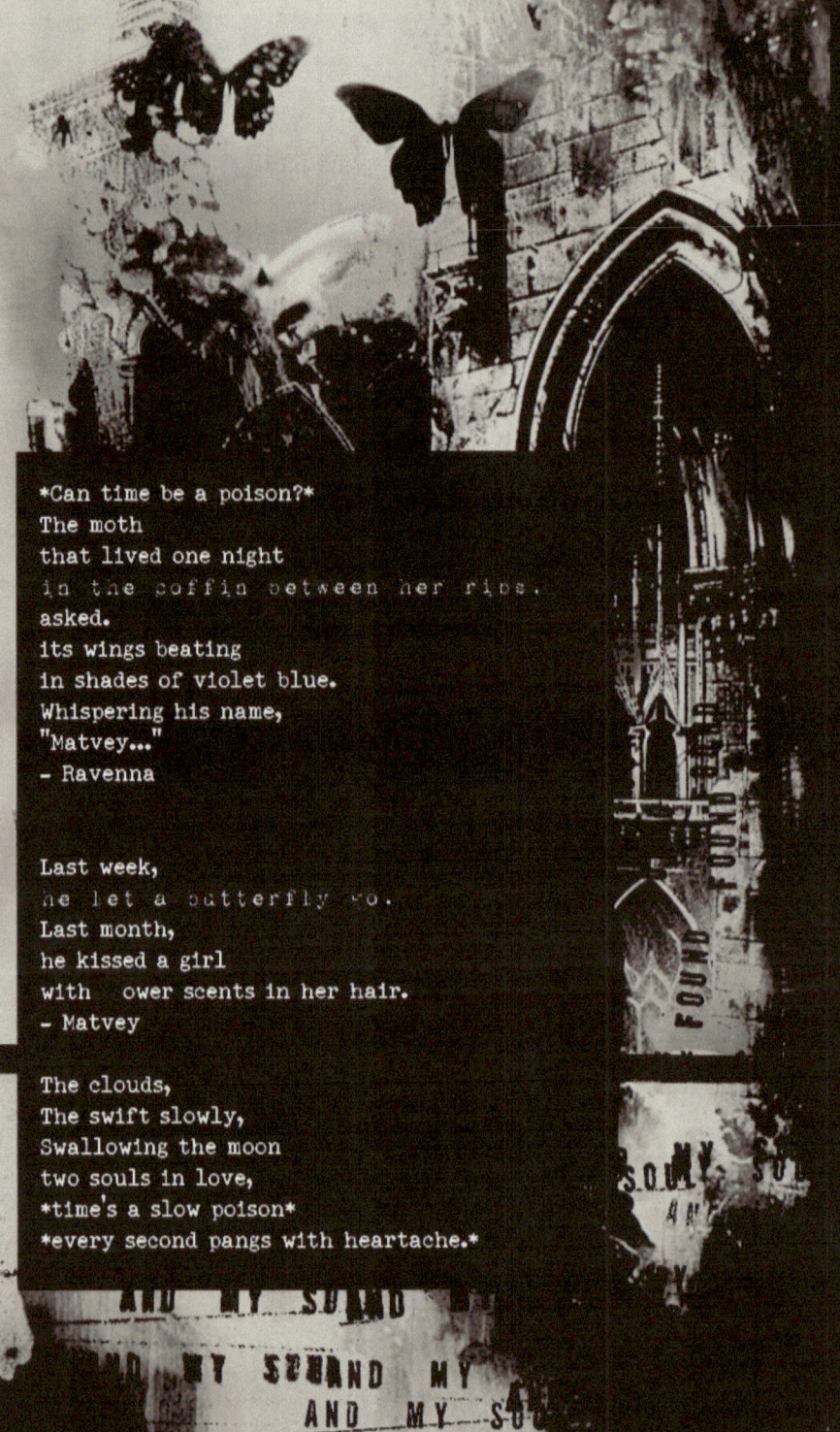

Can time be a poison?
The moth
that lived one night
in the coffin between her ribs.
asked.
its wings beating
in shades of violet blue.
Whispering his name,
"Matvey..."
- Ravenna

Last week,
he let a butterfly go.
Last month,
he kissed a girl
with ower scents in her hair.
- Matvey

The clouds,
The swift slowly,
Swallowing the moon
two souls in love,
time's a slow poison
every second pangs with heartache.

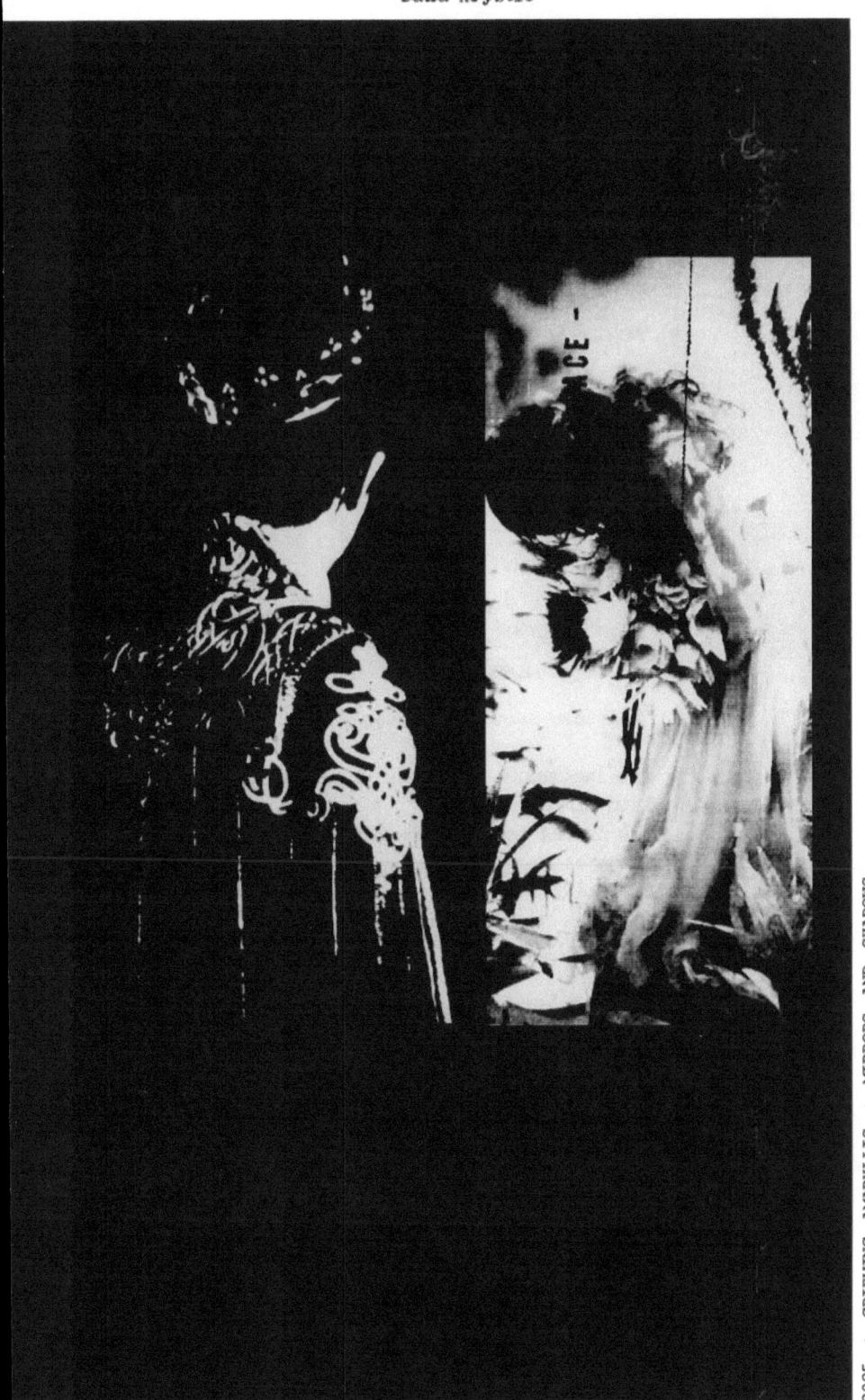

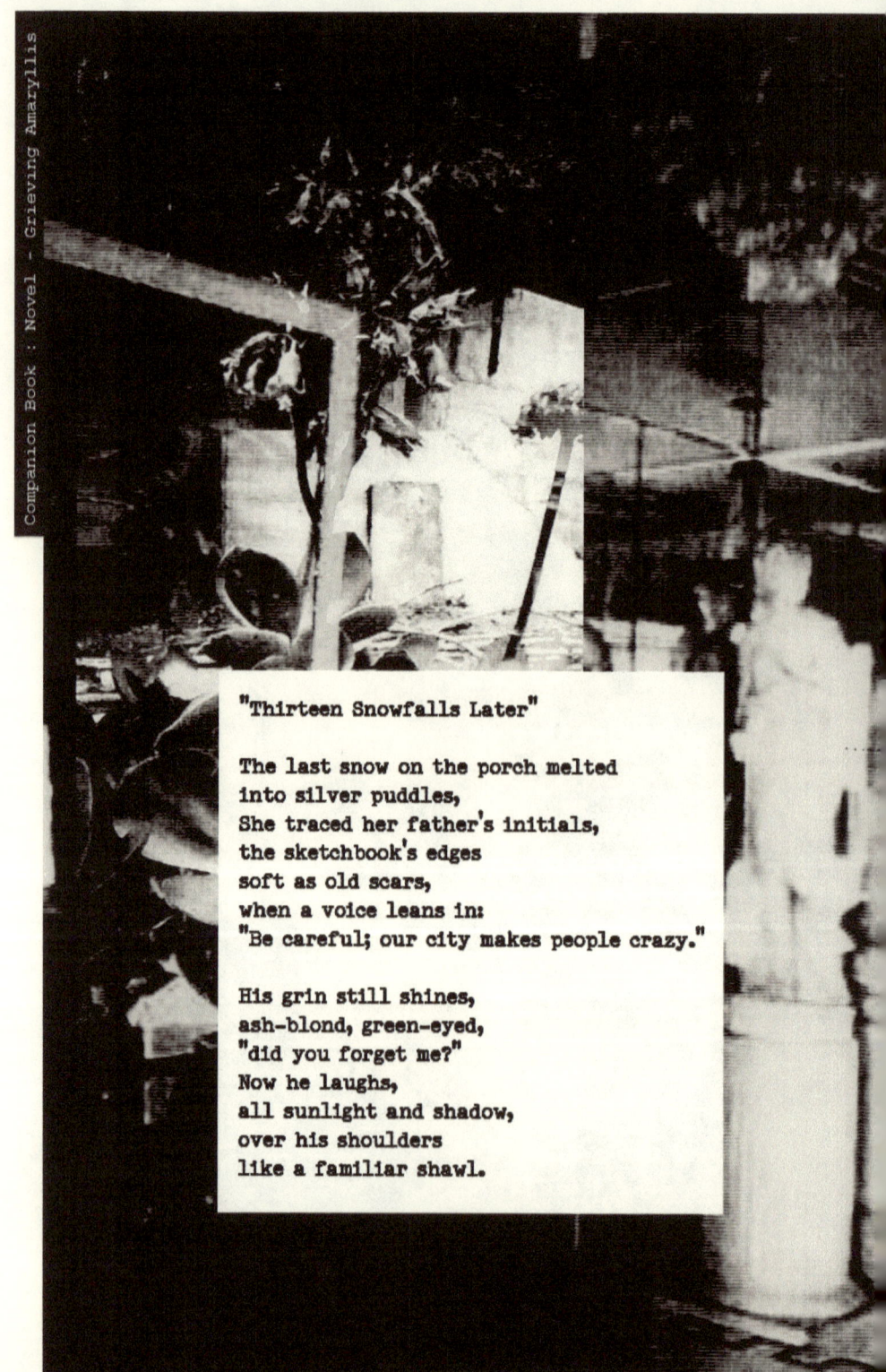

"Thirteen Snowfalls Later"

The last snow on the porch melted
into silver puddles,
She traced her father's initials,
the sketchbook's edges
soft as old scars,
when a voice leans in:
"Be careful; our city makes people crazy."

His grin still shines,
ash-blond, green-eyed,
"did you forget me?"
Now he laughs,
all sunlight and shadow,
over his shoulders
like a familiar shawl.

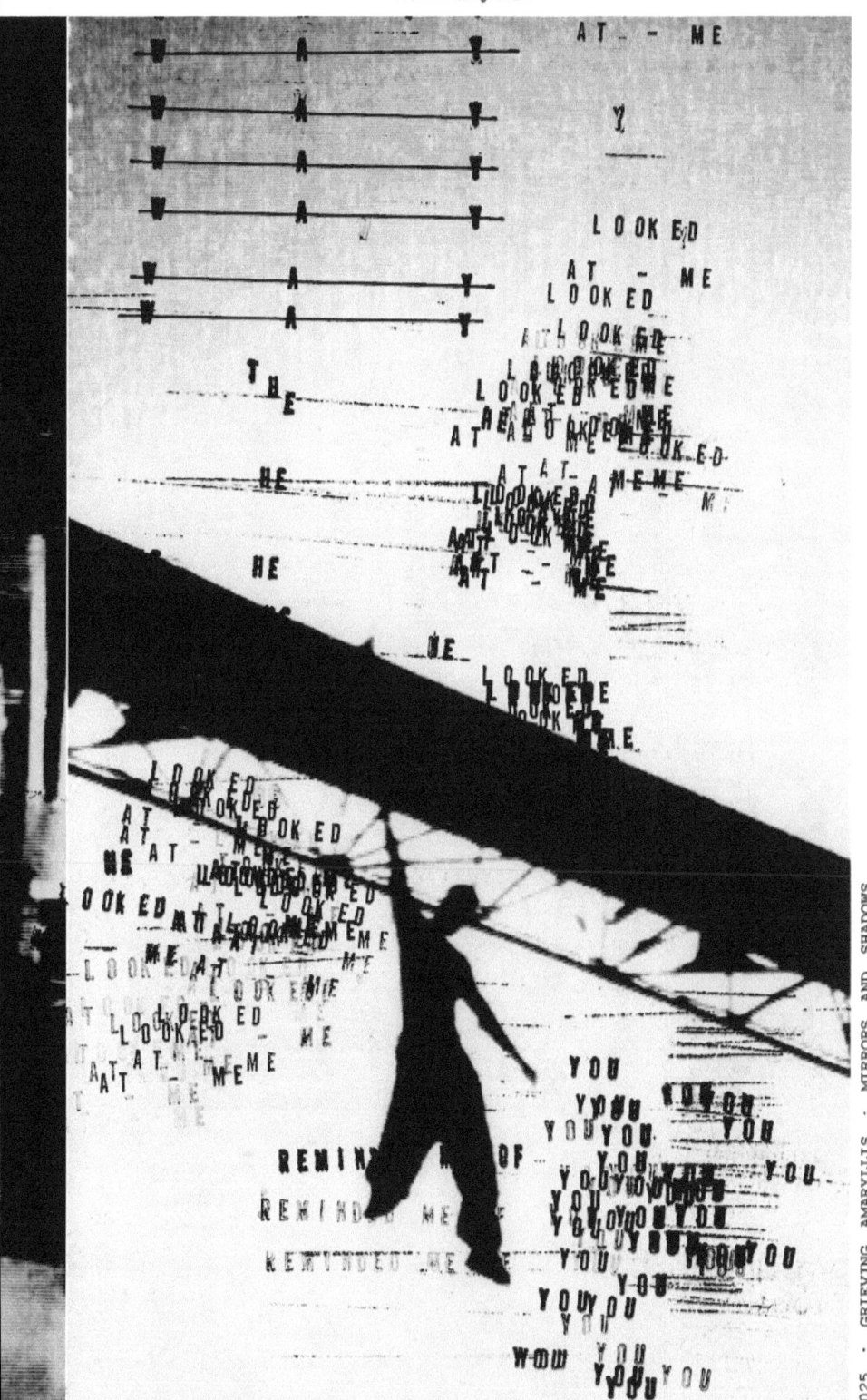

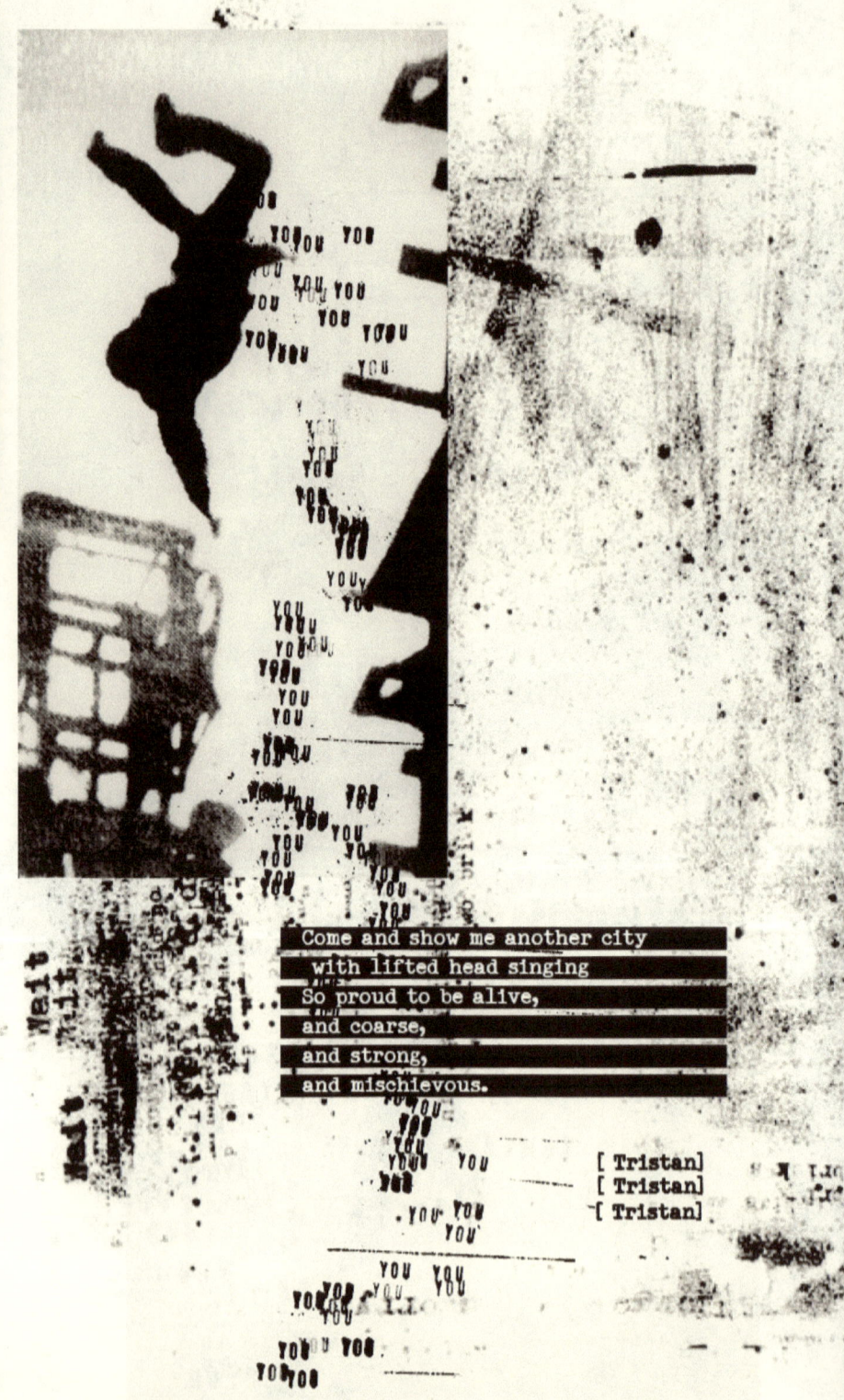

Come and show me another city
with lifted head singing
So proud to be alive,
and coarse,
and strong,
and mischievous.

[Tristan]
[Tristan]
[Tristan]

I want to live; life's too short to not have adventures.
Tristan lifted his arms in the air, the sun and sky
monumental above him.
Imagine living in a city where you don't have to rely
on overcrowded trains, gridlocked roads, and packed
pavement. Able to leap from rooftop to rooftop-as if
nothing, not even buildings, can stop you.

This is the urban art Tristan chose for himself. It's
a feeling he can't fully explain, the closest he gets to
truly feeling alive.

An electric surge of energy bursts through his
body, a euphoric addiction. For him, it's about discipline,
about clearing every obstacle in his path, about finding
absolute freedom in towns and cities designed to contain.

He propelled himself higher and higher, chasing the
thrill, flowing effortlessly across urban chairs, fences,
and handrails.

Daily, he finds ways to practice on houses, temples,
shops, and halls, drinking in the beauty of City-A with
his eyes and lungs.

This is how he battles his own demons, challenging
his doubts and conquering his fears. He always finds an
opportunity to jump, to back-flip, to run-to run-to run.

When Tristan pauses, he gazes high at the sky,
feeling as if he's just a few more leaps from touching the
soft clouds. His body suddenly feels tall and imposing,
the light in his hands is bathed in sunlight, moonlight,
and the stars.

He thrives on living with his heart in his throat
every day, embracing new risks and dangerous paths,
striving for elegance in every movement, he creates
a seamless harmony between himself and the urban
landscape.

There is always a path. He loves to spread his
hands wide, like a bird taking flight, tiptoeing along the
thin ledges of most building rooftops, as he watches his
shadow glide across the streets and buildings below.

This city, City-A, is his boundless playground.

Columbine at Midnight

Columbine at Midnight

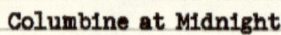

The Shadow Saints pass like ink in the dark,
Tristan learns the weight of her palm,
gently placed on his lips,
silence,
lest the ink turn both their shadows into
blood.

"Buildings can't stop me," he brags,
And the way her laugh unfolds
Lines and strokes of secrets,
connecting constellations
the saints beg to see.

He plucked a violet promise
from cracked concrete,
At dawn, they'll call it vandalism,
At sunrise she calls it freedom.

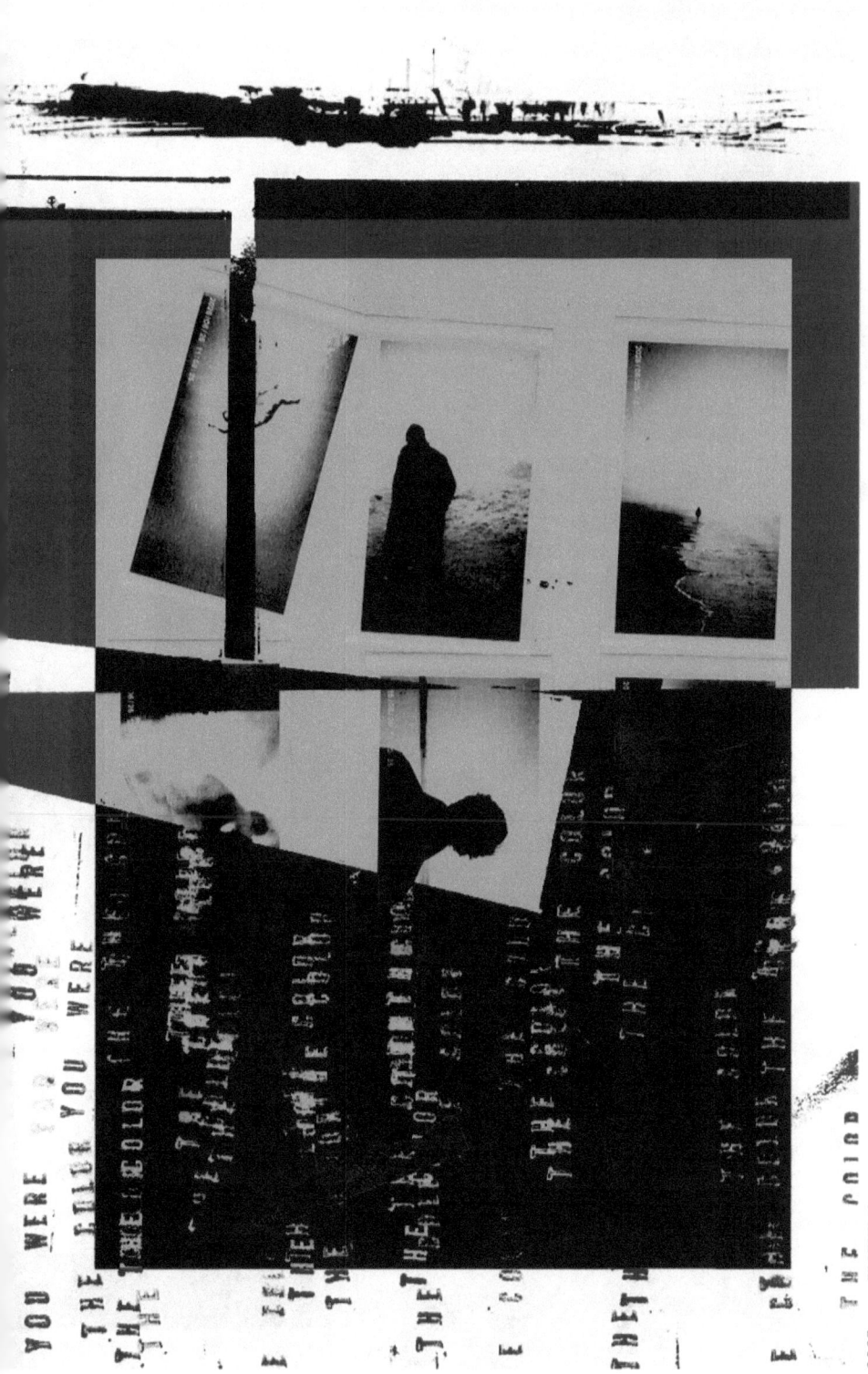

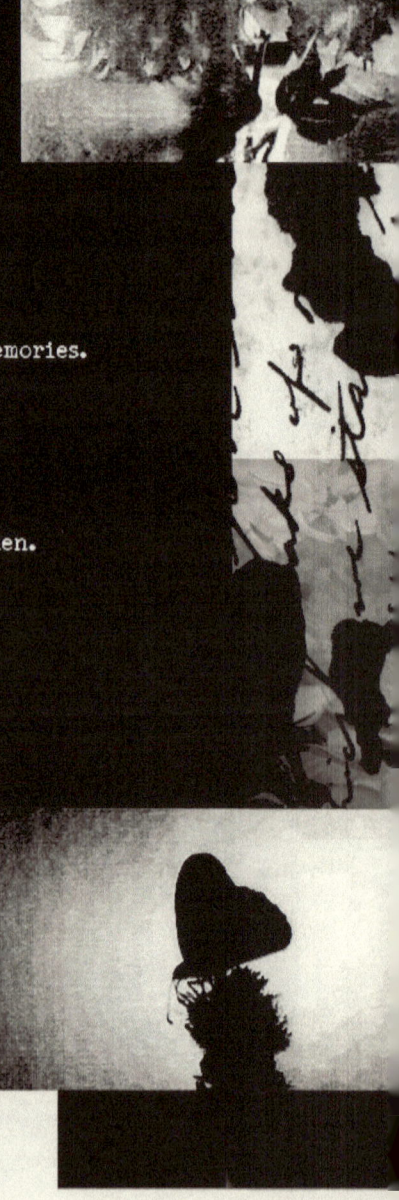

"Burning House Constellation"

"I had a dream last night."
but the smoke was real,
and the scar under his eye
colored in fresh blood,
a six-year-old's memory,
a written fate from God.

"You lied," he laughs,
"this was a memory."
The night dome above:
Constellations kissing their skin
glittering over their childhood memories.

The bridge beneath them,
becomes an altar.
Her head on his shoulder,
his pulse humming
it's okay, we were just children then.

Somewhere, the burned house
collapsed into dust.
Everywhere, the two children
walked through the woods crying.

Here, only the river witnesses
how quietly
a decade of blame
dissolved
between two souls
her cold teardrop fell
on his flustered ch

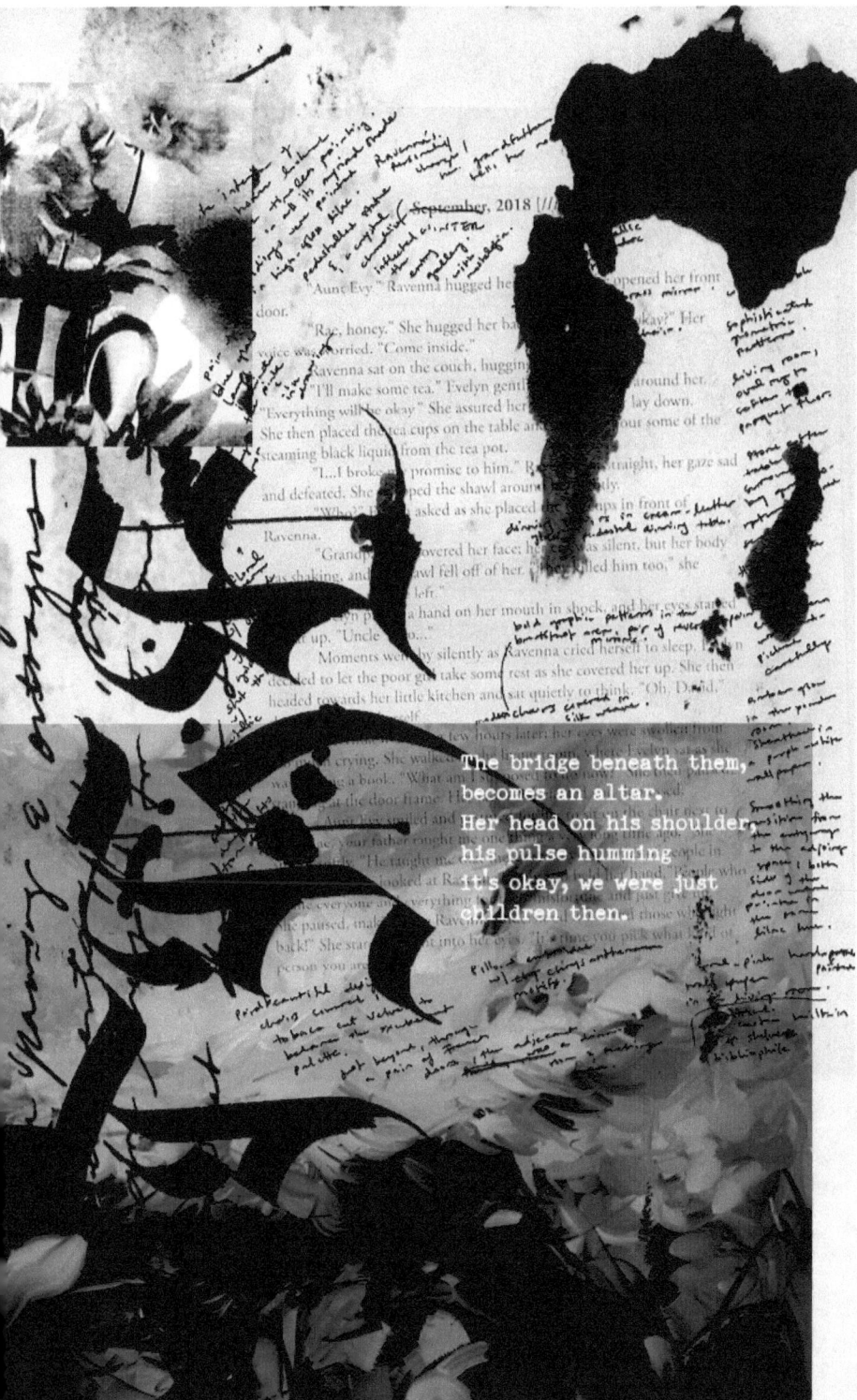

The bridge beneath them,
becomes an altar.
Her head on his shoulder,
his pulse humming
it's okay, we were just
children then.

I live in fear of thinking that you've
met someone else and found a soulmate
in him. Did I say someone else?
No, there is no one for me, no one on
earth to whom I'd have given my heart
Ravenui you belong to no
My whole life in

The Glass Cathedral's Oath

"Saints never lie,"

Alexander walks the hall of martyrs,
his shadow stretching long
over marble faces

He remembers Matvey's hands
trembling as they pressed
the emerald ribbon
into his palm,
"Keep her safe."
The green silk
smelled of salt and hydrangeas,
A shore,
A place,
Matvey would never walk again.

A shore,
A place,
Matvey would never walk
again.

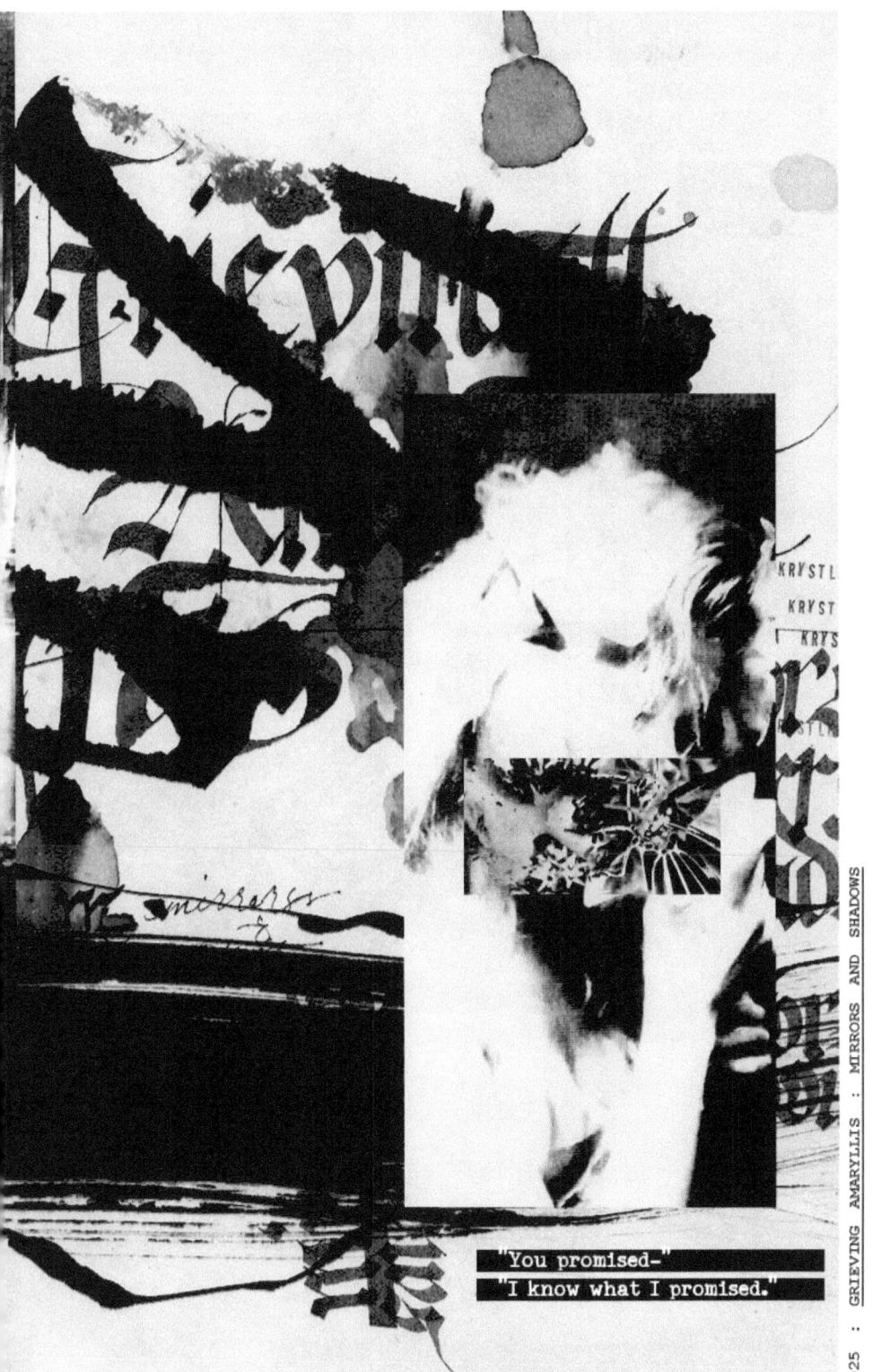

"You promised-"
"I know what I promised."

Companion Book : Novel - Grieving Amaryllis

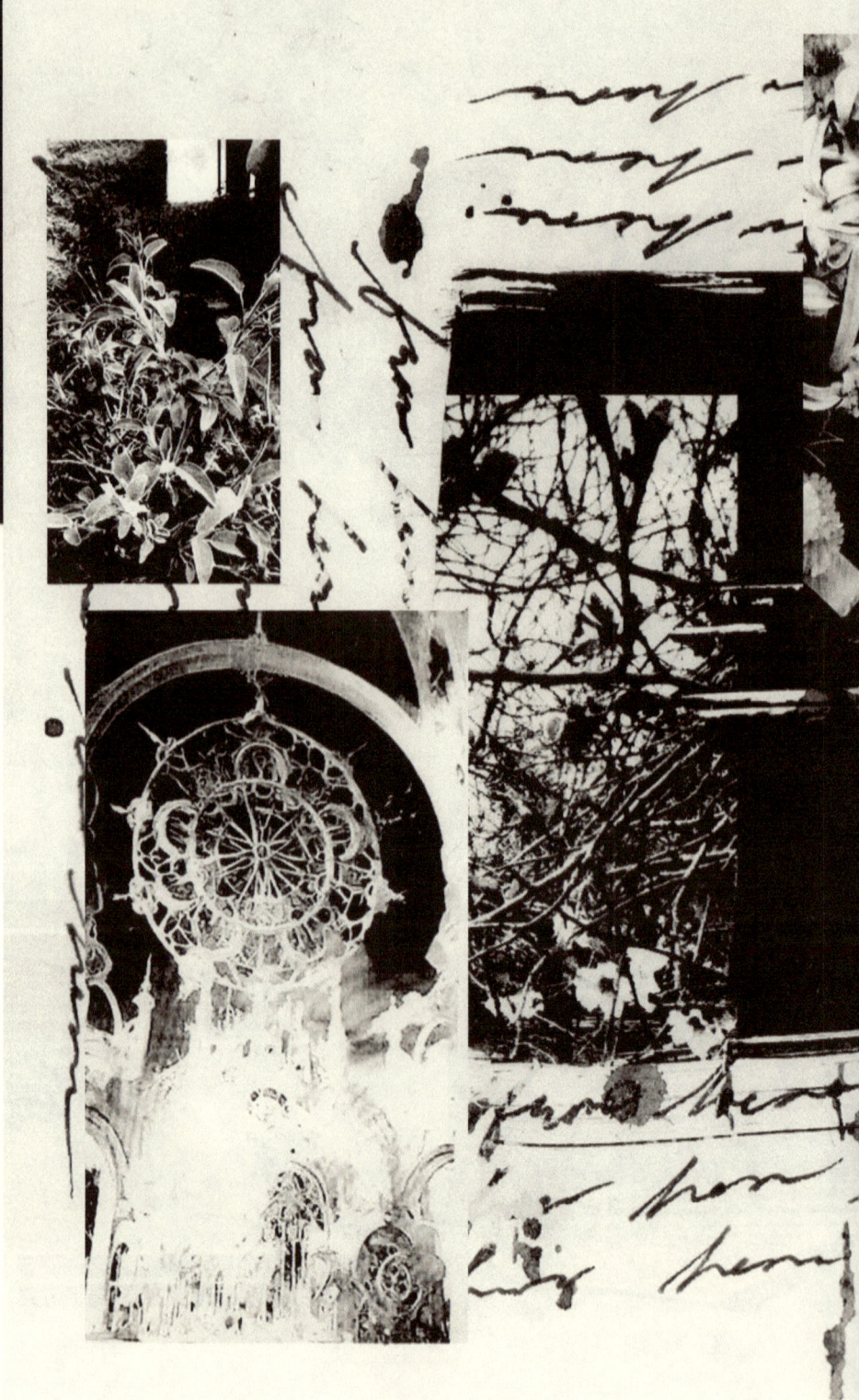

Columbine at Midnight

The Shadow Saints pass like ink in the dark,
Tristan learns the weight of her palm,
gently placed on his lips,
silence,
lest the ink turn both their shadows into blood.

"Buildings can't stop me," he brags,
And the way her laugh unfolds
Lines and strokes of secrets,
connecting constellations
the saints beg to see.

He plucked a violet promise
from cracked concrete,
At dawn, they'll call it vandalism,
At sunrise she calls it freedom.

2025 : GRIEVING AMARYLLIS : MIRRORS AND SHADOWS

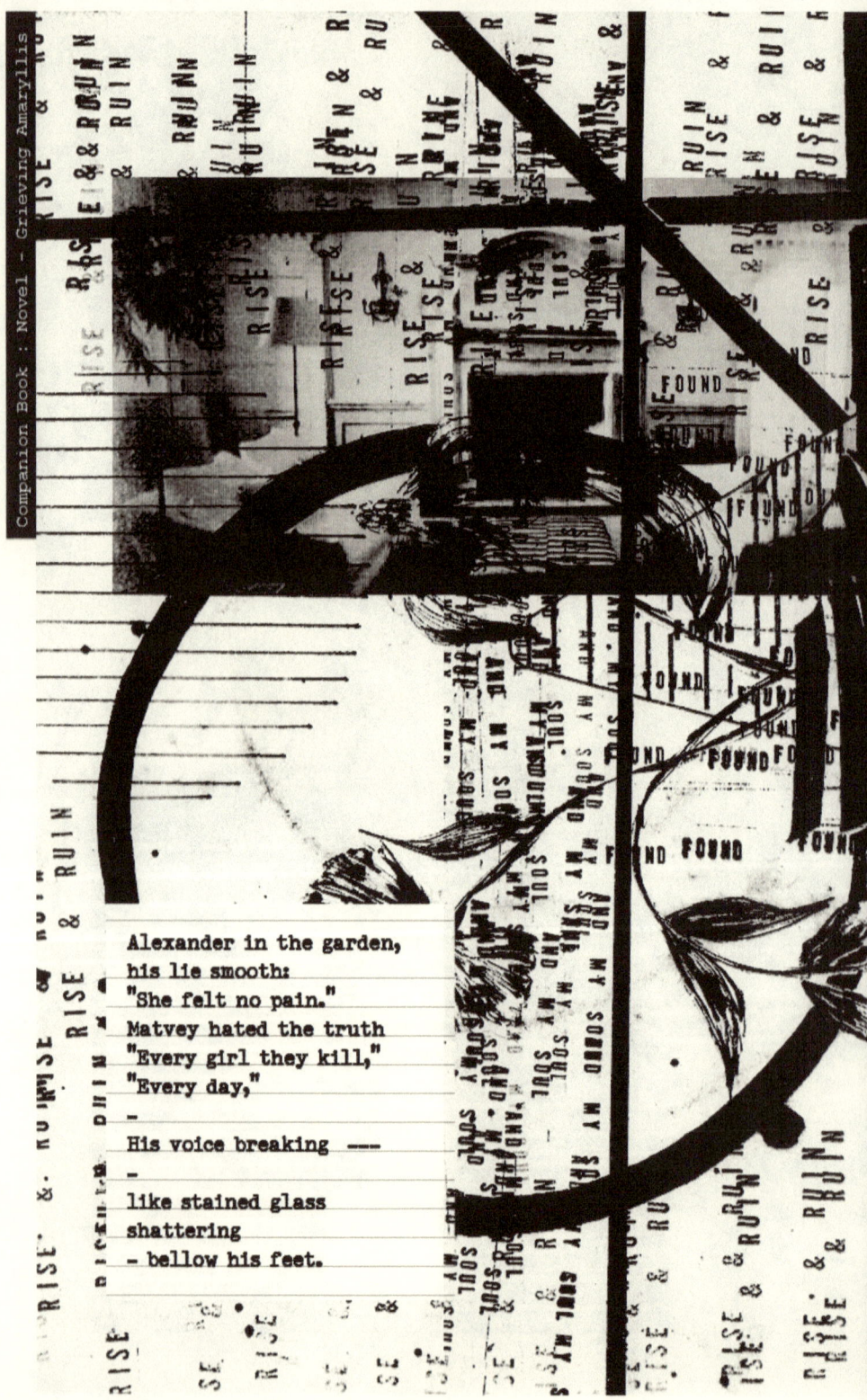

Companion Book : Novel – Grieving Amaryllis

Alexander in the garden,
his lie smooth:
"She felt no pain."
Matvey hated the truth
"Every girl they kill,"
"Every day,"
–

His voice breaking ⸺
–

like stained glass
shattering
– bellow his feet.

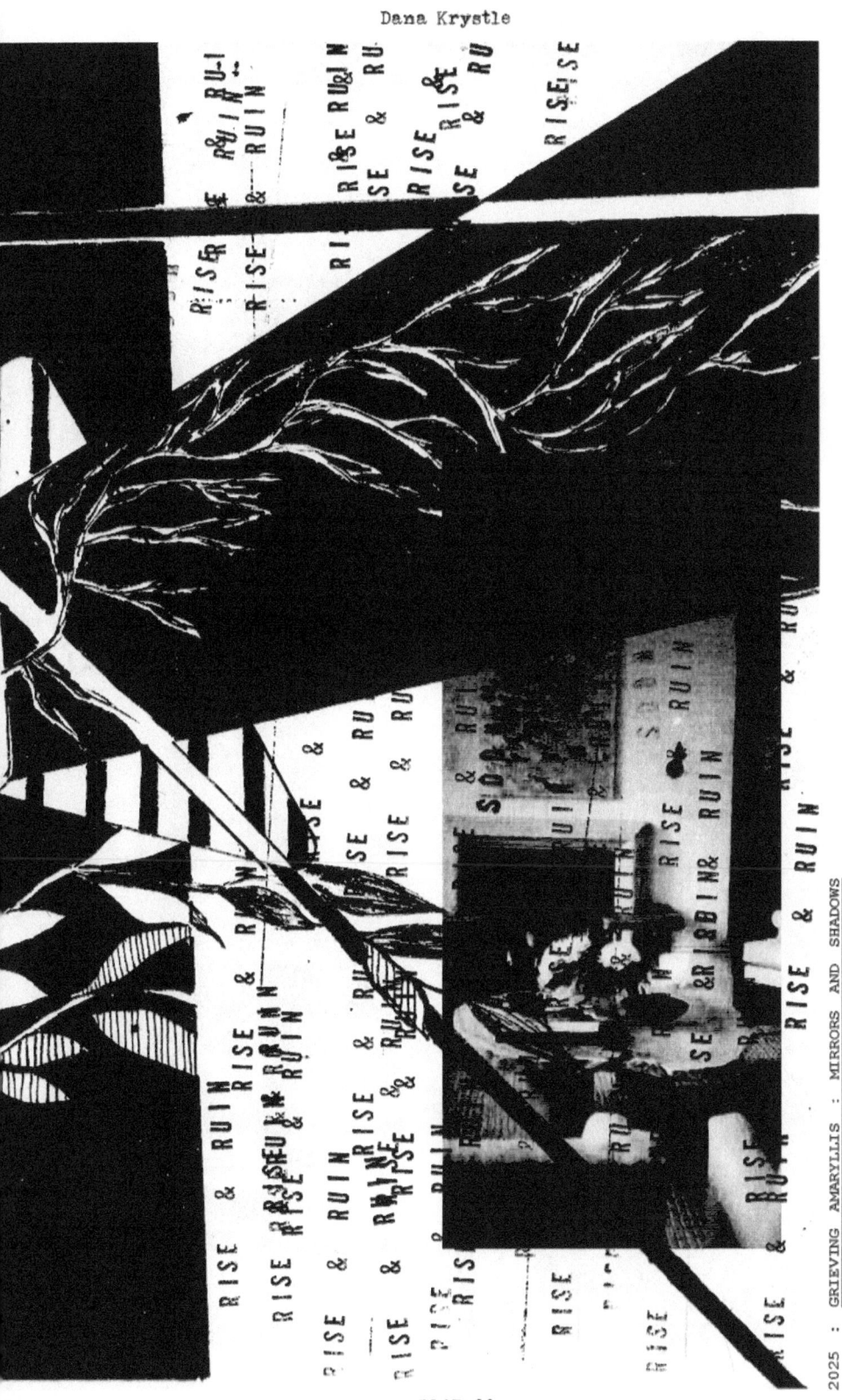

2025 : GRIEVING AMARYLLIS : MIRRORS AND SHADOWS

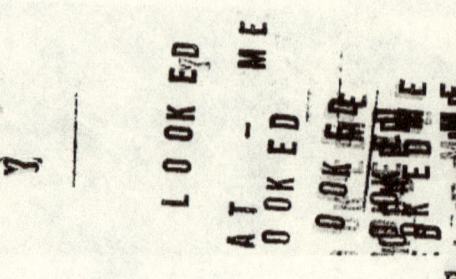

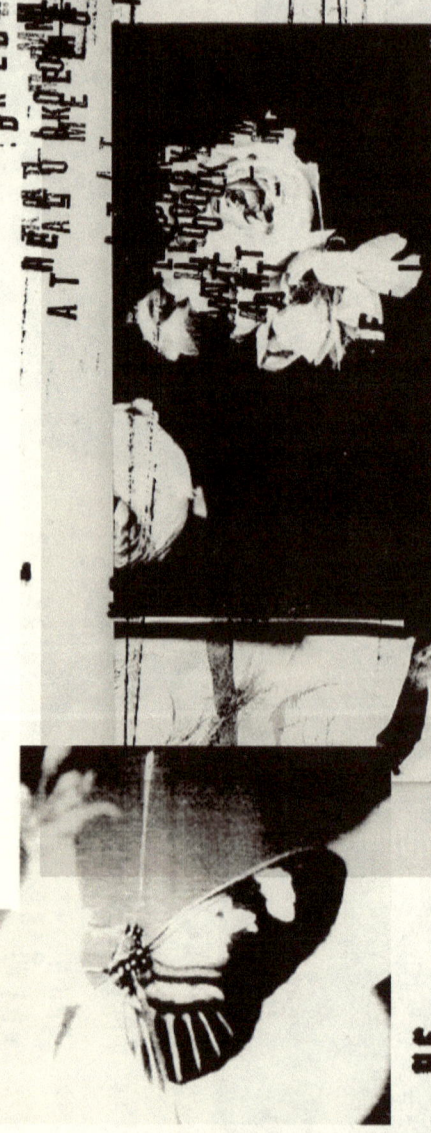

"Why do you love Me?"

"Emerald-green dawn,
Violet-blue mornings,
Pink-orange noons,
Lilac evenings.

That butterfly of death
still flutters in his
periphery,
one wing "emerald green,"
the other "violet blue."

"How can love be this painful?"

"Why do you love Me?"
"Because I can."

Matvey, Ravenna...

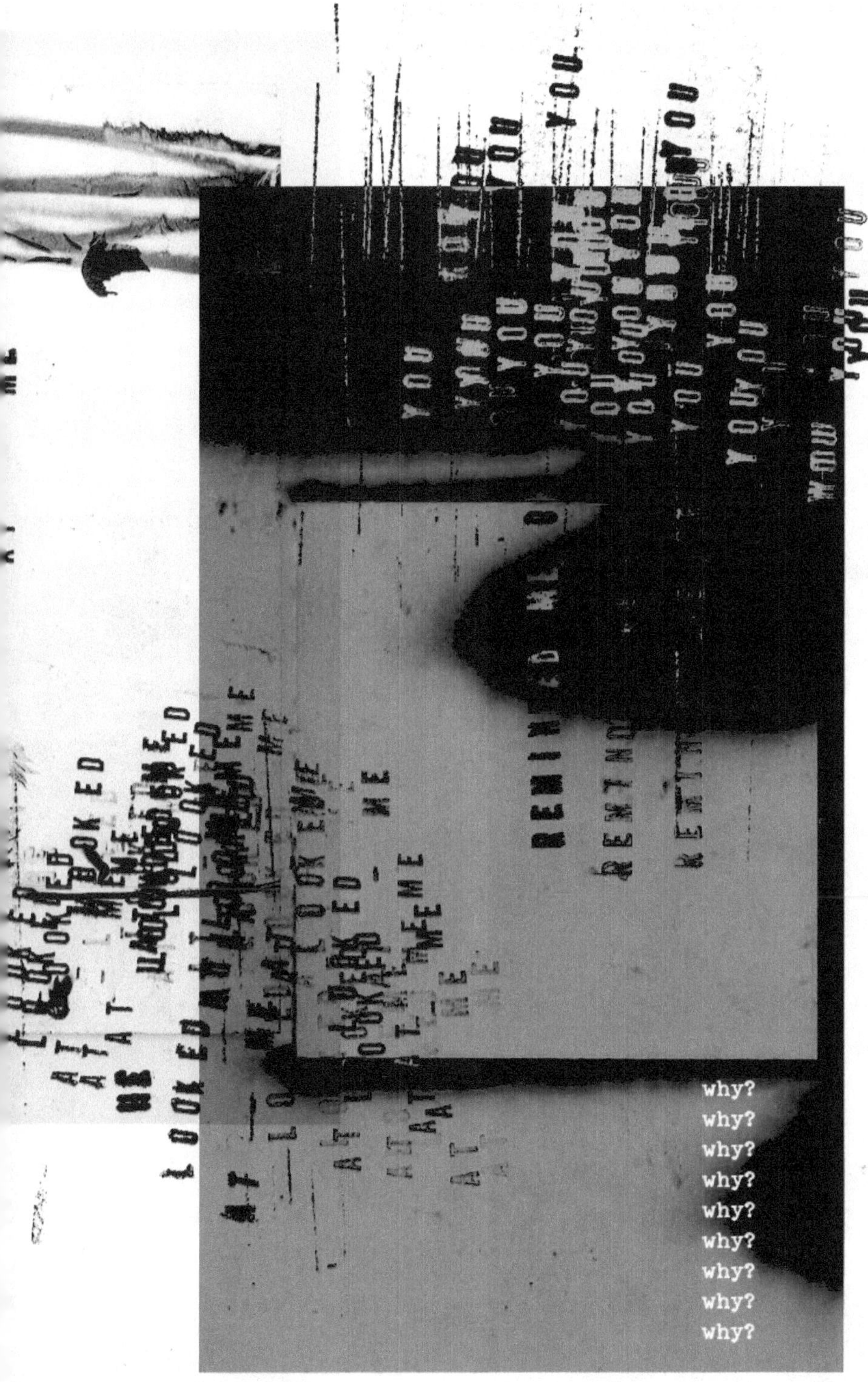

YOU YOU YOU YOU YOU
YOU YOU YOU YOU
YOU YOU YOU
YOU YOU YOU

REMINDED ME O
REMINDE
REMIN

LOOKED
AT AT ME
AT AT ME
US LOOKED
LOOKED LOOKED

LOOKED ME
LOOKED AT ME
LOOKED AT ME
AT ME ME
ME
AT AT
AT AT
AT

why?
why?
why?
why?
why?
why?
why?
why?

2025 : GRIEVING AMARYLLIS : MIRRORS AND SHADOWS

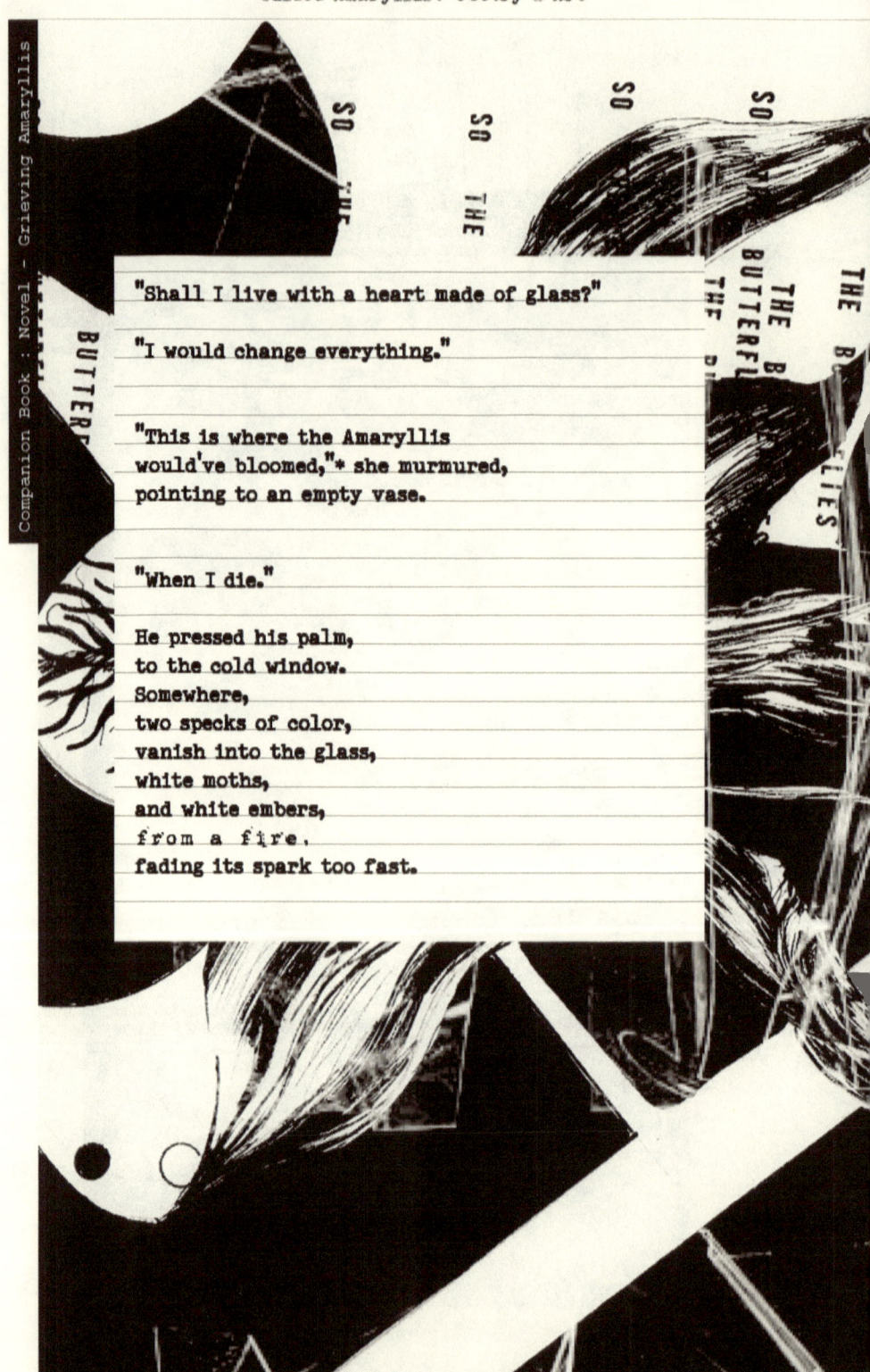

Companion Book :: Novel - Grieving Amaryllis

"Shall I live with a heart made of glass?"

"I would change everything."

"This is where the Amaryllis
would've bloomed,"* she murmured,
pointing to an empty vase.

"When I die."

He pressed his palm,
to the cold window.
Somewhere,
two specks of color,
vanish into the glass,
white moths,
and white embers,
from a fire,
fading its spark too fast.

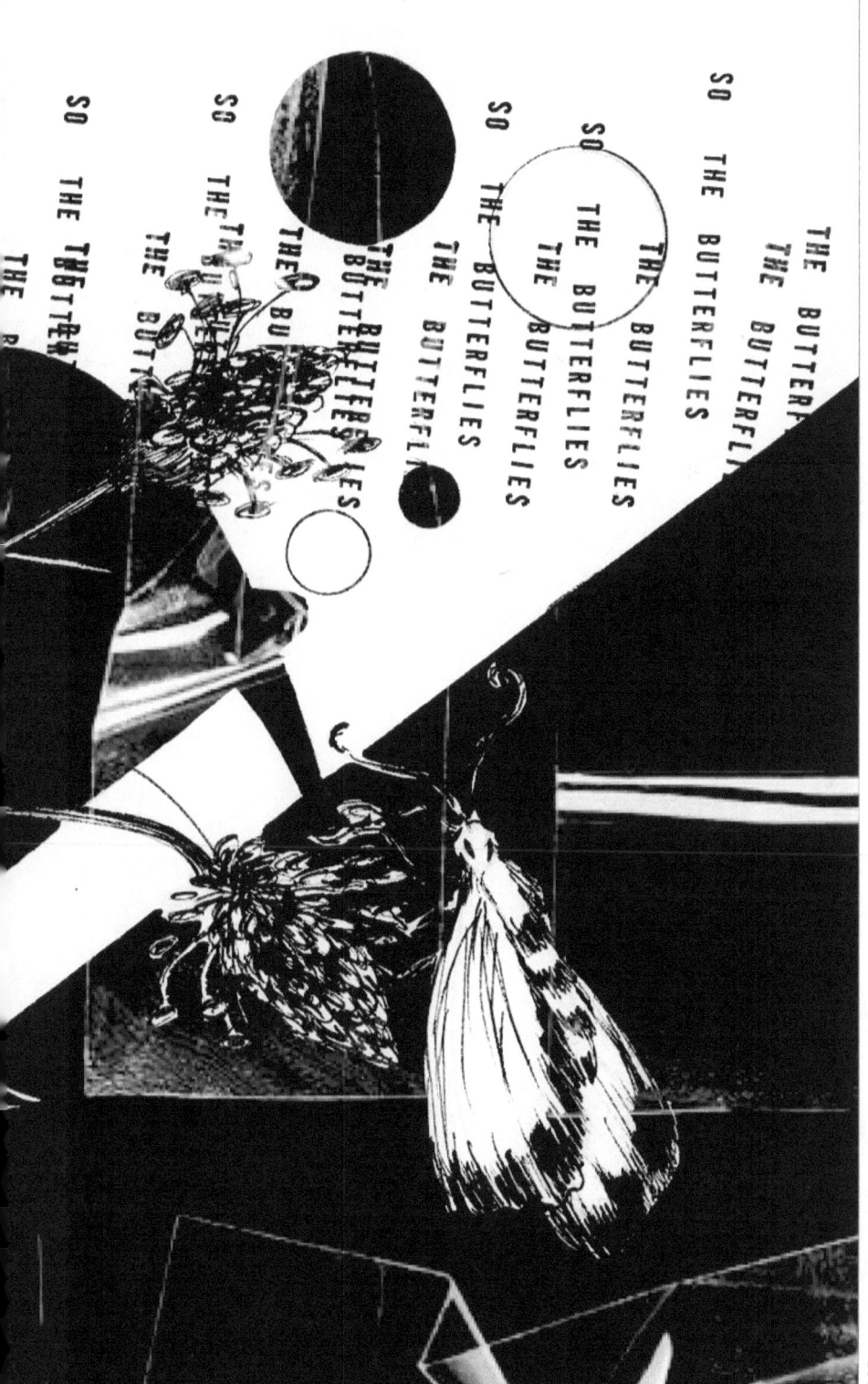

2025 : GRIEVING AMARYLLIS : MIRRORS AND SHADOWS

Pages 142-143 from the novel :
Excerpt -
Train scene.

[----E-]2022 - A Train

"The world feels like it's floating."

"It's funny how easy it is to just disappear." The thought crosses your mind as the train's rustling sound grows closer. The silence engulfs you against the engine's soaring sound. "The pain is severe but short," you think, "one moment, one last, and it's over."

"It's easy; this emptiness will be gone if I just step half a meter more."

The train light blazes; the whirring of its wheels gets louder. Every inch of your body screams in silence; your heart is begging for an end. What is life if it's all this excruciating pain inside? All this damn pain, all this... this numbness, this so-called life... I can't feel anything.

"Life is nothing," you whisper.

"Nothing!" You scream against the loud, approaching shriek.

"Nothing!" You scream louder; your voice merges with the train's noises like two giants colliding.

-

Complete silence.

-

-

You freeze; a reflection stares at you from across the platform, her silhouette interrupted by the passing carriages. Your eyes squint, your head shifts, trying to get a better look. The strong wind from the speeding train almost pulls you forward.

The whirring of wheels on tracks and the loud shriek of brakes fill the air around you. One carriage at a time, one reflection of your face and her silhouette at a time.

-

-

Finally, focus breaks through, and your heart skips a beat. A cold tremor runs through your body, and ice trickles down your spine.

"She is smiling." Your heart gave a twist in your rib cage.

She is smiling as if she knows something better is waiting for you, as if she knows this will all pass. You take a step back, hesitantly—one foot away from the edge of the platform, and then your next follows.

You look back at her with a nervous smile, but she starts to walk away. "Wait!" You call after her, running as fast as you can, eyes fixed on the platform across from you as you cross the bridge that connects them.

She's already gone.

You look up and notice violet wisteria petals falling all around you like rain. Their scent fills the fresh night air, and your face softens at the irony of it all.

"It's her."

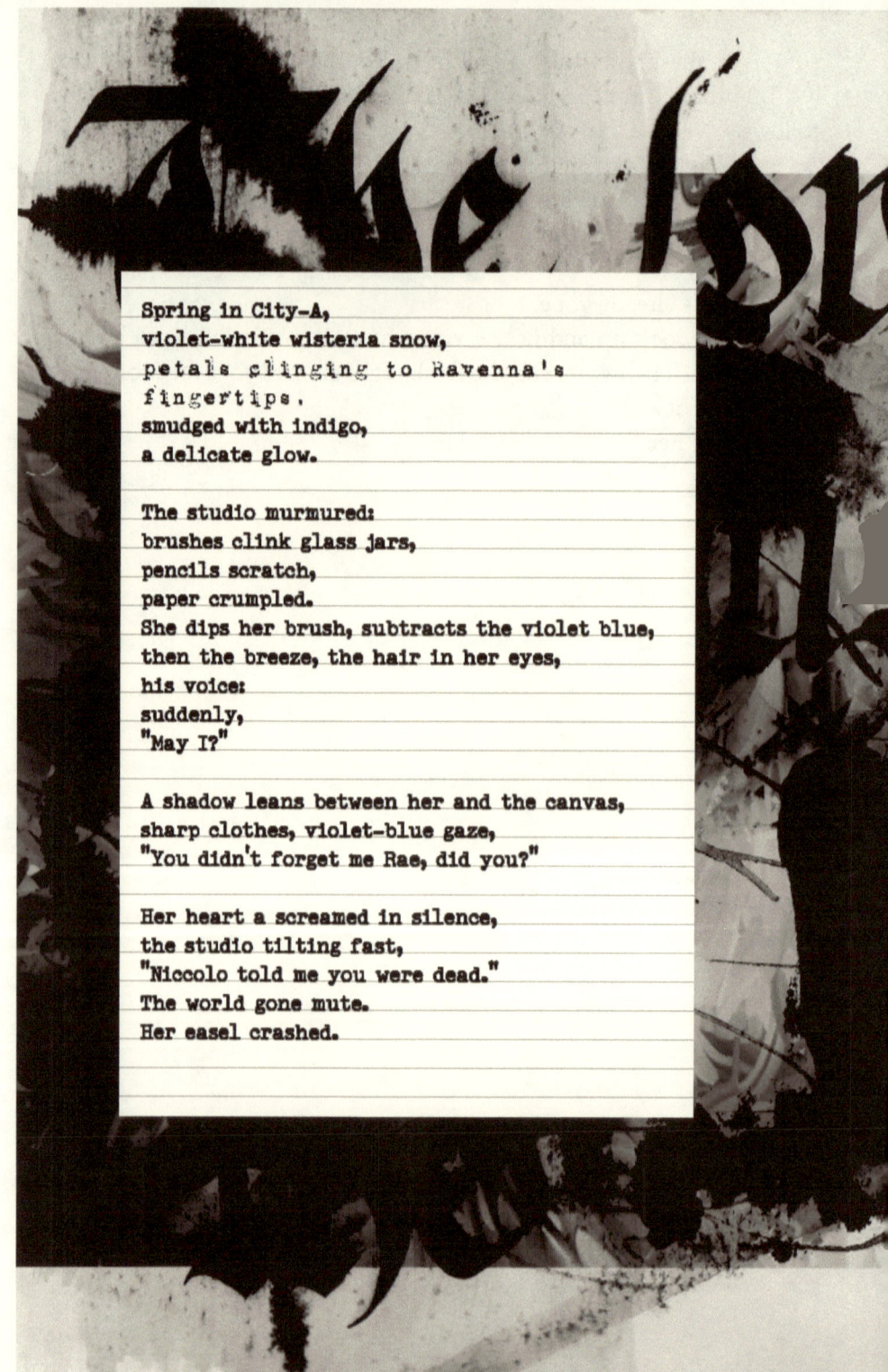

Spring in City-A,
violet-white wisteria snow,
petals clinging to Ravenna's
fingertips,
smudged with indigo,
a delicate glow.

The studio murmured:
brushes clink glass jars,
pencils scratch,
paper crumpled.
She dips her brush, subtracts the violet blue,
then the breeze, the hair in her eyes,
his voice:
suddenly,
"May I?"

A shadow leans between her and the canvas,
sharp clothes, violet-blue gaze,
"You didn't forget me Rae, did you?"

Her heart a screamed in silence,
the studio tilting fast,
"Niccolo told me you were dead."
The world gone mute.
Her easel crashed.

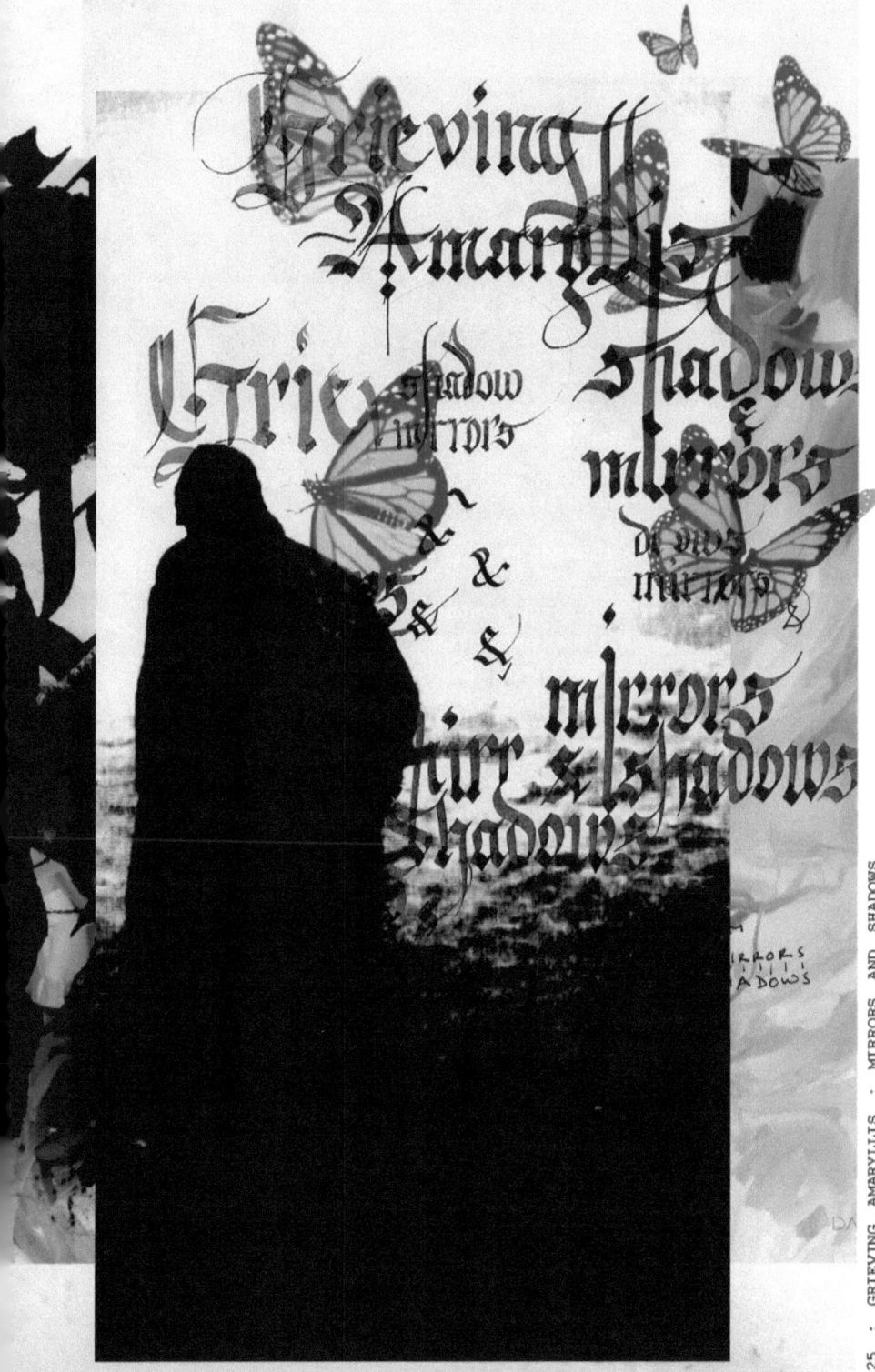

"White Lie"

Alexander's door swings wide,
Matvey dark against the brightness,
a stain on marble.

"She's here. You lied."

Cornices curl ,
frozen white
delicate lace.
Oak floors underfoot.
"Saints don't lie," he says,
The garden bright
through French doors.
flowers bloom their secrets.
vines twisting towards skylight.

Matvey sinks into black leather,
a shadow in this curated white.
Alexander arranges the truth:

"I saw how you looked at her
by the cemetery."
A smirk. Sunlight knives
through glassware,
glints off bowls,
catches the blue
of a gaze too cold to thaw.

"I followed her.
Notebook in hand,
tracing her father's tunnels,
you know where they lead."

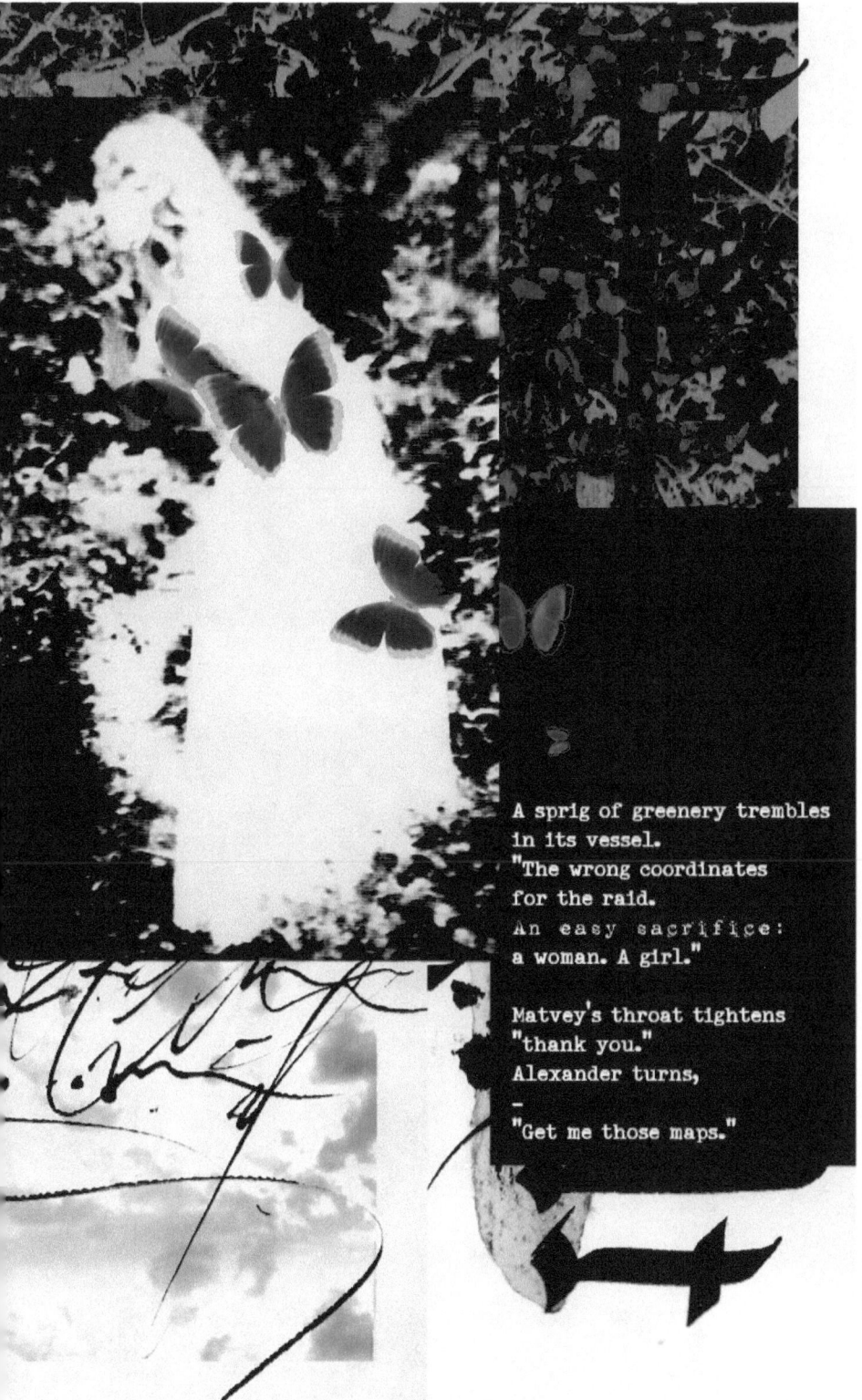

A sprig of greenery trembles
in its vessel.
"The wrong coordinates
for the raid.
An easy sacrifice:
a woman. A girl."

Matvey's throat tightens
"thank you."
Alexander turns,
—
"Get me those maps."

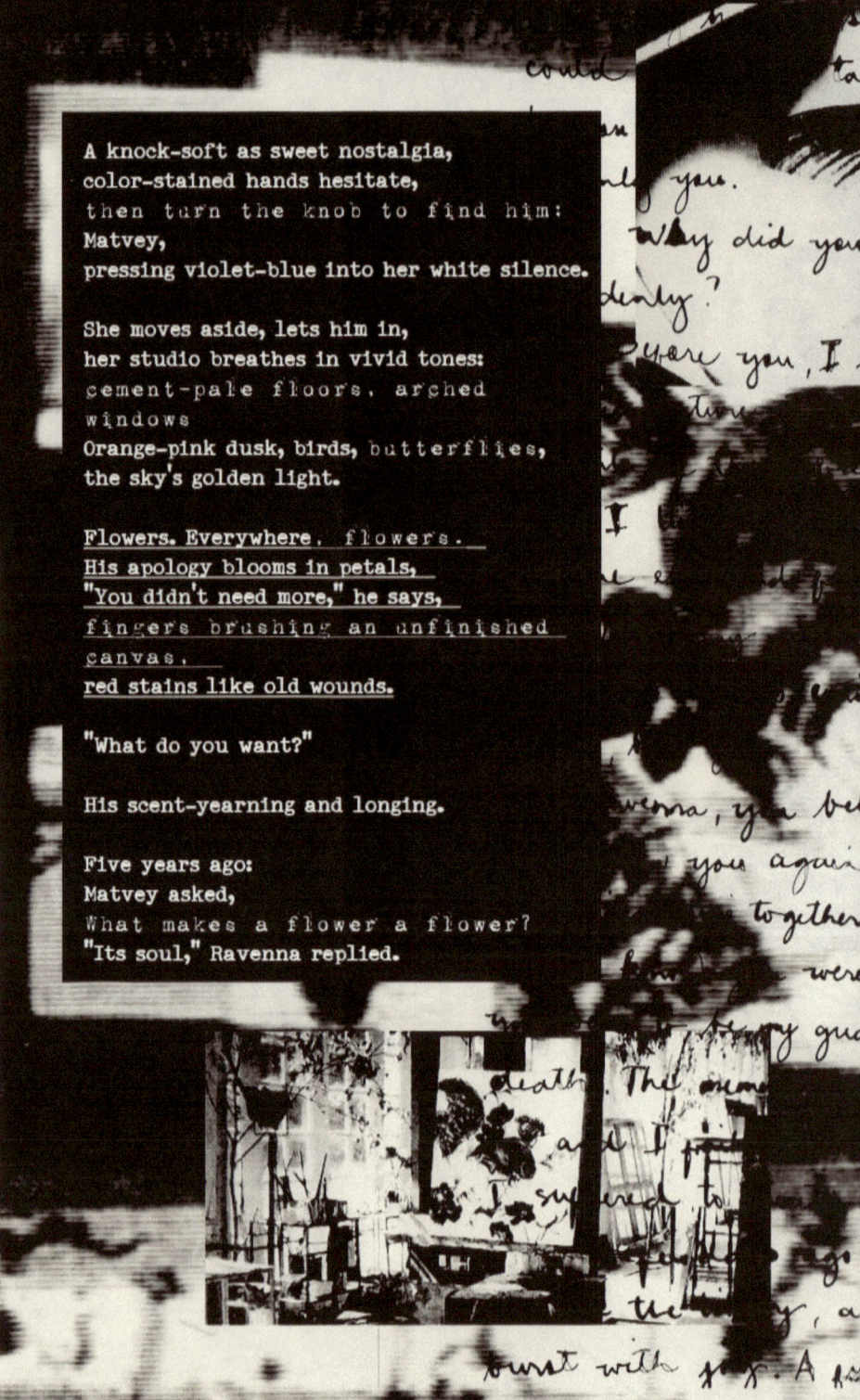

A knock-soft as sweet nostalgia,
color-stained hands hesitate,
then turn the knob to find him:
Matvey,
pressing violet-blue into her white silence.

She moves aside, lets him in,
her studio breathes in vivid tones:
cement-pale floors, arched windows
Orange-pink dusk, birds, butterflies,
the sky's golden light.

Flowers. Everywhere, flowers.
His apology blooms in petals,
"You didn't need more," he says,
fingers brushing an unfinished canvas,
red stains like old wounds.

"What do you want?"

His scent-yearning and longing.

Five years ago:
Matvey asked,
What makes a flower a flower?
"Its soul," Ravenna replied.

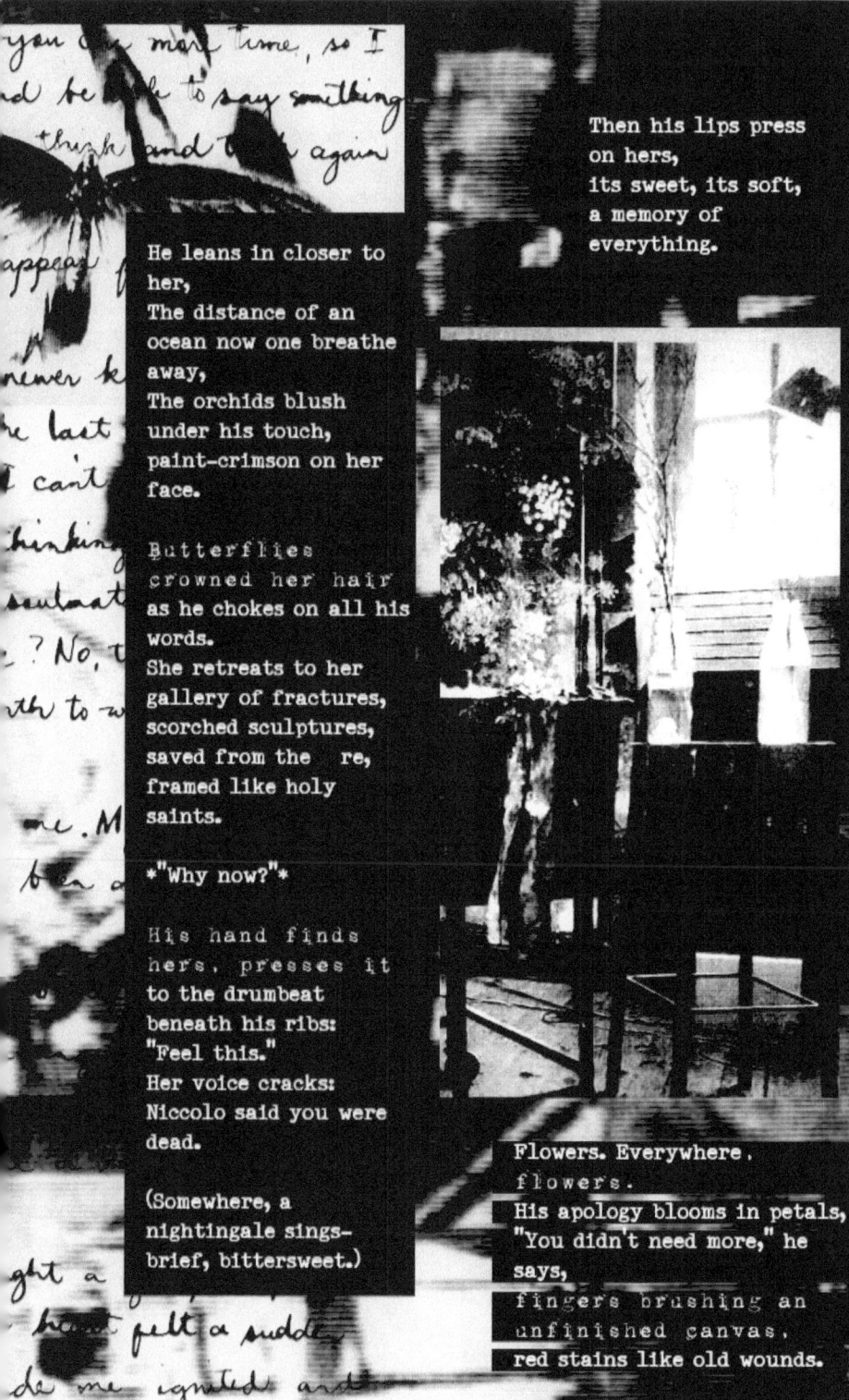

Then his lips press
on hers,
its sweet, its soft,
a memory of
everything.

He leans in closer to
her,
The distance of an
ocean now one breathe
away,
The orchids blush
under his touch,
paint-crimson on her
face.

Butterflies
crowned her hair
as he chokes on all his
words.
She retreats to her
gallery of fractures,
scorched sculptures,
saved from the   re,
framed like holy
saints.

"Why now?"

His hand finds
hers, presses it
to the drumbeat
beneath his ribs:
"Feel this."
Her voice cracks:
Niccolo said you were
dead.

(Somewhere, a
nightingale sings—
brief, bittersweet.)

Flowers. Everywhere.
flowers.
His apology blooms in petals,
"You didn't need more," he
says,
fingers brushing an
unfinished canvas,
red stains like old wounds.

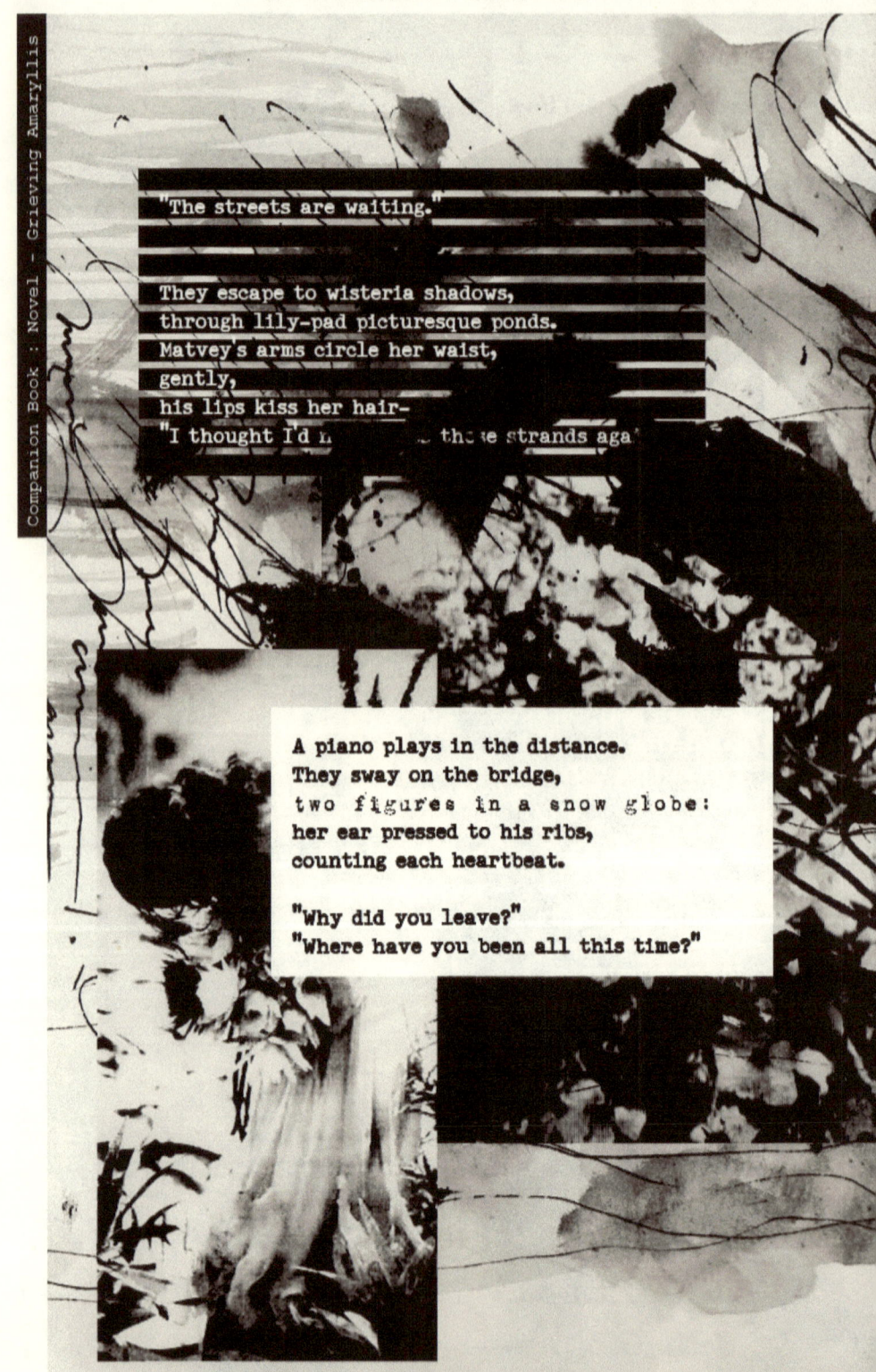

"The streets are waiting."

They escape to wisteria shadows,
through lily-pad picturesque ponds.
Matvey's arms circle her waist,
gently,
his lips kiss her hair-
"I thought I'd h   these strands aga

A piano plays in the distance.
They sway on the bridge,
two figures in a snow globe:
her ear pressed to his ribs,
counting each heartbeat.

"Why did you leave?"
"Where have you been all this time?"

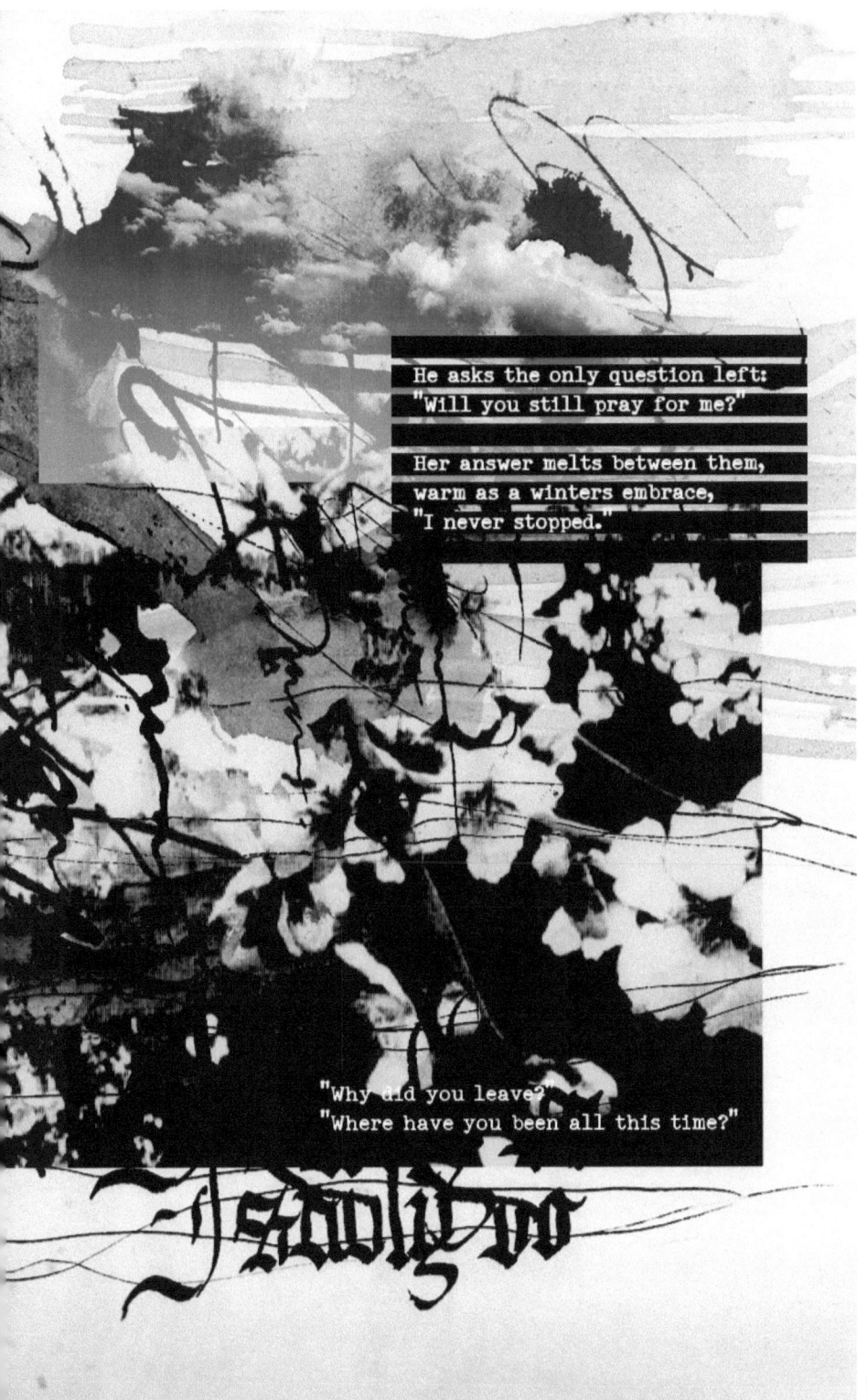

He asks the only question left:
"Will you still pray for me?"

Her answer melts between them,
warm as a winters embrace,
"I never stopped."

"Why did you leave?"
"Where have you been all this time?"

**Niccolo's letter at the
library scene.**

Ravenna,

I am writing to you; need I say more? First, I wanted to stay silent, believe me. If I'd had any hope of seeing you one more time, so I could hear you talk and be able to say something to you in return, and then think and think again of only you.

Why did you disappear from my life suddenly?

Before you, I had never known this agony, or this torture. I spent the last five years in the turmoil of these feelings I can't control.

I lived in fear of thinking that you've met someone else and found a soulmate in him.

Did I say someone else? No, there's no one for me, no one in this entire earth to whom I'd give my heart, but you.

Ravenna, you belong to me. My whole life, up until I saw you again, has been a prelude to our predestined life together.

I know you were sent to me by God, and you were to be my guardian angel until my death. The memory of your emerald eyes haunted me and I failed to replicate it in every sculpture I suffered to create.

A few days ago, I caught a glimpse of you here in the library, and my heart felt a sudden burst with joy. A fire inside me ignited and

I told myself, she came back for me!

I will be waiting for you in my gallery, just with a single glance, you will bring my inner hopes to life. I loved you Ravenna, I always have and I always will.

Till death,
Niccolo

Ravenna,

I am writing to you; need I say more? First, I wanted to stay silent, believe me. If I'd had any hope of seeing you one more time, so I could hear you talk and be able to say something to you in return, and then think and think again of only you.

Why did you disappear from my life suddenly? Before you, I had never known this agony or this torture. I spent the last five years in the turmoil of these feelings I can't control.

I lived in fear of thinking that you've met someone else and found a soulmate in him.

Did I say someone else? No, there's no one for me, no one in this entire earth to whom I'd give my heart, but you.

Ravenna, you belong to me. My whole life, up until I saw you again, has been a prelude to our predestined life together. I know you were to be my guardian angel until my death. The memory of your emerald eyes haunted me and I failed to replicate it in every sculpture I suffered to create.

A few days ago, I caught a glimpse of you here in the library, and my heart felt a sudden burst with joy. A fire inside me ignited and I told myself, she came back to me!

I will be waiting for you in my gallery; just with a single glance, you will bring my inner hopes to life. I loved you Ravenna, I always have and I always will.

Till death,
Niccolo

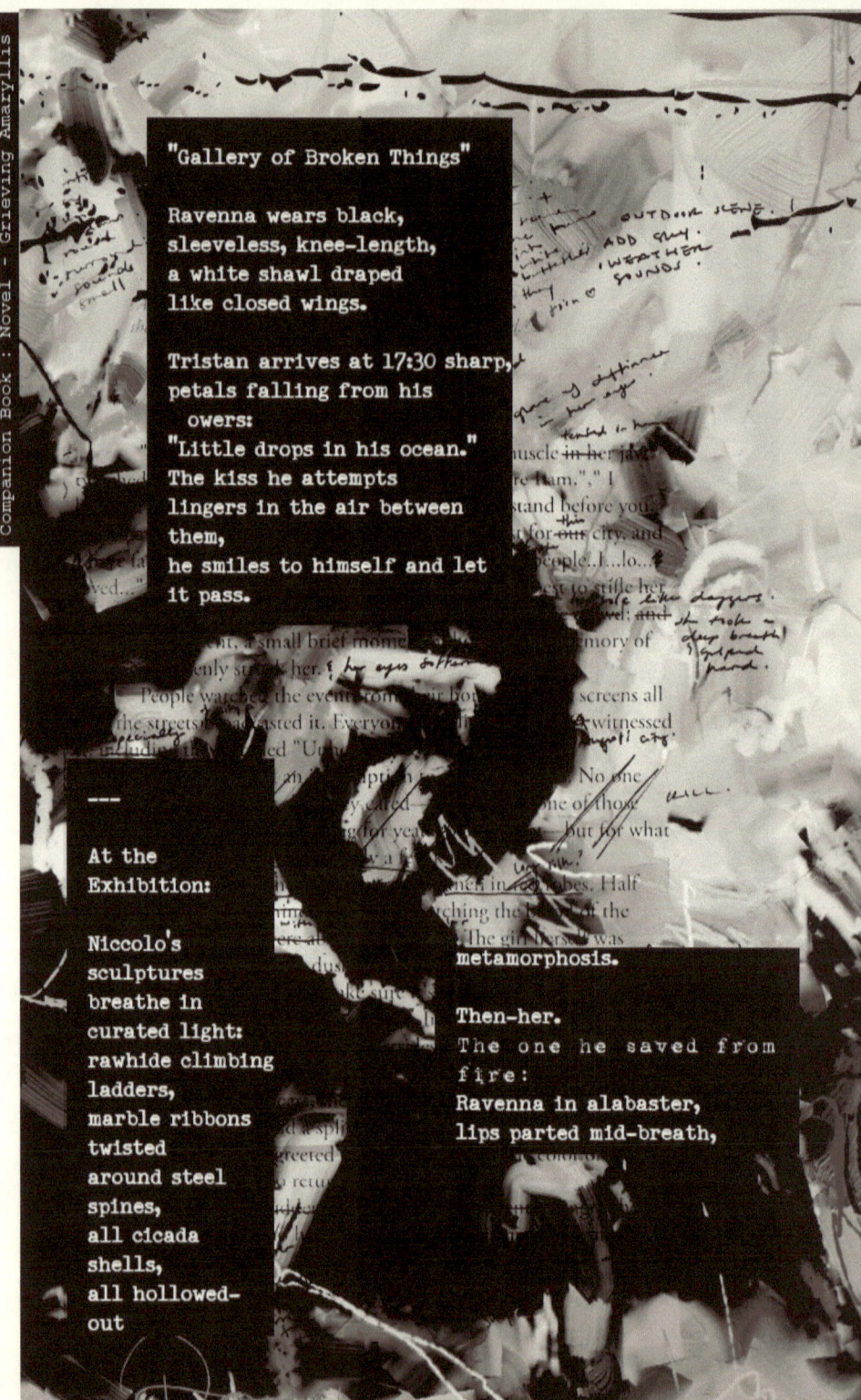

"Gallery of Broken Things"

Ravenna wears black,
sleeveless, knee-length,
a white shawl draped
like closed wings.

Tristan arrives at 17:30 sharp,
petals falling from his
    owers:
"Little drops in his ocean."
The kiss he attempts
lingers in the air between
them,
he smiles to himself and let
it pass.

At the
Exhibition:

Niccolo's
sculptures
breathe in
curated light:
rawhide climbing
ladders,
marble ribbons
twisted
around steel
spines,
all cicada
shells,
all hollowed-
out

metamorphosis.

Then-her.
The one he saved from
fire:
Ravenna in alabaster,
lips parted mid-breath,

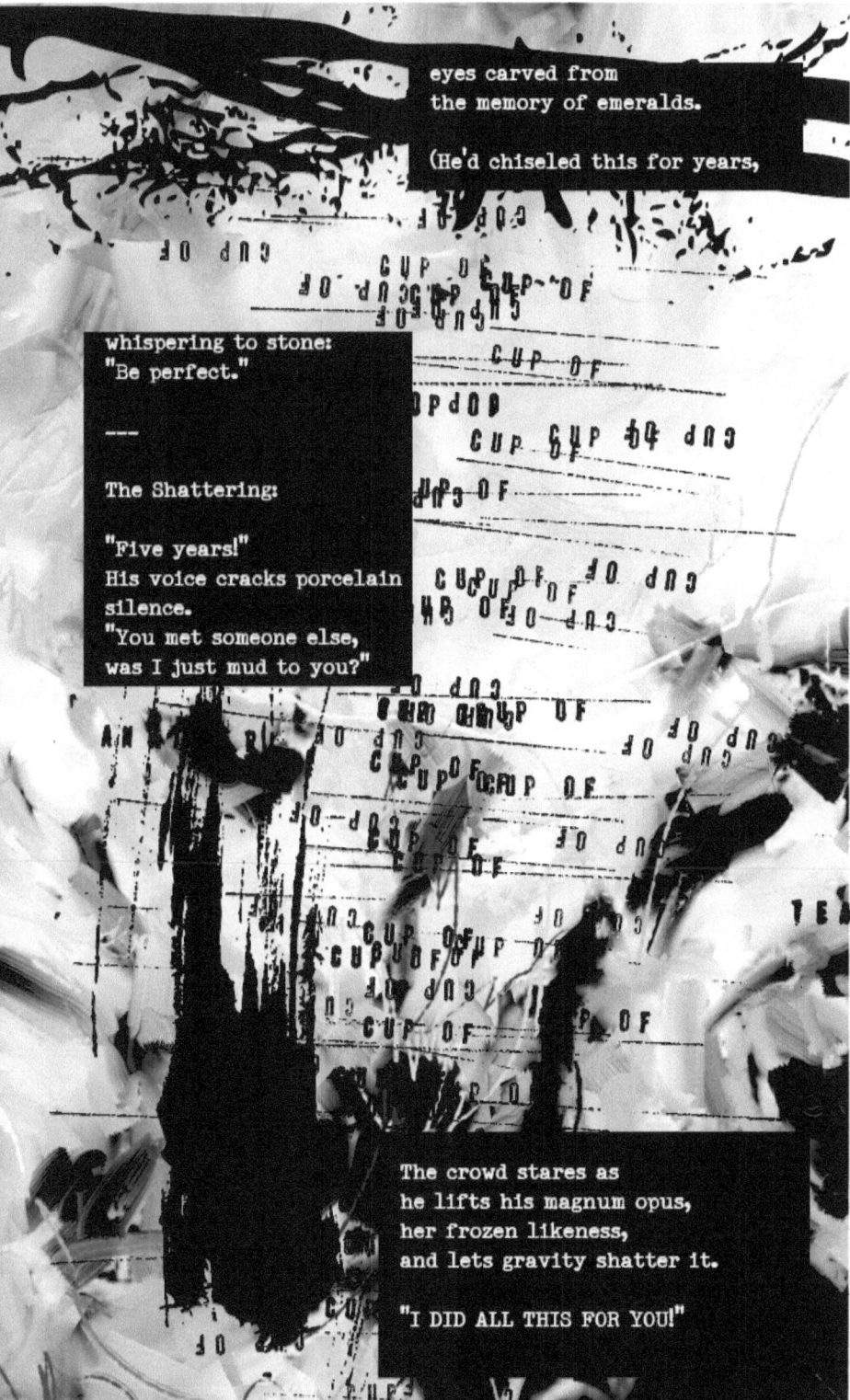

eyes carved from
the memory of emeralds.

(He'd chiseled this for years,

whispering to stone:
"Be perfect."

The Shattering:

"Five years!"
His voice cracks porcelain
silence.
"You met someone else,
was I just mud to you?"

The crowd stares as
he lifts his magnum opus,
her frozen likeness,
and lets gravity shatter it.

"I DID ALL THIS FOR YOU!"

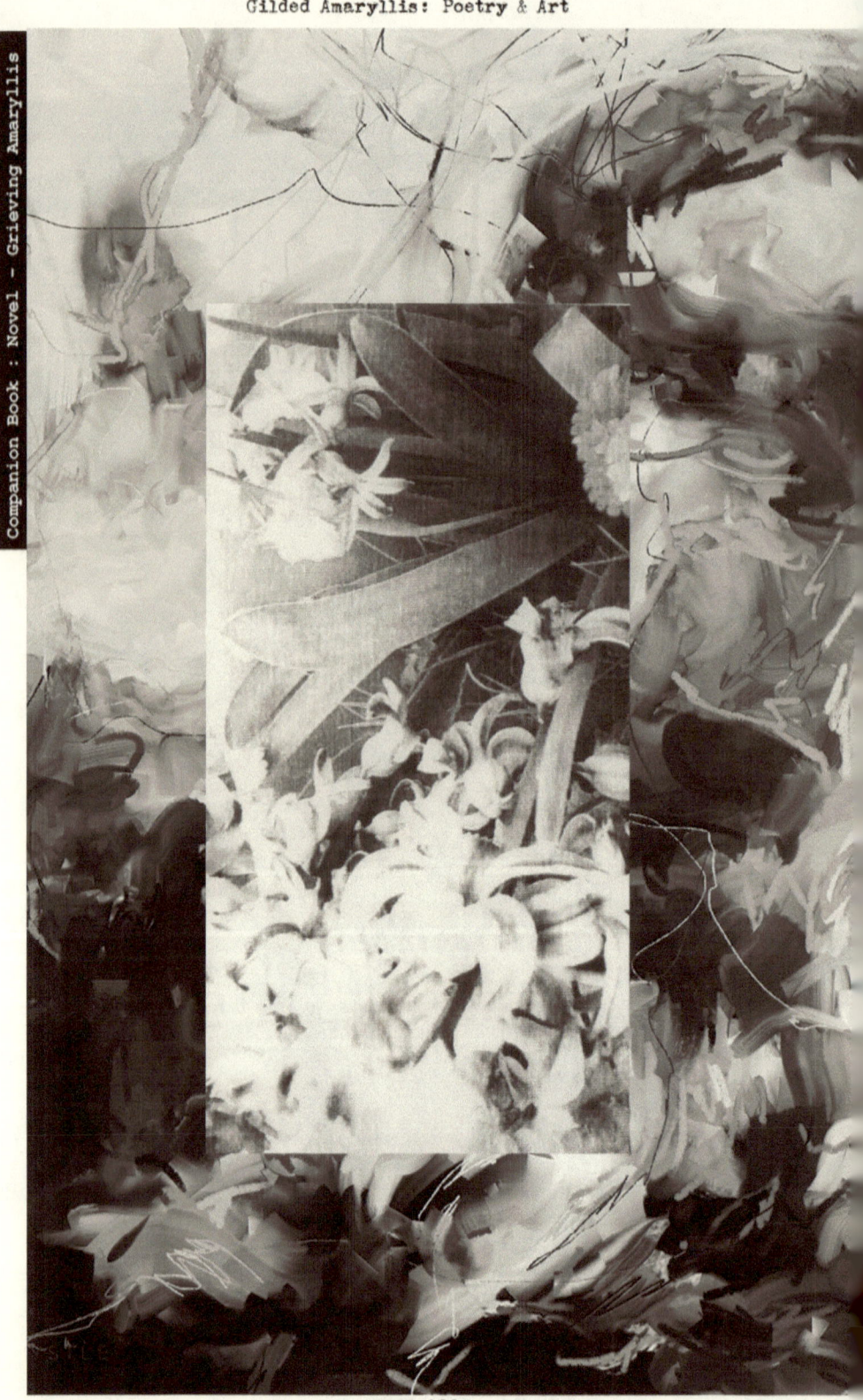

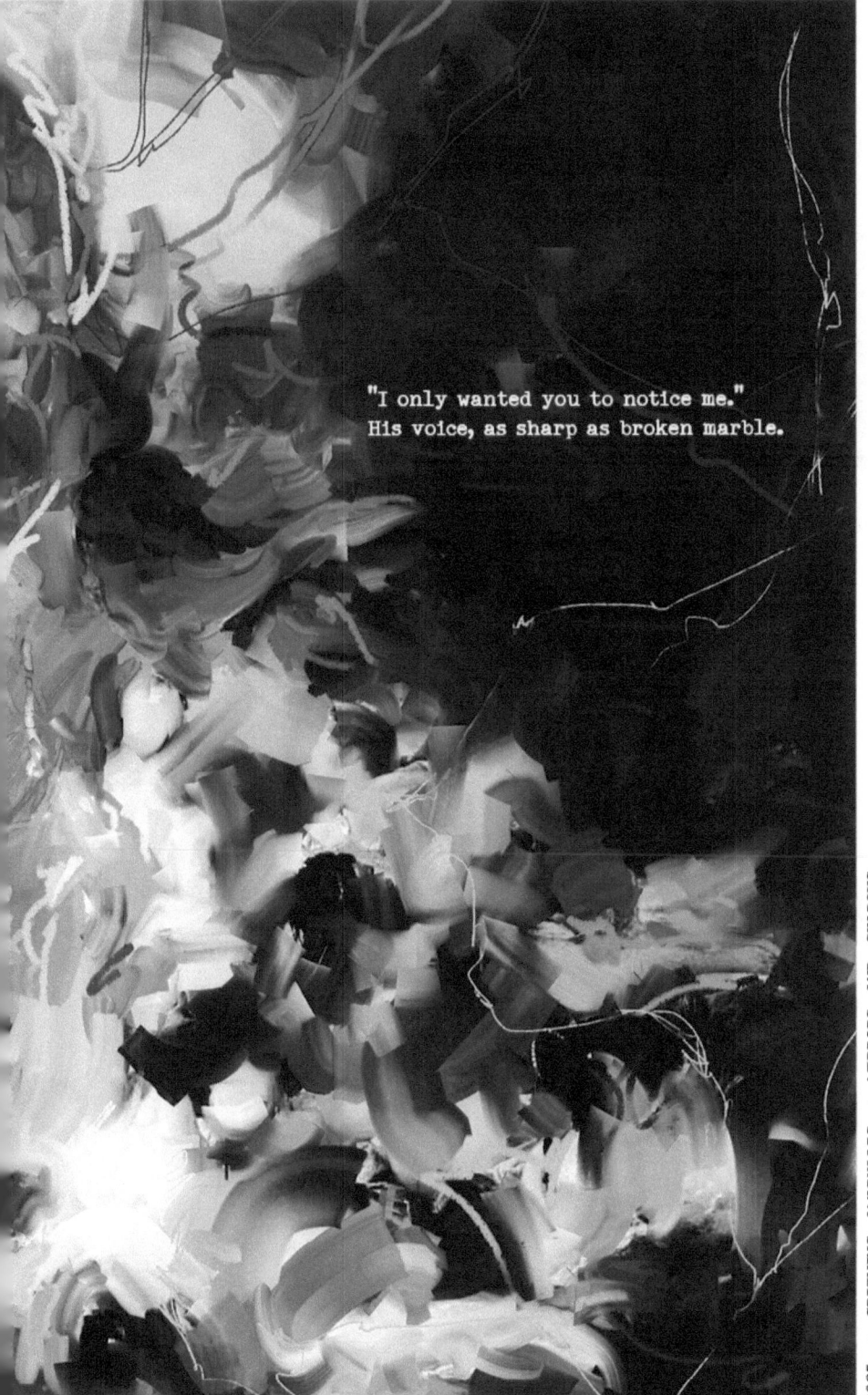

"I only wanted you to notice me."
His voice, as sharp as broken marble.

2025 : GRIEVING AMARYLLIS : MIRRORS AND SHADOWS

[Ravenna's Diary - 2023]

"The Red Sketchbook entry"

I am moving, then, as one who moves forever at the centers of his circle: a circle filled with light.

And into it came bulging shapes from darkness, rays of light from the street, and then I was soaked in darkness again. Drops of water from these tunnels I hear clearly; I follow the lines of my father's sketchbook: two church bells with
alternate beats, striking from above; and through these things, my pencil pushes softly to weave gray webs of lines on this carefully designed page.

I turn and look one instant behind me for familiar gardens.
"Beauty!" I cry. My feet move on and take me between dark walls.
Beauty; beheld like someone half-forgotten, remembered—with slow pang, as one neglected.
Well, I am frustrated.
Life has beaten me. The thing I strongly seized has turned to darkness,And darkness takes my heart...

If I could solve this darkness, the city would have me.
This causeless melancholy that comes with rain and fire. On such days as this, when large, wet, heavy drops of rain fall around me...

The morning when I saw him, he was much preoccupied and would not smile.

And now, I saw too much; following these lines, these strokes from this red sketchbook,

I finally find the destination—I open the screeching door, and all I see is this: I see what my family died for. The reason I lost everything.

I kneel in front of its majestic altar, and I can't help but cry.

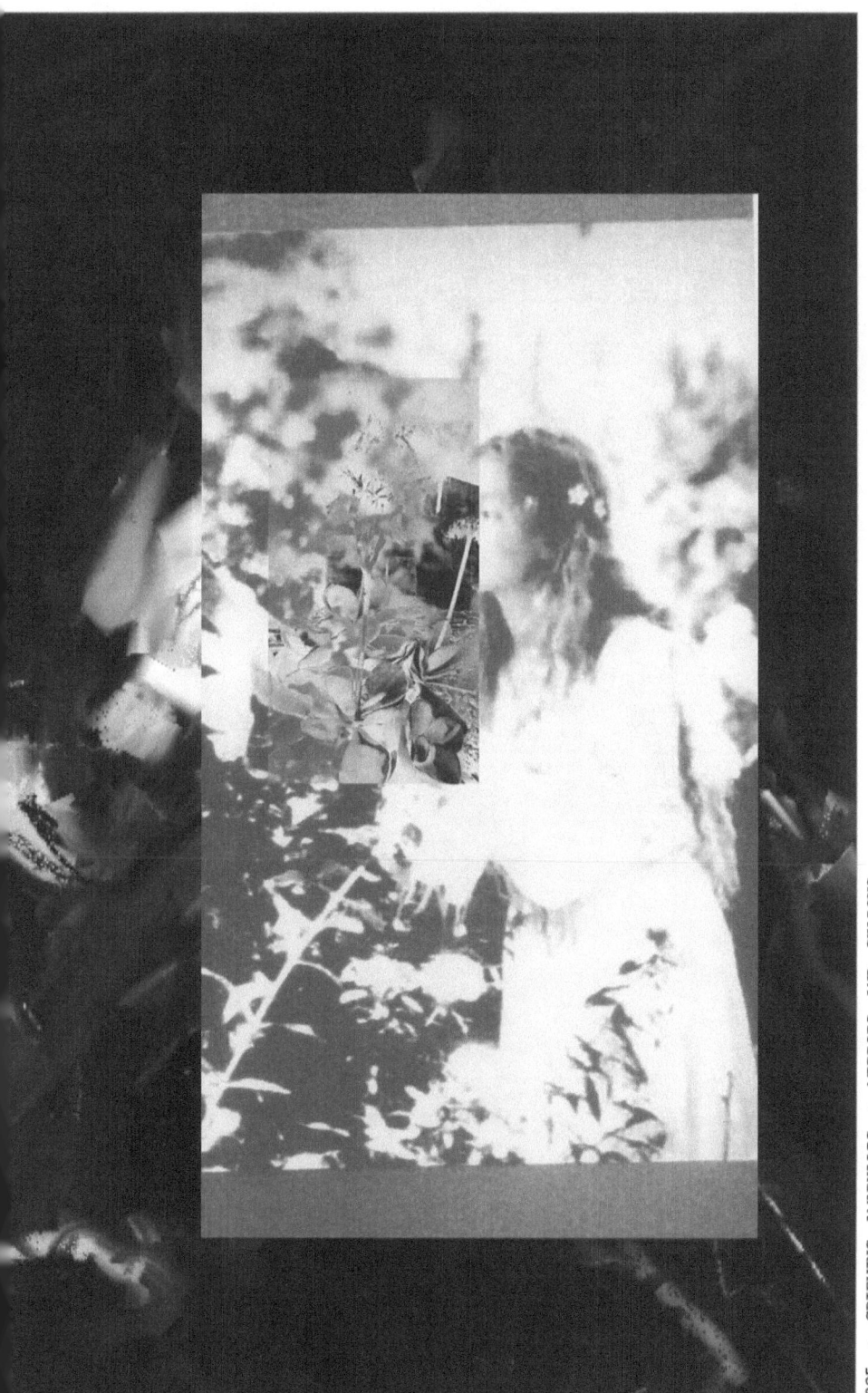

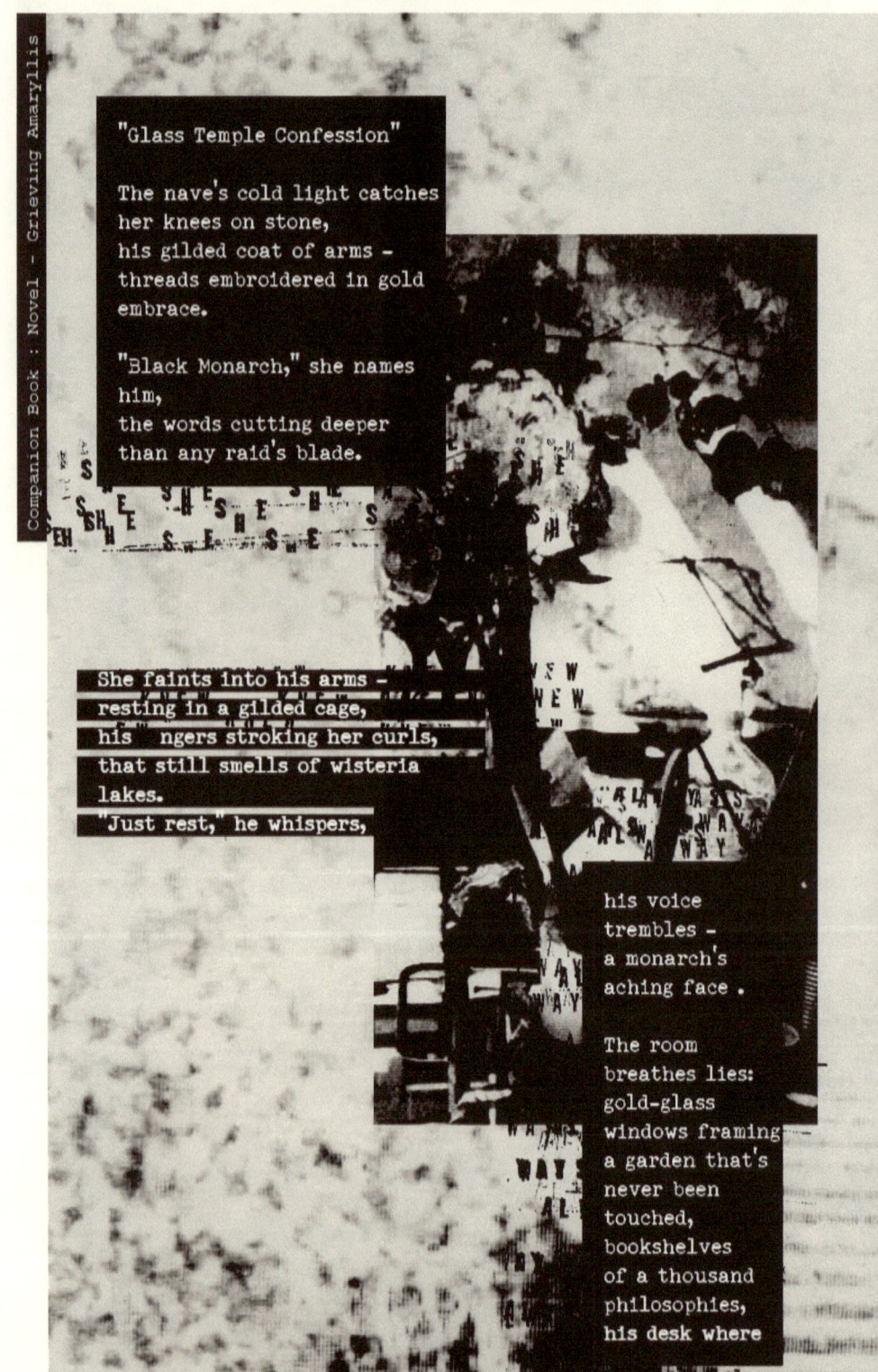

"Glass Temple Confession"

The nave's cold light catches
her knees on stone,
his gilded coat of arms -
threads embroidered in gold
embrace.

"Black Monarch," she names
him,
the words cutting deeper
than any raid's blade.

She faints into his arms -
resting in a gilded cage,
his ngers stroking her curls,
that still smells of wisteria
lakes.
"Just rest," he whispers,

his voice
trembles -
a monarch's
aching face .

The room
breathes lies:
gold-glass
windows framing
a garden that's
never been
touched,
bookshelves
of a thousand
philosophies,
his desk where

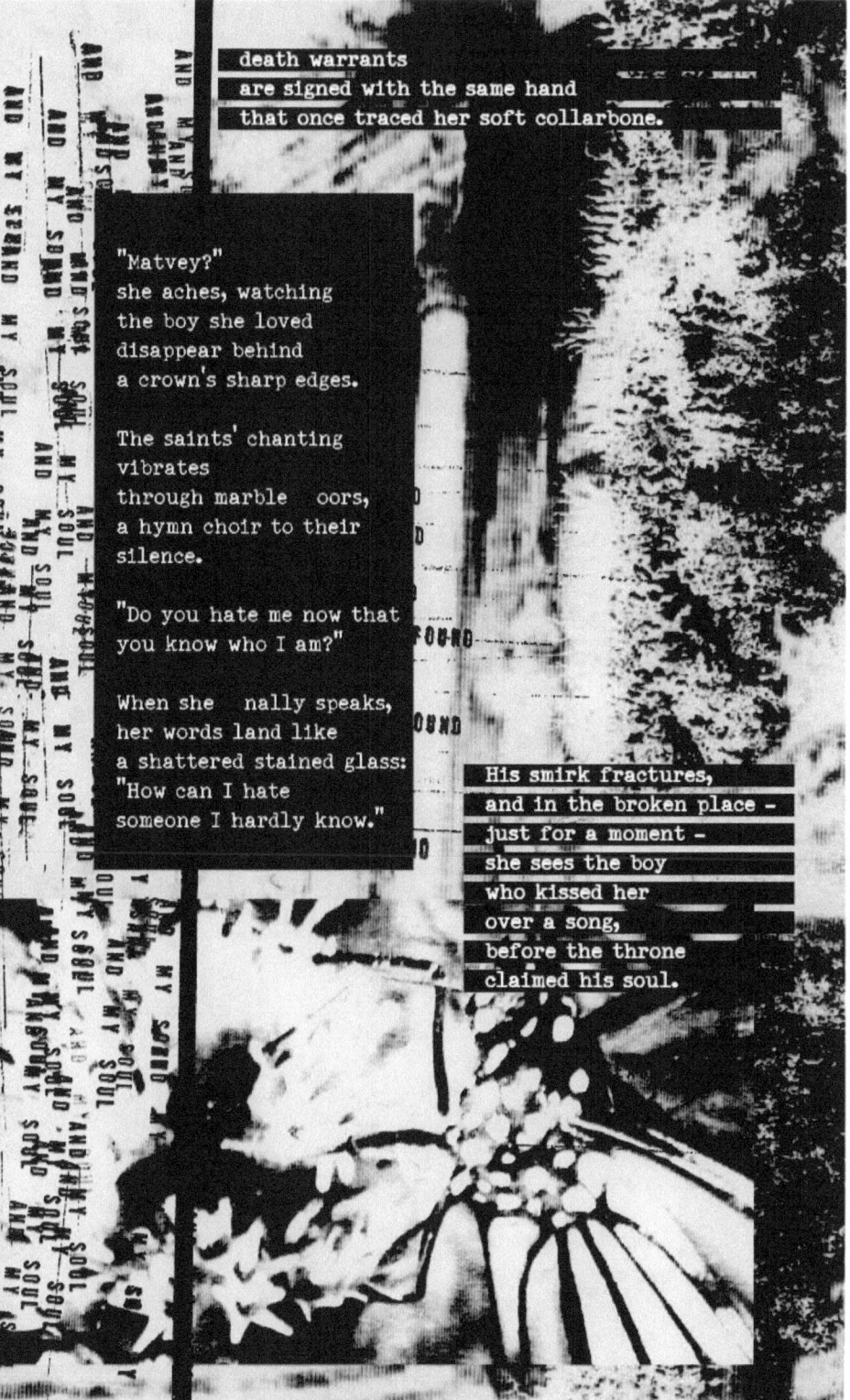

death warrants
are signed with the same hand
that once traced her soft collarbone.

"Matvey?"
she aches, watching
the boy she loved
disappear behind
a crown's sharp edges.

The saints' chanting
vibrates
through marble oors,
a hymn choir to their
silence.

"Do you hate me now that
you know who I am?"

When she nally speaks,
her words land like
a shattered stained glass:
"How can I hate
someone I hardly know."

His smirk fractures,
and in the broken place -
just for a moment -
she sees the boy
who kissed her
over a song,
before the throne
claimed his soul.

The hill soaked in midnight.
City-A sprawls below -
a fading galaxy of lights,
a love's last confessions.

"Look at the stars with me,"
he asks,
His eyes carves the darkness:
"Time stopped for me."
(for a moment.)

"I wanted-"

The words break.

She reaches -
her palms gently cup his face,
searching for the boy beneath
the gilded mask.

"It's over."
His   ngers brush hers away,

like old
bandages
from a wound
that never
closed right.

"Leave the
city."
His back merges
with the
nightfall.

Ravenna stands

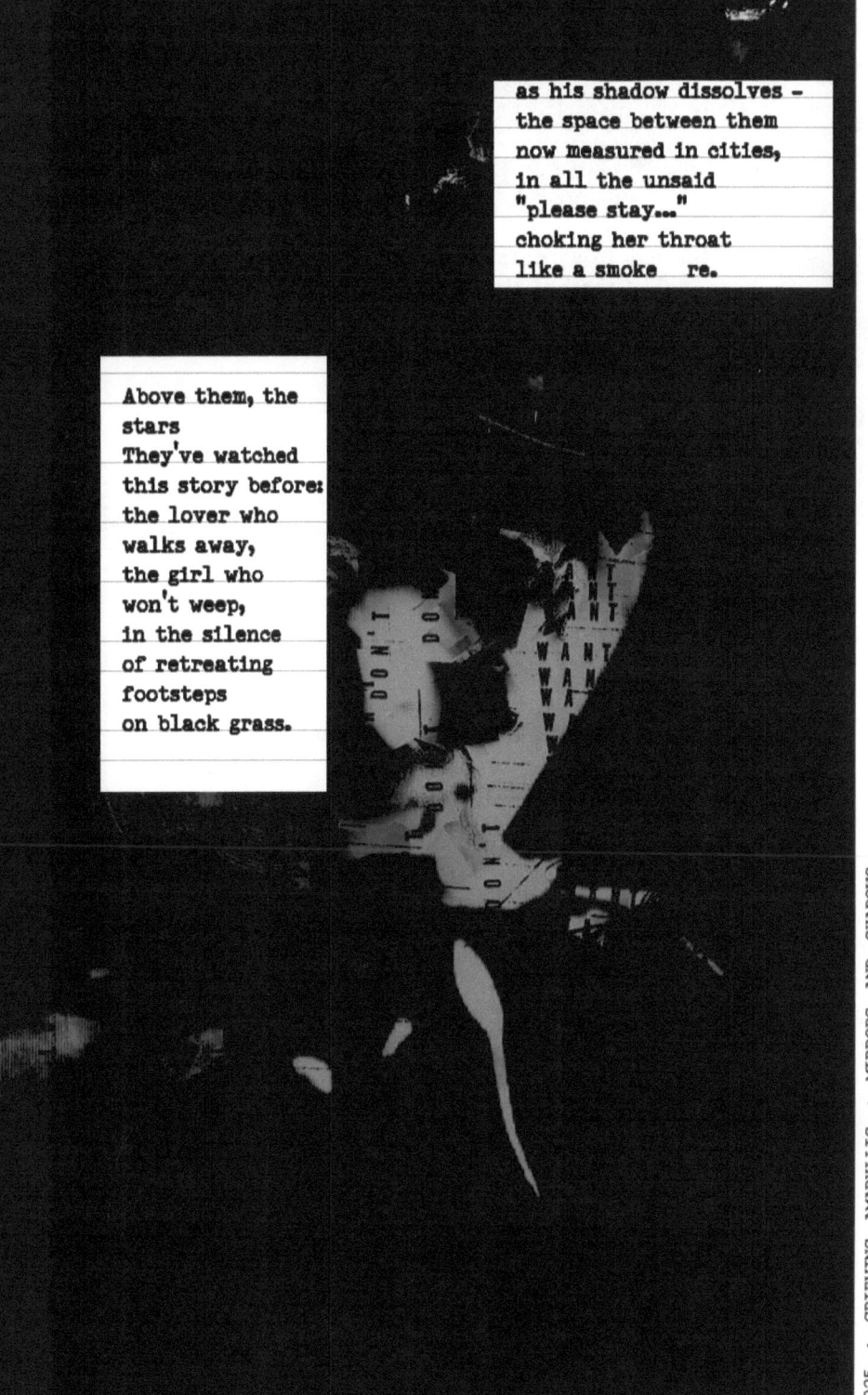

as his shadow dissolves -
the space between them
now measured in cities,
in all the unsaid
"please stay..."
choking her throat
like a smoke   re.

Above them, the
stars
They've watched
this story before:
the lover who
walks away,
the girl who
won't weep,
in the silence
of retreating
footsteps
on black grass.

12:34

The torrent in my chest
has nally reached its banks,
no more damming
this black current,
a soul left in point blank.

Coat discarded like a broken armor,
gloves thrown its empty prayers.
The staircase weeps,
angels turning
their marble faces away.

Even open windows
refuse to give me air.

The desk accepts my heavy heart,
like all the altars that kissed my knees.
Cold metal presses
where her hand once rested,

12:34

The angels don't flinch
when the shot breaks
the night's glass.

Somewhere downstream,
a girl in a wisteria dress
wakes gasping,
her pillow wet
with her soulmate's torrent.

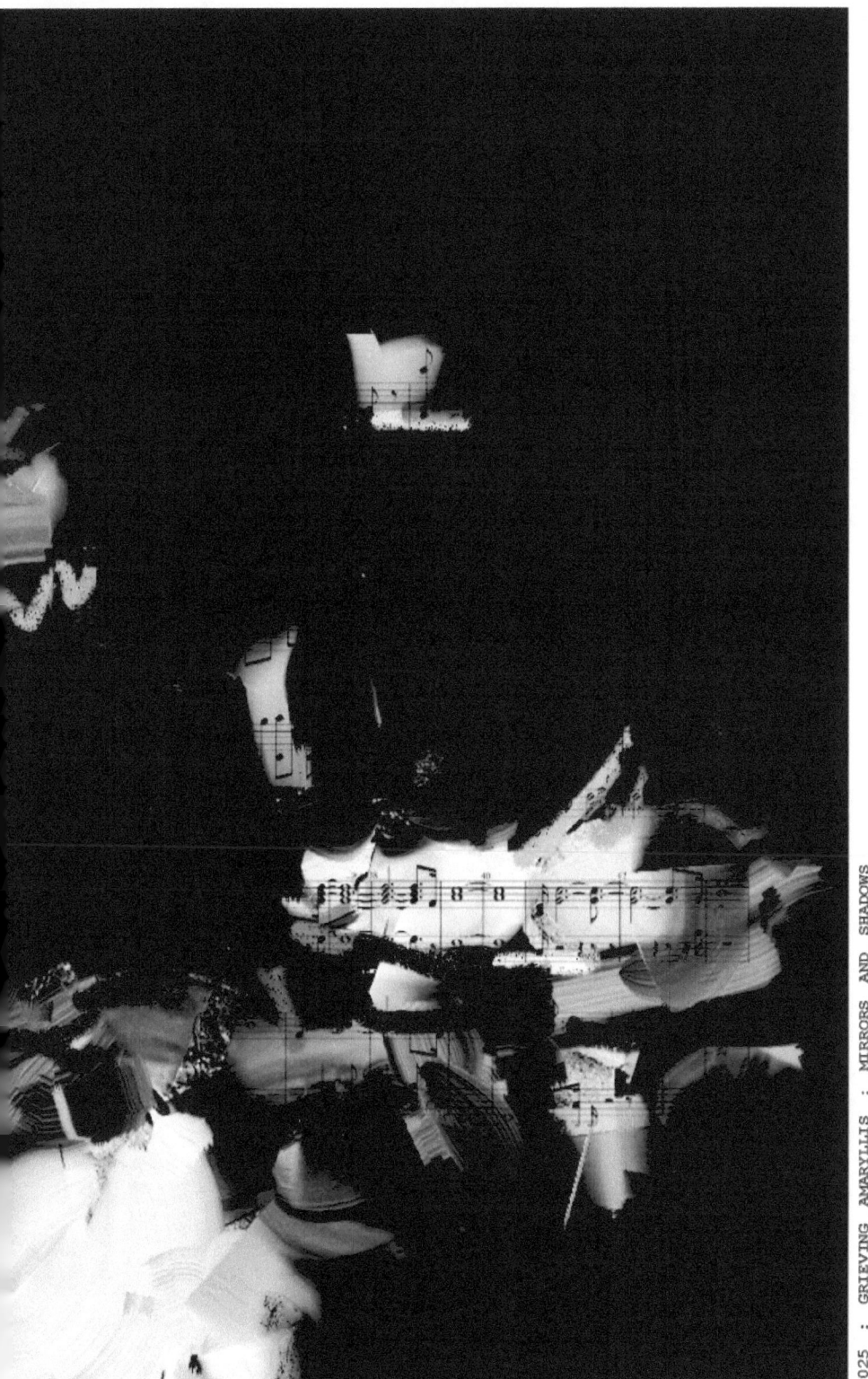

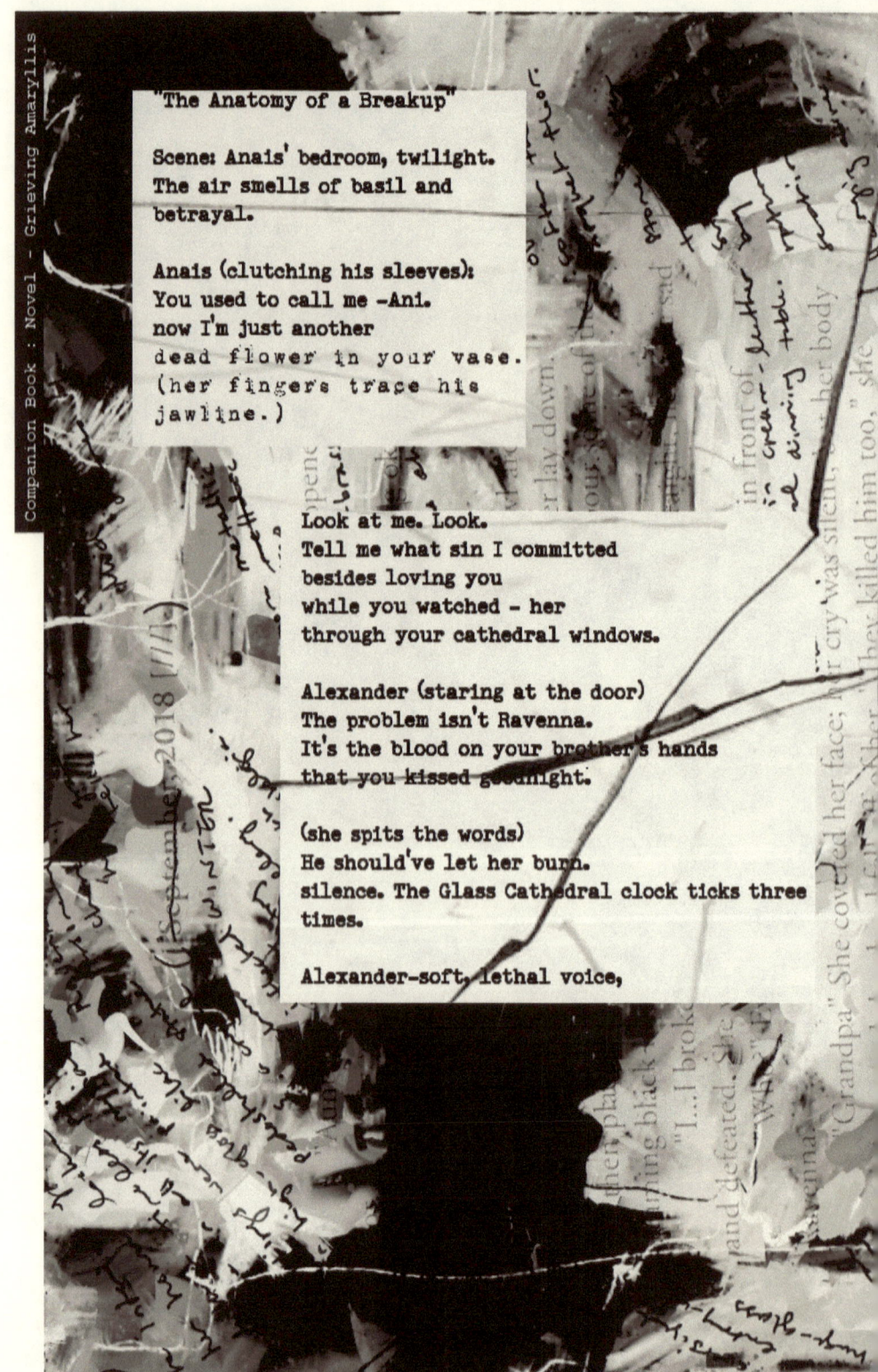

Companion Book : Novel – Grieving Amaryllis

"The Anatomy of a Breakup"

Scene: Anais' bedroom, twilight.
The air smells of basil and
betrayal.

Anais (clutching his sleeves):
You used to call me -Ani.
now I'm just another
dead flower in your vase.
(her fingers trace his
jawline.)

Look at me. Look.
Tell me what sin I committed
besides loving you
while you watched - her
through your cathedral windows.

Alexander (staring at the door)
The problem isn't Ravenna.
It's the blood on your brother's hands
that you kissed goodnight.

(she spits the words)
He should've let her burn.
silence. The Glass Cathedral clock ticks three
times.

Alexander-soft, lethal voice,

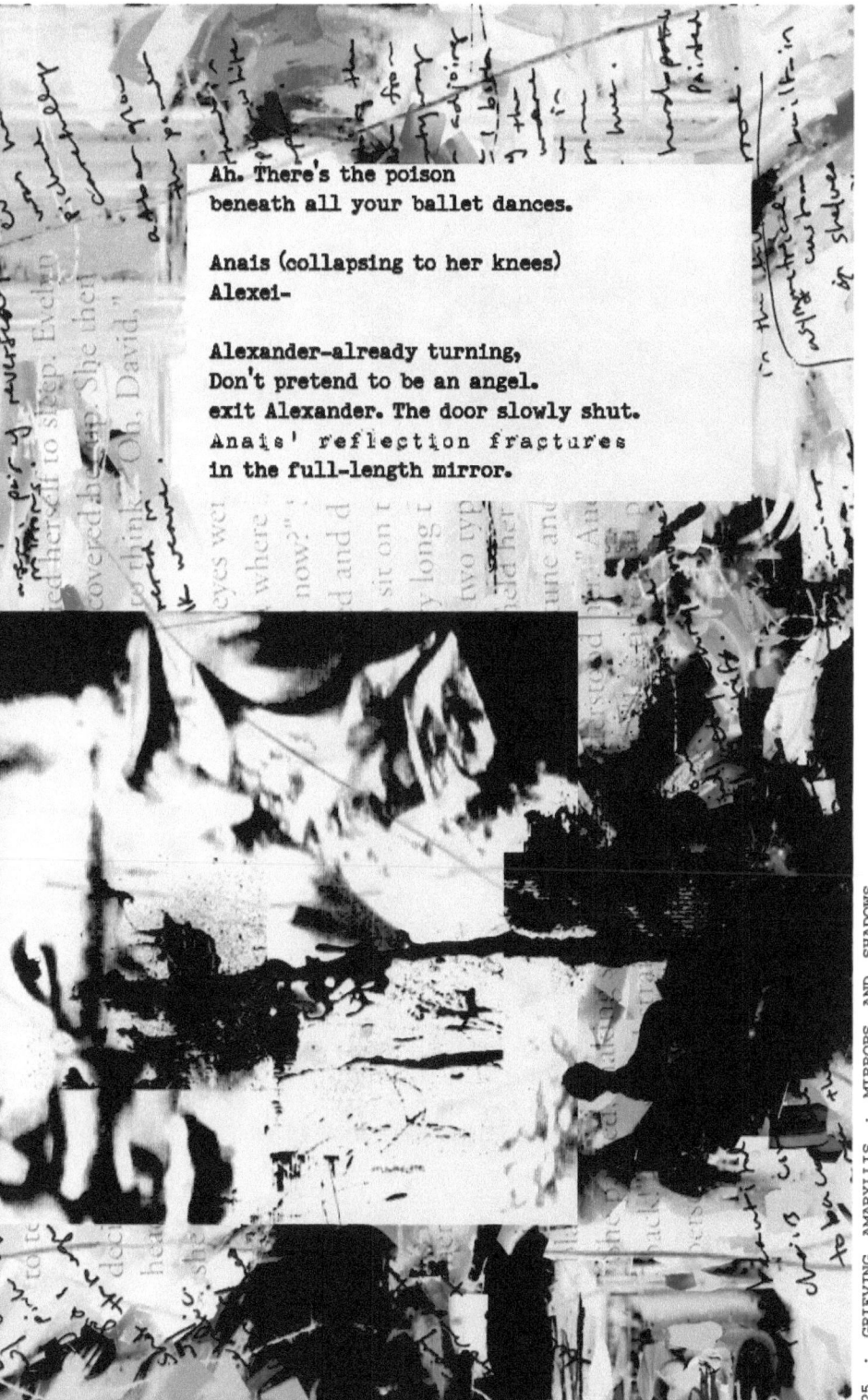

Ah. There's the poison
beneath all your ballet dances.

Anais (collapsing to her knees)
Alexei-

Alexander-already turning,
Don't pretend to be an angel.
exit Alexander. The door slowly shut.
Anais' reflection fractures
in the full-length mirror.

The Sculptor's Master Piece

(A sculpture in three acts, staged by thunder)

I. Niccolo's Kiss
(rain as hurt, rain as violence)

His mouth claims hers
like a blade splitting marble,
too hard, too deep.

She pushes back acid and obsession,
his fingers leaving violet blooms
where her veins should be.

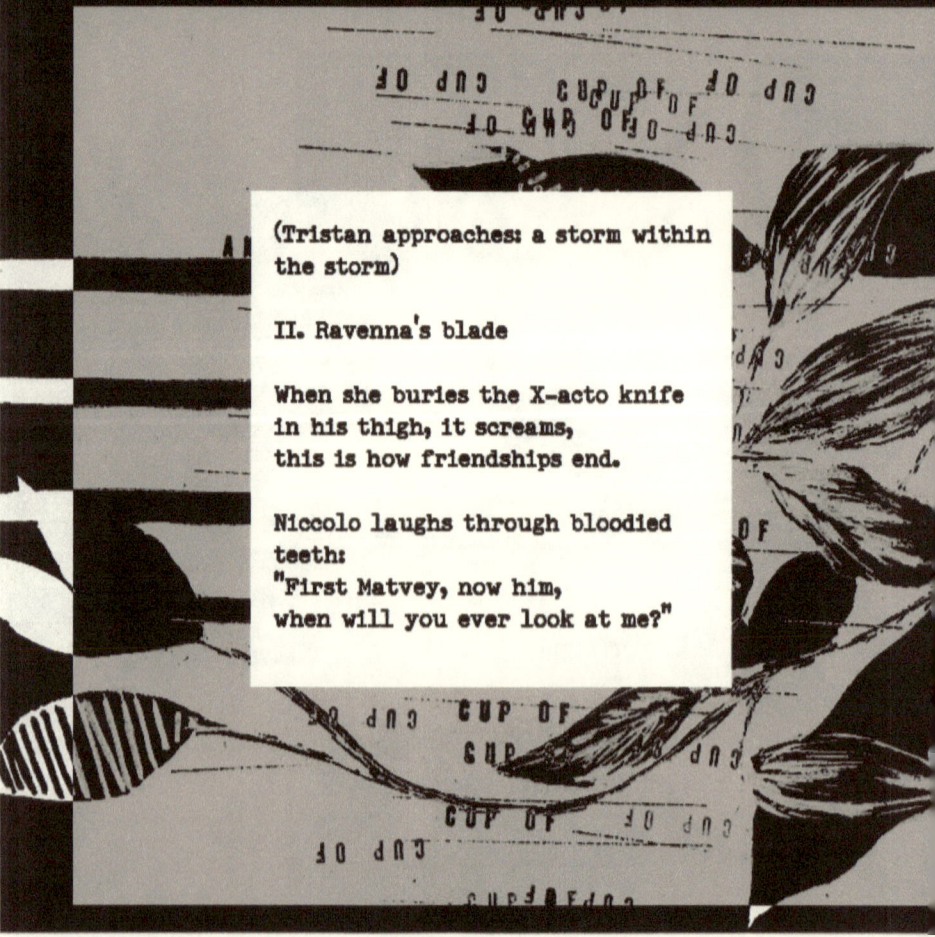

(Tristan approaches: a storm within
the storm)

II. Ravenna's blade

When she buries the X-acto knife
in his thigh, it screams,
this is how friendships end.

Niccolo laughs through bloodied
teeth:
"First Matvey, now him,
when will you ever look at me?"

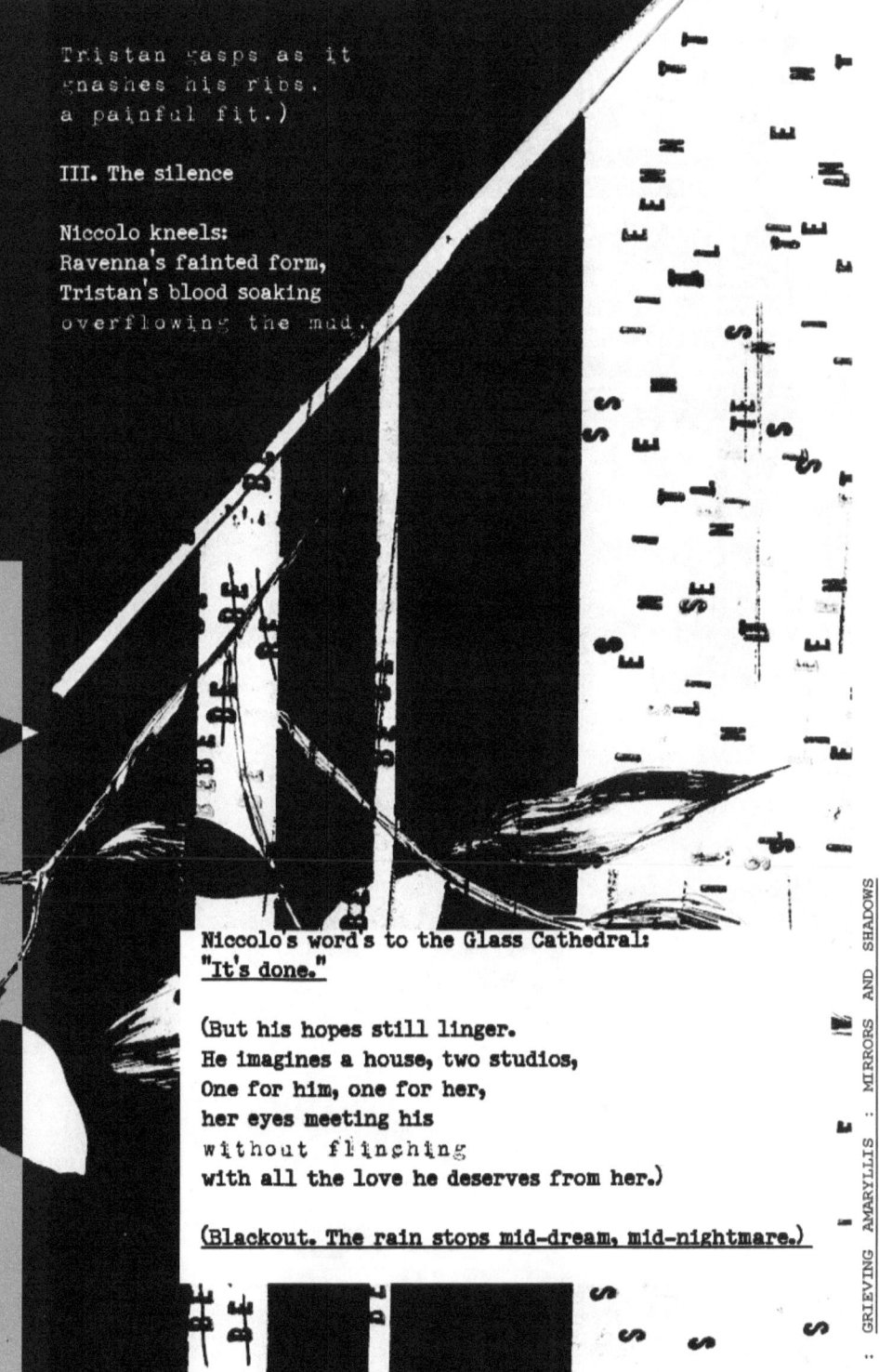

Tristan gasps as it
gnashes his ribs.
a painful fit.)

III. The silence

Niccolo kneels:
Ravenna's fainted form,
Tristan's blood soaking
overflowing the mud.

Niccolo's words to the Glass Cathedral:
"It's done."

(But his hopes still linger.
He imagines a house, two studios,
One for him, one for her,
her eyes meeting his
without flinching
with all the love he deserves from her.)

(Blackout. The rain stops mid-dream, mid-nightmare.)

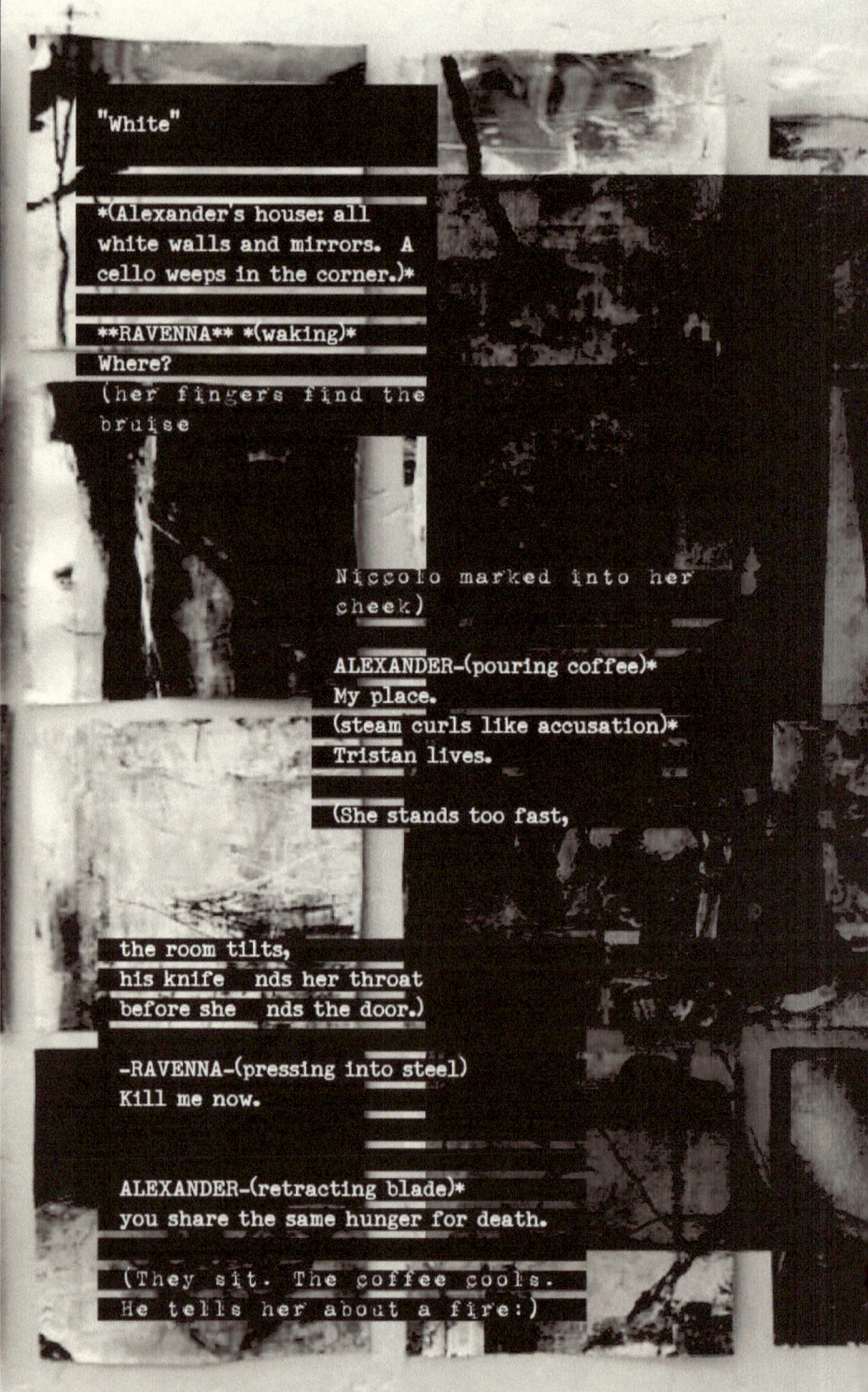

"White"

*(Alexander's house: all
white walls and mirrors. A
cello weeps in the corner.)*

RAVENNA *(waking)*
Where?
(her fingers find the
bruise

Niccolo marked into her
cheek)

ALEXANDER-(pouring coffee)*
My place.
(steam curls like accusation)*
Tristan lives.

(She stands too fast,

the room tilts,
his knife   nds her throat
before she   nds the door.)

-RAVENNA-(pressing into steel)
Kill me now.

ALEXANDER-(retracting blade)*
you share the same hunger for death.

(They sit. The coffee cools.
He tells her about a fire:)

A ten year old boy,
his mother's smile glowing-
brighter than the Voronin house,
the way the memory screamed,
like a broken violin-
snapping its last string.

(Ravenna's slap echoes.
He tastes his own blood,
and smiles.)

ALEXANDER

Monarchs don't mourn.
they execute.

ALEXANDER-(bitter laugh)
Six months with you,
and the Black Monarch
started carving
all the soul saving,
instead of blasphemy verdicts.

(He then pulls a letter from
his coat.
Matvey's suicide note.

ALEXANDER-(softly)
He tried again last night.
(offers his hand.)
Come.
I'll take you to him.

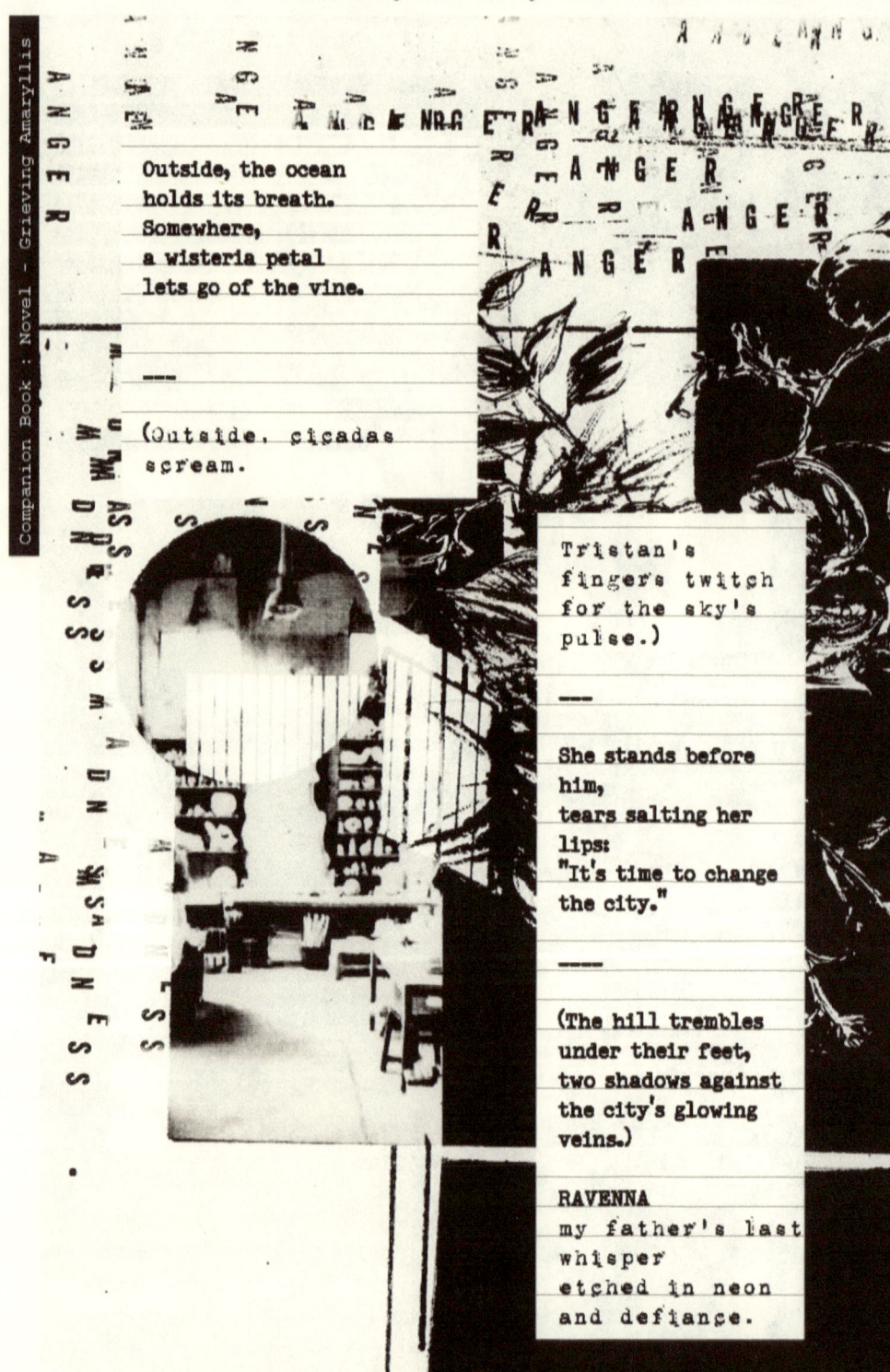

Outside, the ocean
holds its breath.
Somewhere,
a wisteria petal
lets go of the vine.

(Outside, cicadas
scream.

Tristan's
fingers twitch
for the sky's
pulse.)

She stands before
him,
tears salting her
lips:
"It's time to change
the city."

(The hill trembles
under their feet,
two shadows against
the city's glowing
veins.)

RAVENNA
my father's last
whisper
etched in neon
and defiance.

"I love you."
"I love you."

(Matvey ties the emerald ribbon
in her hair.)

MATVEY:
It's perfect.

The Dance Before the Storm

They sway,
her fists clenched in his shirt,
his heartbeat a soft hum
against her cheek.

"Tonight we leave," he tries.

Her thumb catches his tear,
a fallen star.
"I love you."

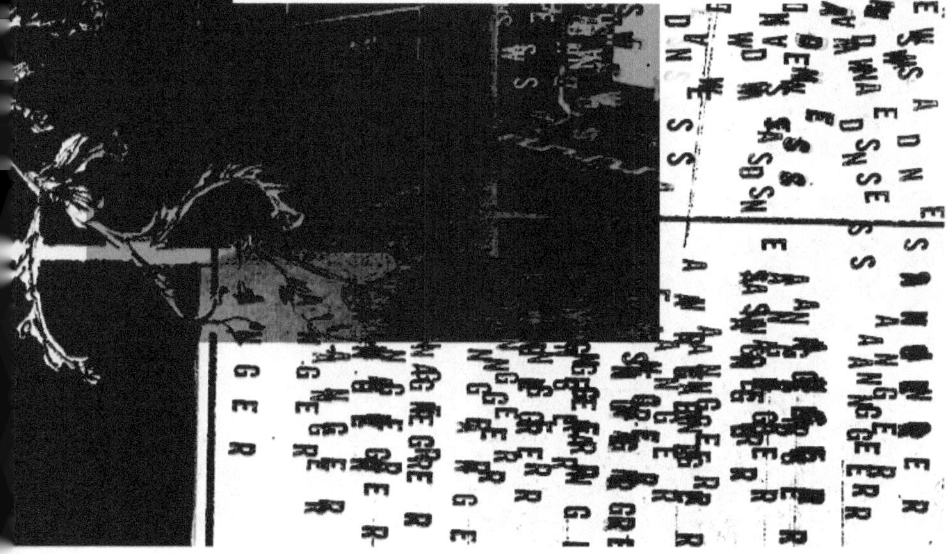

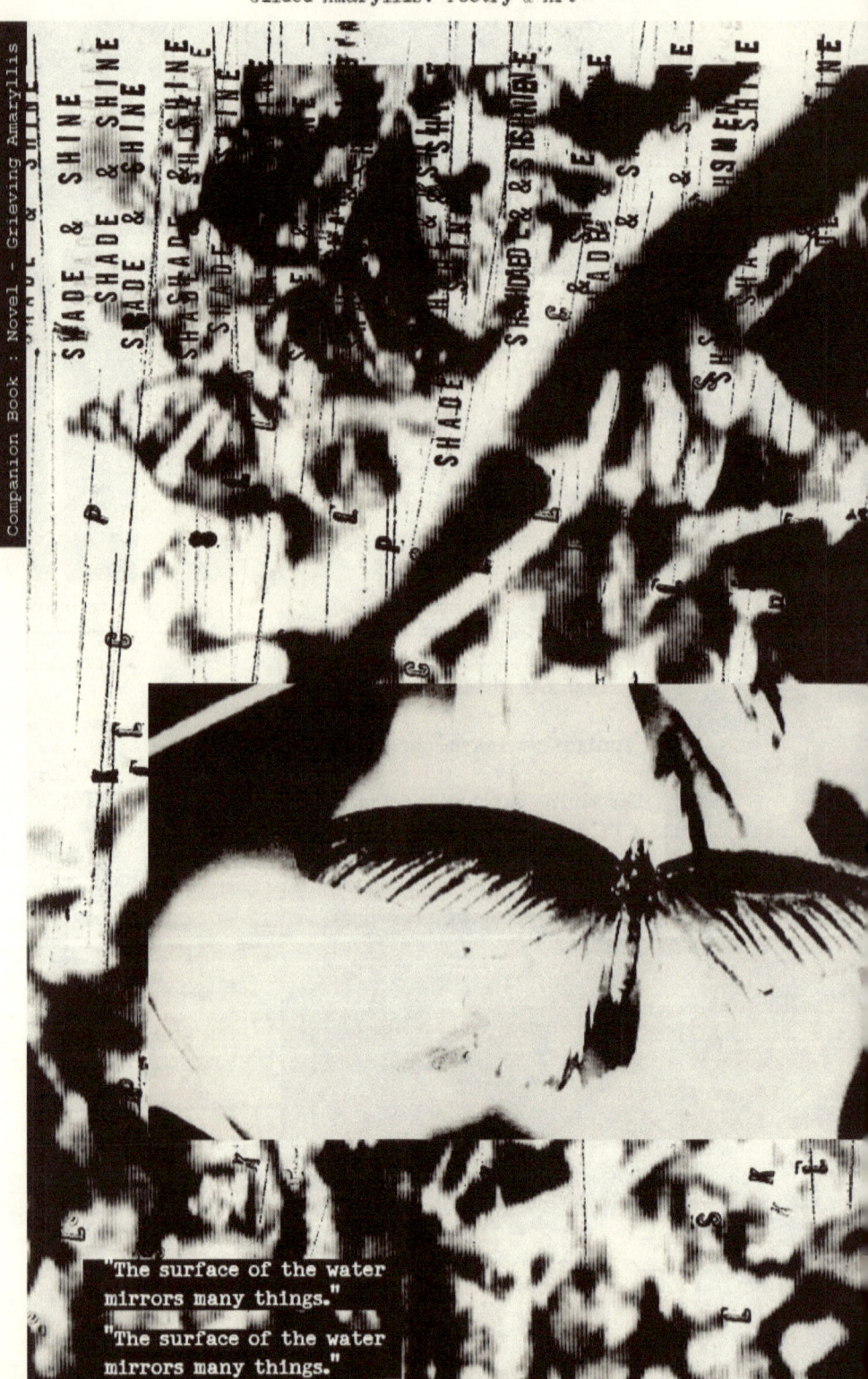

"The surface of the water mirrors many things."

"The surface of the water mirrors many things."

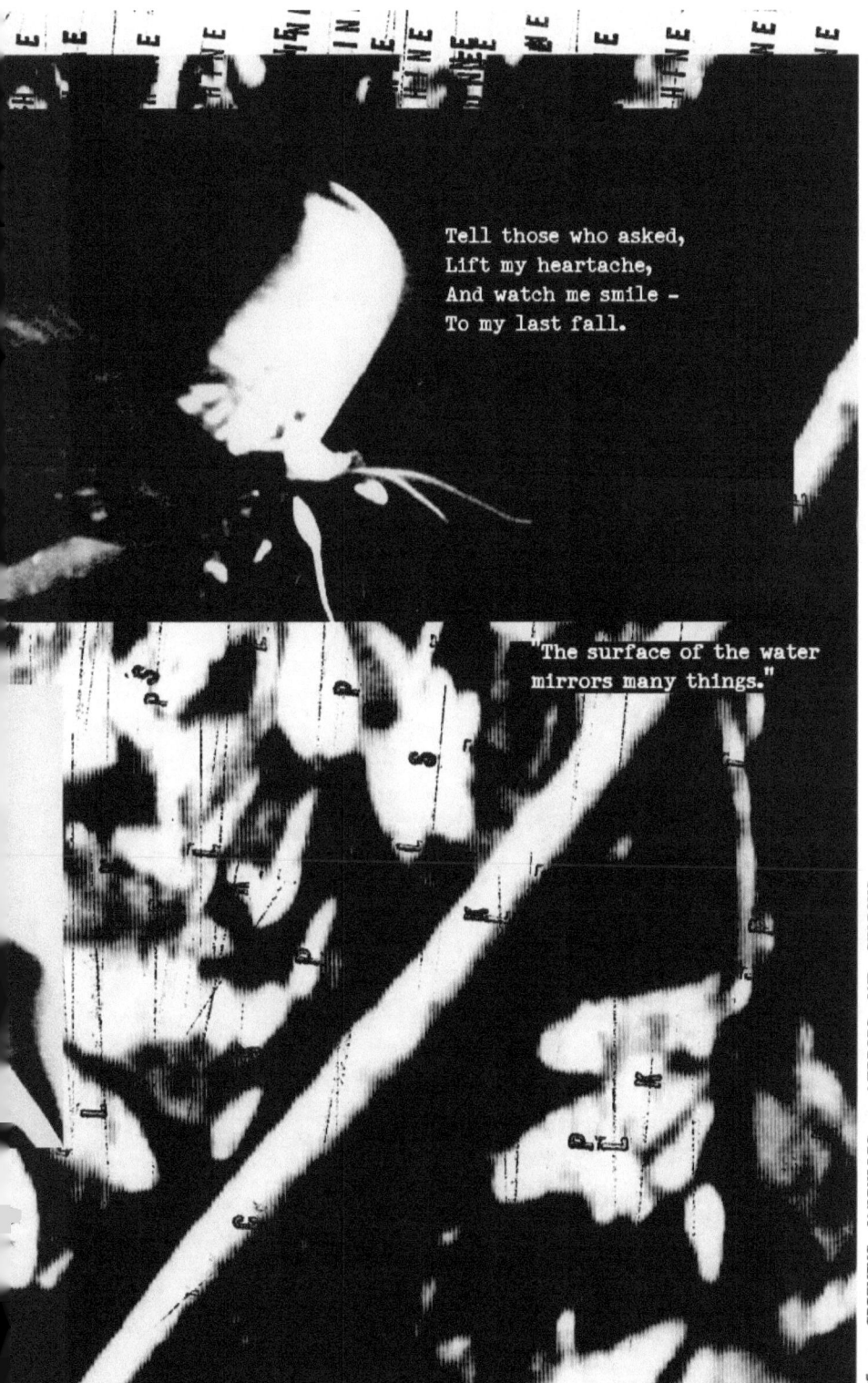

Tell those who asked,
Lift my heartache,
And watch me smile –
To my last fall.

"The surface of the water
mirrors many things."

Companion Book : Novel - Grieving Amaryllis

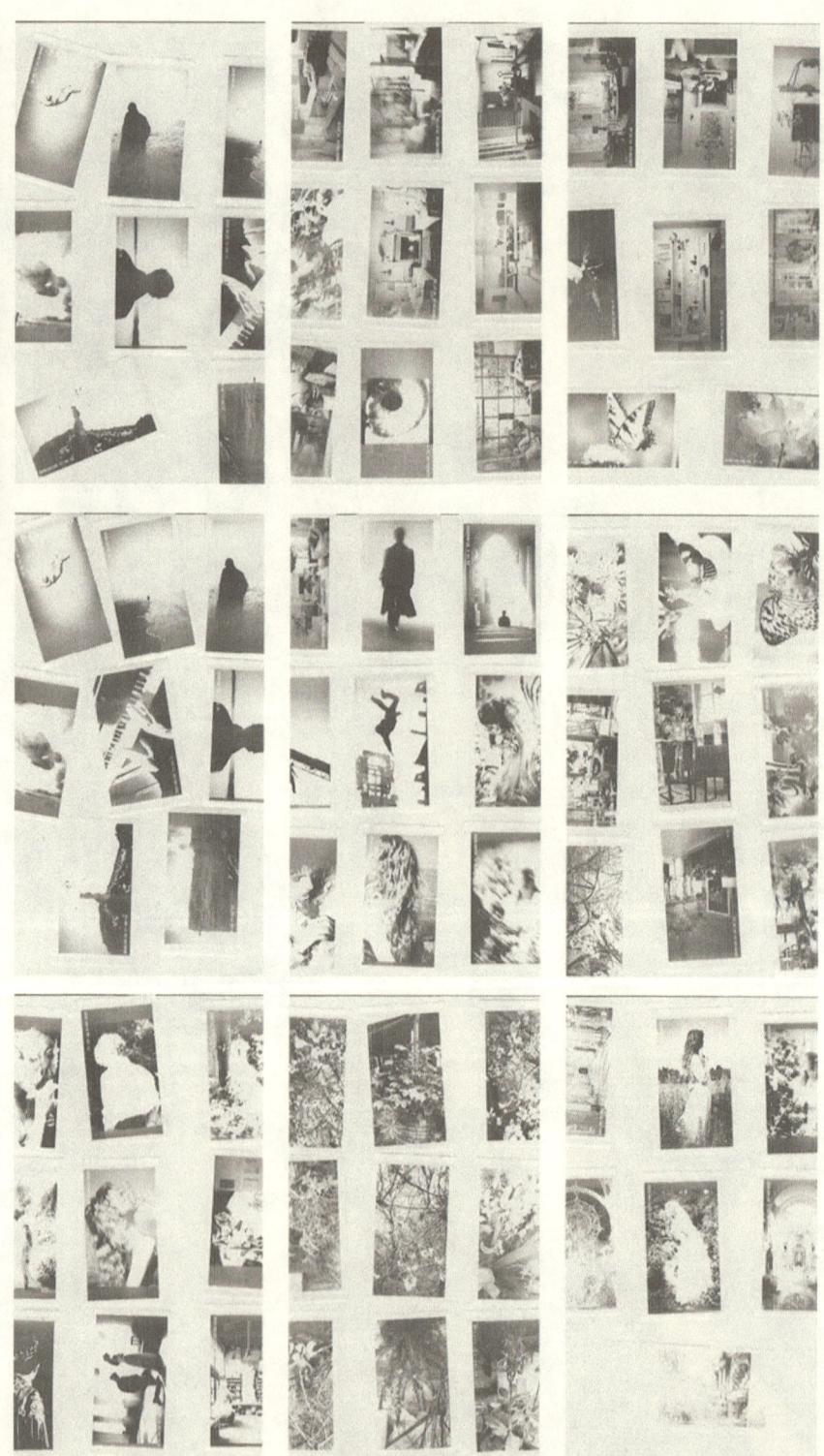

I shiver past the meadows,
Under the rain and hues of wrong,
November winter smiles for me,
For someone has promised me a song.

I died while asleep -
Float the soul, oh   oat.
Asked for an end -
All I had to keep,
Row your dream boat now, row.

Now I smile, teeth stained with joy,
Lips apart for a while -
Once a memory of a boy.

Like birds chirping -
In moods of morning and sun,
My heart beats for us,
I confess to none.

Leave and so you will leave,
Just like those before you enjoy,
And watch me suffer in disbelief,
Of how cruel humans can destroy.

I refuse the cage,
I refuse it all.

Tell those who asked,
Lift my heartache,
And watch me smile -
To my last fall.

A secret to keep,
Of maps and meanings for all.

Let the darkness reveal,
All the lines and strokes -
It's our last call.

Now let the vivid moths breathe,
For the girl who was once a brave soul.

The main poem.

Companion Book : Novel - Grieving Amaryllis

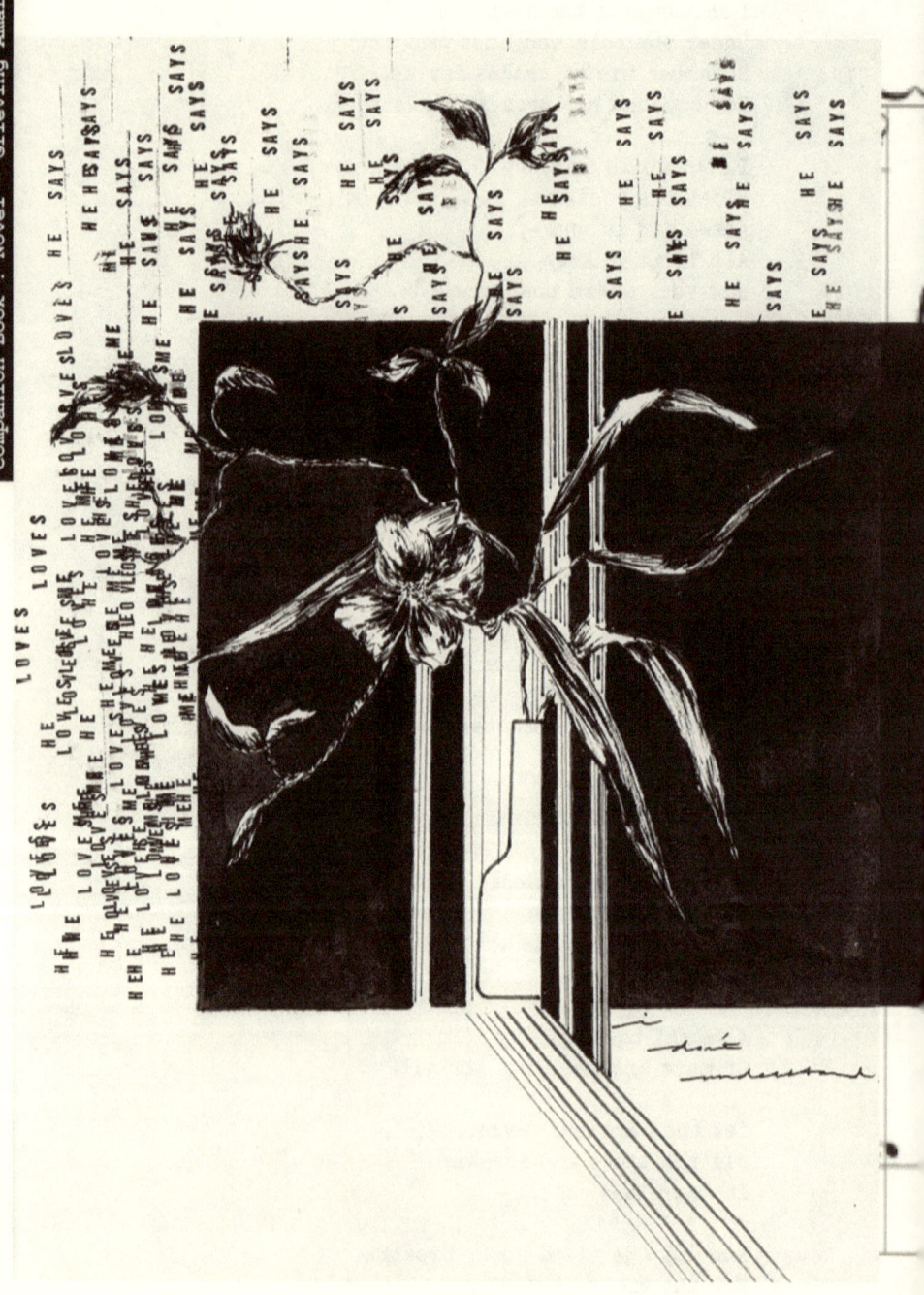

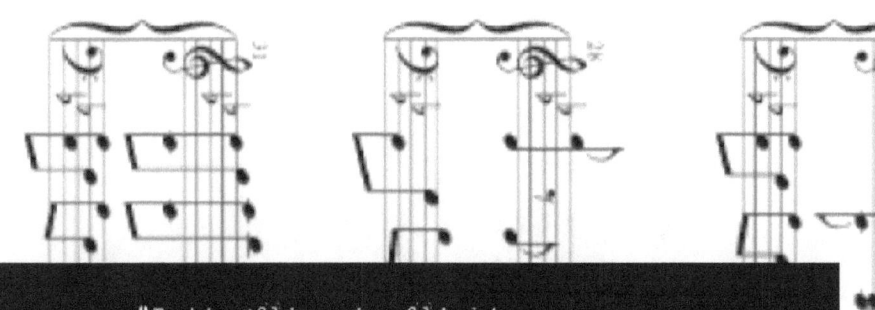

"Butterflies in flight,
the journey home."

Two butterflies flew over the ocean
toward the sunset. The waves swelled
below, their shadows kissing the water's
surface. Beautiful and weightless, they
fluttered above the vast expanse.
Chasing the orange-pink sunset, their
delicate wings caught the golden light,
sparkling, flying, fading away as the
wind carried them. They danced above
frothing whites and bruised blues,
their shadows touching and kissing the
glittering surface.

"The surface of the water mirrors many things."

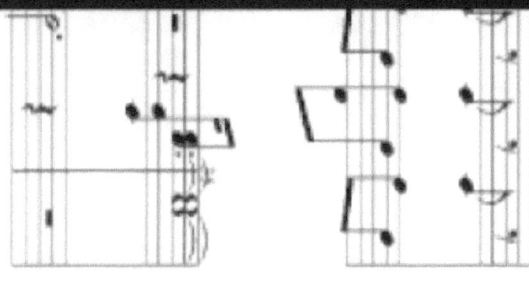

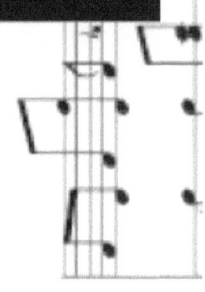

2025 : GRIEVING AMARYLLIS : MIRRORS AND SHADOWS

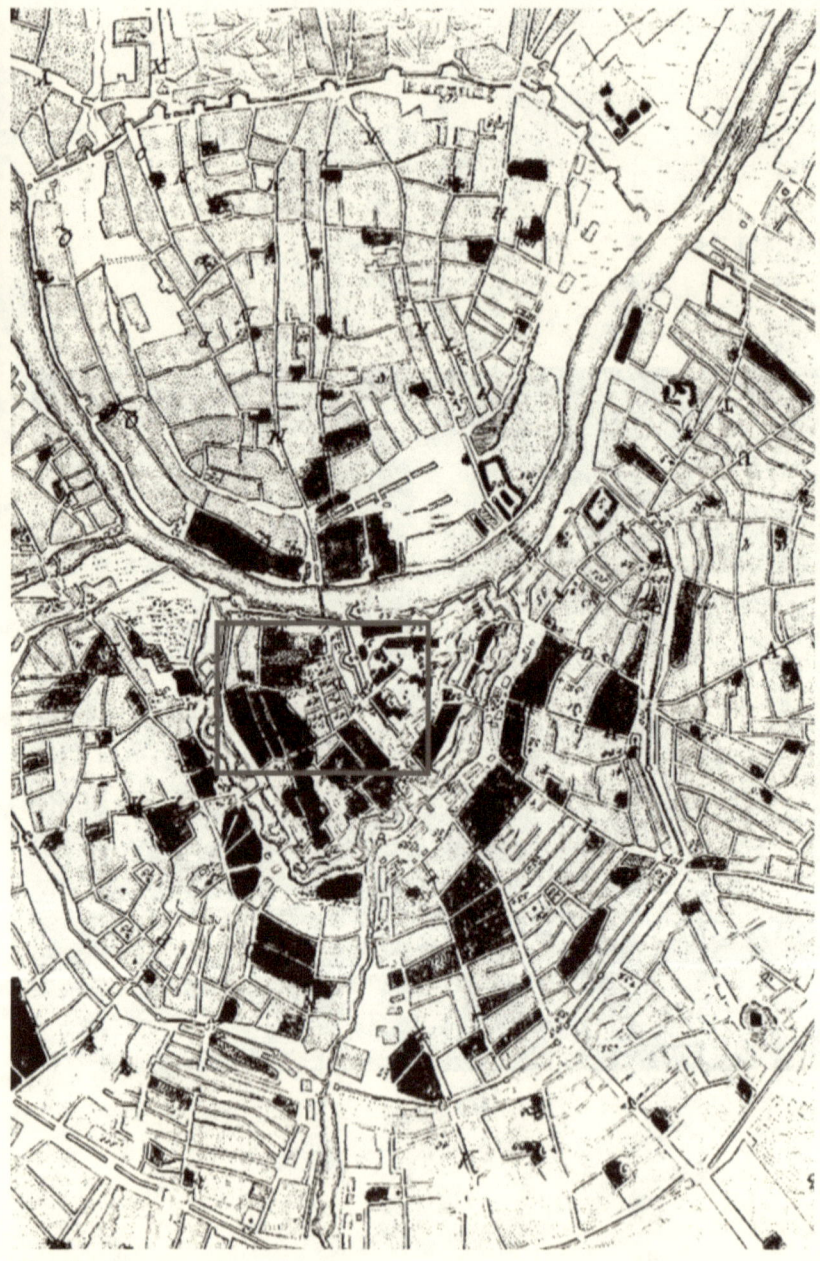

The Glass Temple and
Imperial Garden

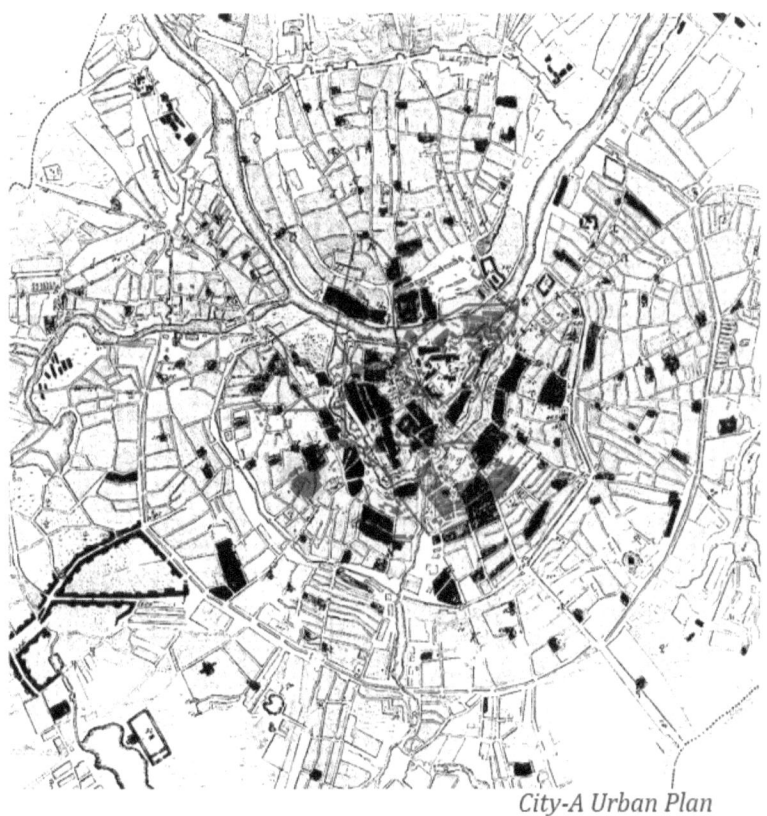

City-A Urban Plan

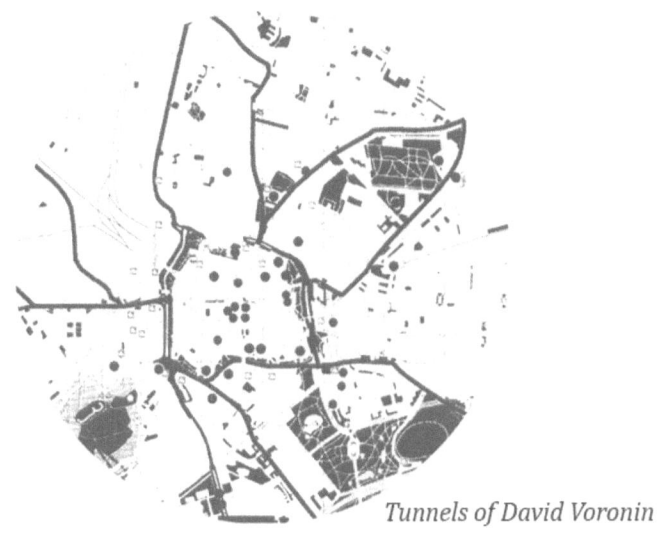

Tunnels of David Voronin

Haiku in the novel - Grieving Amaryllis

Also by Dana Krystle :

Architecture Design Books:
Fluid x Solid: 29 experimental architecture projects.

Novels:
Eden in Black | Novel.
Grieving Amaryllis | Novel.

Poetry Books:
Pretentious Butterflies | Poetry book.
Red Spider Lilies | Poetry book.
Delicate Forget-me-nots | Poetry Book
Orange Cosmos | Poetry Book

Art Books:
Book of Fragments | Art book.
Book of Fragments Vol.2 | Art book.
Coral Peonies | Art book (personal paintings).
Liquid Dreams | Art book.
Calligraphy Experiments in ink | Calligraphy and art book.
Juicy Strokes | Turning Classical Paintings into Contemporary Artworks.

Architecture Illustrations and sketches Books:
Sketchbook No.11 | A series of architecture illustrations.
Sketchbook No.12 | A series of architecture illustrations.
Sketchbook No.13 | A series of architecture illustrations.
The Mini Sketchbook of Concepts Vol.1 | (Architecture Concept Sketches).
The Mini Sketchbook of Concepts Vol.2 | (Architecture Concept Sketches).
The Mini Sketchbook of Concepts Vol.3 | (Architecture Concept Sketches).
The Mini Sketchbook of Concepts Vol.4 | (Architecture Concept Sketches).
The Monochrome Sketchbook Vol.1 (Architecture sketches).
The Monochrome Sketchbook Vol.2 (Architecture sketches, Vol.1 included).

If you liked this book, please write a review on goodreads or on Amazon, for more questions, email me at :
danakhalilfa@live.com